**ABERDEENSHIRE LIBRARY
AND INFORMATION SERVICE
MELDRUM MEG WAY, OLDMELDRUM**

THE LAST DANCE

ALSO BY ED McBAIN

THE 87TH PRECINCT NOVELS

Cop Hater • The Mugger • The Pusher (1956) The Con Man • Killer's Choice (1957) Killer's Payoff • Killer's Wedge • Lady Killer (1958) 'Til Death • King's Ransom (1959) Give the Boys a Great Big Hand • The Heckler • See Them Die • (1960) Lady, Lady, I Did It! (1961) The Empty Hours • Like Love (1962) Ten Plus One (1963) Ax (1964) He Who Hesitates • Doll (1965) Eighty Million Eyes (1966) Fuzz (1968) Shotgun (1969) Jigsaw (1970) Hail, Hail, the Gang's All Here (1971) Sadie When She Died • Let's Hear It for the Deaf Man (1972) Hail to the Chief (1973) Bread (1974) Blood Relatives (1975) So Long As You Both Shall Live (1976) Long Time No See (1977) Calypso (1979) Ghosts (1980) Heat (1981) Ice (1983) Lightning (1984) Eight Black Horses (1985) Poison • Tricks (1987) Lullaby (1989) Vespers (1990) Widows (1991) Kiss (1992) Mischief (1993) And All Through the House (1994) Romance (1995) Nocturne (1997) The Big Bad City (1999)

THE MATTHEW HOPE NOVELS

Goldilocks (1978) Rumpelstiltskin (1981) Beauty and the Beast (1982) Jack and the Beanstalk (1984) Snow White and Rose Red (1985) Cinderella (1986) Puss in Boots (1987) The House That Jack Built (1988) Three Blind Mice (1990) Mary, Mary (1993) There Was a Little Girl (1994) Gladly the Cross-Eyed Bear (1996) The Last Best Hope (1998)

OTHER NOVELS

The Sentries (1965) Where There's Smoke • Doors (1975) Guns (1976) Another Part of the City (1986) Downtown (1991)

AND BY EVAN HUNTER

NOVELS

The Blackboard Jungle (1954) Second Ending (1956) Strangers When We Meet (1958) A Matter of Conviction (1959) Mothers and Daughters (1961) Buddwing (1964) The Paper Dragon (1966) A Horse's Head (1967) Last Summer (1968) Sons (1969) Nobody Knew They Were There (1971) Every Little Crook and Nanny (1972) Come Winter (1973) Streets of Gold (1974) The Chisholms (1976) Love, Dad (1981) Far From the Sea (1983) Lizzie (1985) Criminal Conversation (1994) Privileged Conversation (1996)

SHORT STORY COLLECTIONS

Happy New Year, Herbie (1963) The Easter Man (1972)

CHILDREN'S BOOKS

Find the Feathered Serpent (1952) The Remarkable Harry (1959) The Wonderful Button (1961) Me and Mr Stenner (1976)

SCREENPLAYS

Strangers When We Meet (1959) The Birds (1962) Fuzz (1972) Walk Proud (1979)

TELEPLAYS

The Chisholms (1979) The Legend of Walks Far Woman (1980) Dream West (1986)

THE LAST DANCE

A Novel of the 87th Precinct

Ed McBain

Hodder & Stoughton

Copyright © 2000 by Hui Corp.

First published in Great Britain in 2000 by Hodder and Stoughton
A division of Hodder Headline

The right of Ed McBain to be identified as the Author
of the Work has been asserted by him in accordance with the Copyright,
Designs and Patents Act 1988.

10 9 8 7 6 5 4 3 2 1

A CIP catalogue record for this title is available
from the British Library.

ISBN 0 340 72805 1

Typeset by Palimpsest Book Production Limited,
Polmont, Stirlingshire
Printed and bound in Great Britain by
Clays Ltd, St Ives plc, Bungay, Suffolk

Hodder and Stoughton
A division of Hodder Headline
338 Euston Road
London NW1 3BH

This, yet another time, is for my wife—
DRAGICA DIMITRIJEVIĆ-HUNTER

The city in these pages is imaginary.
The people, the places are all fictitious.
Only the police routine is based on established
investigatory technique.

Chapter One

"He had heart trouble," the woman was telling Carella.

Which perhaps accounted for the tiny pinpricks of blood on the dead man's eyeballs. In cases of acute right-heart failure, you often found such hemorrhaging. The grayish-blue feet sticking out from under the edge of the blanket were another matter.

"Told me he hadn't been feeling good these past few days," the woman was saying. "I kept telling him to go see the doctor. Yeah, I'll go, I'll go, don't worry, like that, you know? So I stopped by this morning to see how he was, found him just this way. In bed. Dead."

"So you called the police," Meyer said, nodding.

Because he'd expected to go out on a narcotics plant this morning, he was wearing blue jeans, a sweat shirt, and Reeboks. Instead, he'd caught this one with Carella and here he was. On a fishing expedition with a woman he felt was lying. Burly and bald, he posed his question with wide, blue-eyed innocence, just as if it did not conceal a hand grenade.

"Yes," she said, "I called the police. That was the first thing I did."

"Knew straight off he was dead, is that right?"

"Well ... yes. I could see he was dead."

"You didn't take his pulse or anything like that, did you?" Carella asked.

Looking trimmer and fitter than he had in a long while—he had deliberately lost six pounds since his fortieth birthday—he was dressed casually this morning in dark blue trousers, a gray corduroy jacket, a plaid sports shirt and a dark blue knit tie. He had not anticipated this particular squeal at a little past ten in the morning. In fact, he had scheduled a ten-fifteen squadroom interview with a burglary victim. Instead, here he was, talking to a woman he, too, felt was lying.

"No," she said. "Well, yes. Well, not his pulse. But I leaned over him. To see if he was still breathing. But I could see he was dead. I mean ... well, look at him."

The dead man was lying on his back, covered with a blanket, his eyes and his mouth open, his tongue protruding. Carella glanced at him again, a faint look of sorrow and pain momentarily knifing his eyes. In these moments, he felt particularly vulnerable, wondering as he often did if he was perhaps unsuited to a job that brought him into frequent contact with death.

"So you called the police," Meyer said again.

"Yes. Told whoever answered the phone ..."

"Was this 911 you called? Or the precinct number direct?"

"911. I don't know the precinct number. I don't live around here."

"Told the operator you'd come into your father's apartment and found him dead, is that right?"

"Yes."

"What time was this, Miss?"

"A little after ten this morning. It's Mrs, by the way," she said almost apologetically.

Carella looked at his watch. It was now twenty minutes to eleven. He wondered where the medical examiner was.

Couldn't touch anything in here till the ME pronounced the victim dead. He wanted to see the rest of the body. Wanted to see if the legs matched the feet.

"Mrs Robert Keating," the woman said. "Well, *Cynthia* Keating, actually."

"And your father's name?" Meyer asked.

"Andrew. Andrew Hale."

Better to let Meyer stay with it for now, Carella thought. He had noticed the same things Carella had, was equally familiar with the telltale signs of a hanging, which this one resembled a great deal, but you couldn't hang yourself lying flat on your back in bed with no noose around your neck.

"How old was he, can you tell us?"

"Sixty-eight."

"And you say he had heart trouble?"

"Two heart attacks in the past eight years."

"Serious?"

"Oh yes."

"Bypasses?"

"No. Two angioplasties. But his condition was very grave. He almost lost his life each time."

"And he continued having trouble, is that it?"

"Well ... no."

"You said he had heart trouble."

"Two serious heart attacks in eight years, yes, that's heart trouble. But he wasn't restricted in his activities or anything."

"Good morning, gentlemen," a voice said from the bedroom doorway. For a moment, the detectives couldn't tell whether the man standing there was Carl Blaney or Paul Blaney. Not very many people knew that Carl Blaney and Paul Blaney were twin brothers. Most of the detectives in this city had spoken to them separately, either on the phone or in person at the morgue, but they assumed the similarity of their surnames and the fact that they both worked for

3

the Medical Examiner's Office were attributable to mere coincidence. As every working cop knew, coincidence was a major factor in police work.

Both Blaneys were five feet, nine inches tall. Paul Blaney weighed a hundred and eighty pounds, whereas his brother Carl weighed a hundred and sixty-five. Carl still had all of his hair. Paul was going a bit bald at the back of his head. Both Paul and Carl had violet eyes, although neither was related to Elizabeth Taylor.

"Carl," the man in the doorway said, clearing up any confusion at once. He was wearing a lightweight topcoat, a plaid muffler draped loose around his neck. He took off the coat and muffler and threw them over a straight-backed chair just inside the bedroom door.

"You are?" he asked Cynthia.

"His daughter," she said.

"I'm sorry for your trouble," he told her, managing to sound as if he actually meant it. "I'd like to examine your father now," he said. "Would you mind stepping outside, please?"

"Yes, of course," she said, and started for the doorway, and then stopped, and asked, "Shall I call my husband?"

"Might be a good idea," Carella said.

"He works nearby," she said to no one in particular and then went out into the kitchen. They could hear her dialing the wall phone there.

"What's it look like?" Blaney asked.

"Asphyxia," Carella said.

Blaney was already at the bed, leaning over the dead man as if about to kiss him on the lips. He noticed the eyes at once. "This what you mean?" he asked. "The petechiae?"

"Yes."

"By no means conclusive evidence of death by asphyxia," Blaney said flatly. "You should know that, Detective. This how he was found? On his back this way?"

"According to the daughter."

"Couldn't have accidentally smothered then, could he?"

"I guess not."

"You have any reason to disbelieve her?"

"Just the blood spots. And the blue feet."

"Oh? Do we have blue feet as well?" Blaney asked, and looked toward the foot of the bed. "Are we suspecting death by hanging then? Is that it?"

"The daughter says he had a history of heart disease," Carella said. "Maybe it was heart failure. Who knows?"

"Who knows indeed?" Blaney asked the dead man's feet. "Let's see what else we've got here, shall we?" he said, and threw back the blanket.

The dead man was wearing a white shirt open at the throat, gray flannel trousers fastened with a black belt. No shoes or socks.

"Goes to bed with all his clothes on, I see," Blaney said dryly.

"Barefoot though," Carella said.

Blaney grunted, unbuttoned the shirt, and slid a stethoscope onto the dead man's chest, not expecting to find a heart beat, and not surprised when he didn't. He removed all the man's garments—he was also wearing striped boxer shorts—and noticed at once the grayish-blue coloration of the corpse's legs, forearms, and hands. "*If* he was hanged," he told Carella, "and I'm not saying he was, then it was in an upright position. And *if* he was moved to the bed here, and I'm not saying he was, then it wasn't too soon after he died. Otherwise the postmortem lividity would have faded from the extremities and moved to the back and buttocks. Let's take a look," he said and rolled the dead man onto his side. His back was pale, his ass as white as a full moon. "Nope," he said, and rolled the corpse onto his back again. The man's penis was swollen and distended. "Postmortem lividity," Blaney explained. "Settling of tissue fluids." There were dried stains in the corpse's undershorts. "Probably semen," Blaney said. "We don't know why, but a seminal discharge is commonplace in cases of asphyxia. Has nothing whatever to do with any sexual activity. Rigor mortis in the seminal vesicles causes it." He looked at Carella. Carella merely nodded. "No rope burns," Blaney said, examining the neck, "no imprint of a noose, no blisters from pinching or squeezing of the skin. A knot may have caused this," he said, indicating a small bruise under the chin. "Did you find any kind of noose?"

"We haven't really made a search yet," Carella said.

"Well, it certainly *looks* like a hanging," Blaney said, "but who knows?"

"Who knows indeed?" Carella echoed, as if they were going through a familiar vaudeville routine.

"If I were you, I'd talk to the daughter some more," Blaney said. "Let's see what the autopsy shows. Meanwhile, he's dead and he's yours."

The mobile crime unit arrived some ten minutes later, after the body and Blaney were both gone. Carella told them to keep a special lookout for fibers. The chief technician told him they were *always* on the lookout for fibers, what did he mean by a *special* lookout? Carella cut his eyes toward where Meyer was talking to Cynthia Keating across the room. The chief technician still didn't know why a special lookout for fibers was necessary, but he didn't ask Carella anything else.

It was starting to rain.

The mandatory date for turning on the heat in this city was October fifteenth—birthdate of great men, Carella thought, but did not say. This was already the twenty-ninth but too many buildings took their time complying with the law. The rain and the falling temperature outside combined to make it a little chilly in the apartment. The technicians, who had just come in from the cold, kept their coats on. Carella put his coat back on before ambling over to where Meyer was idly and casually chatting up the dead man's daughter. They both wanted to know if she'd found the body exactly where she'd said she'd found it, but they weren't asking that just yet.

"... or did you just drop by?" Meyer said.

"He knew I was coming."

"Did he know what time?"

"No. I just said I'd be by sometime this morning."

"But he was still in bed when you got here?"

The key question.

"Yes," she said.

No hesitation on her part.

"Wearing all his clothes?" Carella asked.

She turned toward him. Bad Cop flashed in her eyes. Too many damn television shows these days, everyone knew all the cop tricks.

"Yes," she said. "Well, not his shoes and socks."

"Did he always sleep with his clothes on?" Carella asked.

"No. He must have gotten up and ..."

"Yes?" Meyer said.

She turned to look at him, suspecting Good Cop, but not yet certain.

"Gone back to bed again," she explained.

"I see," Mayer said, and turned to Carella as if seeking approval of this perfectly reasonable explanation of why a man was in bed with all his clothes on except for his shoes and socks.

"Maybe he felt something coming on," Cynthia said further.

"Something coming on?" Meyer said, encouraging her.

"Yes. A heart attack. People know when they're coming."

"I see. And you figure he might have gone to lie down."

"Yes."

"Didn't call an ambulance or anything," Carella said. "Just went to lie down."

"Yes. Thinking it might pass. The heart attack."

"Took off his shoes and socks and went to lie down."

"Yes."

"Was the door locked when you got here?" Carella asked.

"I have a key."

"Then it was locked."

"Yes."

"Did you knock?"

"I knocked, but there was no answer. So I let myself in."

"And found your father in bed."

"Yes."

"Were his shoes and socks where they are now?"

"Yes."

"On the floor there? Near the easy chair?"

"Yes."

"So you called the police," Meyer said for the third time.

"Yes," Cynthia said, and looked at him.

"Did you suspect foul play of any sort?" Carella asked.

"No. Of course not."

"But you called the police," Meyer said.

"Why is that important?" she snapped, suddenly tipping to what was going on here, Good Cop becoming Bad Cop in the wink of an eye.

"He's merely asking," Carella said.

"No, he's not merely asking, he seems to think it's important. He keeps asking me over and over again did I call the police, did I call the police, when you *know* I called the police, otherwise you wouldn't *be* here!"

8

"We have to ask certain questions," Carella said gently.

"But why that particular question?"

"Because some people wouldn't necessarily call the police if they found someone dead from apparent natural causes."

"Who would they call? Necessarily?"

"Relatives, friends, even a lawyer. Not necessarily the police, is all my partner's saying," Carella explained gently.

"Then why doesn't he *say* it?" Cynthia snapped. "Instead of asking me all the time did I call the *police?*"

"I'm sorry, ma'am," Meyer said in his most abject voice. "I didn't mean to suggest there was anything peculiar about your calling the police."

"Well, your *partner* here seems to think it was peculiar," Cynthia said, thoroughly confused now. "*He* seems to think I should have called my husband or my girlfriend or my priest or anybody *but* the police, what *is* it with you two?"

"We simply have to investigate every possibility," Carella said, more convinced than ever that she was lying. "By all appearances, your father died in bed, possibly from a heart attack, possibly from some other cause, we won't know that until the autopsy results are ..."

"He was an old man who'd suffered two previous heart attacks," Cynthia said. "What do you *think* he died of?"

"I don't know, ma'am," Carella said. "Do you?"

Cynthia looked him dead in the eye.

"My husband's a lawyer, you know," she said.

"Is your mother still alive?" Meyer asked, ducking the question and its implied threat.

"He's on the way here now," she said, not turning to look at Meyer, her gaze still fastened on Carella, as if willing him to melt before her very eyes. Green, he noticed. A person could easily melt under a green-eyed laser beam.

"Is she?" Meyer asked.

"She's alive," Cynthia said. "But they're divorced."

"Any other children besides you?"

She glared at Carella a moment longer, and then turned to Meyer, seemingly calmer now. "Just me," she said.

"How long have they been divorced?" Meyer asked.

"Five years."

"What was his current situation?"

"What do you mean?"

"Your father. Was he living with anyone?"

"I have no idea."

"Seeing anyone?"

"His private life was his own business."

"How often did you see your father, Mrs Keating?"

"Around once a month."

"Had he been complaining about his heart lately?" Carella asked.

"Not to me, no. But you know how old men are. They don't take care of themselves."

"Was he complaining about his heart to anyone at *all*?" Meyer asked.

"Not that I know of."

"Then what makes you think he died of a heart attack?" Carella asked.

Cynthia looked first at him, and then at Meyer, and then at Carella again.

"I don't think I like either *one* of you," she said and walked out into the kitchen to stand alone by the window.

One of the technicians had been hovering. He caught Carella's eye now. Carella nodded and went over to him.

"Blue cashmere belt," the technician said. "Blue cashmere fibers over the door hook there. What do you think?"

"Where's the belt?"

"Near the chair there," he said, and indicated the easy chair near the room's single dresser. A blue bathrobe was draped over the back of the chair. The belt to the robe was on the floor, alongside the dead man's shoes and socks.

"And the hook?"

"Back of the bathroom door."

Carella glanced across the room. The bathroom door was open. A chrome hook was screwed into the door, close to the top.

"The robe has loops for the belt," the technician said. "Seems funny it's loose on the floor."

"They fall off all the time," Carella said.

"Sure, I know. But it ain't every day we get a guy dead in bed who looks like maybe he was hanged."

"How strong is that hook?"

"It doesn't have to be," the technician said. "All a hanging does is interrupt the flow of blood to the brain. That can be done by the weight of the head alone. We're talking an average of ten pounds. A *picture* hook can support that."

"You should take the detective's exam," Carella suggested, smiling.

"Thanks, but I'm already Second Grade," the technician said. "Point is, the belt coulda been knotted around the old man's neck and then thrown over the hook to hang him. That's if the fibers match."

"And provided he didn't customarily hang his robe over that hook."

"You looking for a hundred excuses to prove he died of natural causes? Or you looking for one that says it could've been homicide?"

"Who said anything about homicide?"

"Gee, excuse me, I thought that's what you were looking for, Detective."

"How about a suicide made to look like natural causes?"

"That'd be a good one," the technician agreed.

"When will you have the test results?"

"Late this afternoon sometime?"

"I'll call you."

"My card," the technician said.

"Detective?" a man's voice said.

Carella turned toward the kitchen doorway where a burly man in a dark gray coat with a black velvet collar was standing. The shoulders of the coat were damp with rain, and his face was raw and red from the cold outside. He wore a little mustache under his nose, and he had puffy cheeks, and very dark brown eyes.

"I'm Robert Keating," he said, walking toward Carella, but not extending his hand in greeting. His wife stood just behind him. They had obviously talked since he'd come into the apartment. There was an anticipatory look on her face, as if she expected her husband to punch one of the detectives. Carella certainly hoped he wouldn't.

"I understand you've been hassling my wife," Keating said.

"I wasn't aware of that, sir," Carella said.

"I'm here to tell you that better not be the case."

Carella was thinking it better not be the case that your wife came in here and found her father hanging from the bathroom door and took him down and carried him to the bed. That had better not be the case here.

"I'm sorry if there was any misunderstanding, sir," he said.

"There had better *not* be any misunderstanding," Keating said.

"Just so there won't be," Carella said, "let me make our intentions clear. If your father-in-law died of a heart attack, you can bury him in the morning, and you'll never see us again as long as you live. But if he died for some other reason, then we'll be trying to find out why, and you're liable to see us around for quite a while. Okay, sir?"

"This is a crime scene, sir," the technician said. "Want to clear the premises, please?"

"What?" Keating said.

*   *   *

12

At four-thirty that afternoon, Carella called the lab down-town and asked to talk to Detective/Second Grade Anthony Moreno. Moreno got on the phone and told him the fibers they'd lifted from the hook on the bathroom door positively matched sample fibers from the robe's blue cashmere belt.

Not ten minutes later, Carl Blaney called Carella to tell him that the autopsy findings in the death of Andrew Henry Hale were consistent with postmortem appearances in asphyxial deaths.

Carella wondered if Cynthia Keating's husband would accompany her to the squadroom when they asked her to come in.

Robert Keating turned out to be a corporate lawyer who was wise enough to recognize that the police wouldn't be dragging his wife in unless they had reason to believe a crime had been committed. He'd called a friend of his who practiced criminal law, and the man was here now, demanding to know what his client was doing in a police station, even though he'd already been informed that Mrs Keating had been *invited* here, and had arrived of her own volition, escorted only by her husband.

Todd Alexander was a stout little blond man wearing a navy blue sports jacket over a checkered vest and gray flannel trousers. He looked as if he might be more at home attending a yachting meet than standing here in one of the city's grubbier squadrooms, but his manner was that of a man who had dealt with countless bogus charges brought by hundreds of reckless police officers, and he seemed completely unruffled by the present venue or the circumstances that necessitated his being here.

"So tell me what this is all about," he demanded. "In twenty-five words or less."

Carella didn't even blink.

"We have a necropsy report indicating that Andrew Hale died of asphyxia," he said. "Is that twenty-five words or less?"

"Twelve," Meyer said. "But who's counting?"

"Evidence would seem to indicate that the belt from Mr Hale's cashmere robe was knotted and looped around his neck," Carella said, "and then dropped over the hook on the bathroom door in order to effect hanging, either suicidal or homicidal."

"What's that got to do with my client?"

"Your client seems to think her father died in bed."

"Is that what you told them?"

"I told them I found him in bed."

"Dead?"

"Yes," Cynthia said.

"Has Mrs Keating been informed of her rights?" Alexander asked.

"We haven't asked her any questions yet," Carella said.

"She just told me . . ."

"That was at the scene."

"You haven't talked to her since she arrived here?"

"She got here literally three minutes before you did."

"Has she been charged with anything?"

"No."

"Why is she here?"

"We want to ask her some questions."

"Then read her her rights."

"Sure."

"Don't sound so surprised, Detective. She's in custody, you're throwing around words like homicide, I want her to hear her rights. Then we'll decide whether she wants to answer any questions."

"Sure," Carella said again, and began the recitation he knew by heart. "In keeping with the Supreme Court decision in the case of Miranda versus Escobedo," he intoned, and advised her that she had the right to remain silent, asking her every step along the way if she understood what he was saying, told her she had the right to consult a lawyer, which she already had done, told her they would obtain a lawyer for her if she didn't have one, which no longer applied, told her that if she decided to answer questions with or without her lawyer present, she could call off the questioning at any time, do you understand, and finally asked if she wished to answer questions at this time, to which she responded, "I have nothing to hide."

"Does that mean yes?" Carella asked.

"Yes. I'll answer any questions you have."

"Where's that autopsy report?" Alexander asked.

"Right there on my desk."

Alexander picked it up, looked at it briefly . . .

"Who signed it?" he asked.

"Carl Blaney."

. . . seemed abruptly bored by it, and tossed it back onto the desk again.

"Did you also speak to Blaney in person?" he asked.

"Yes, I did."

"Did he have anything to add to his findings?"

"Only that because the ligature around the neck was soft and wide, there was only a faint impression of the loop on the skin. But the knot caused a typical abrasion under the chin."

"All right, ask your questions," Alexander said. "We haven't got all day here."

"Mrs Keating," Carella said, "what time did you get to your father's apartment this morning?"

"A little after ten."

"Did you call the Emergency Service number at ten-oh-seven A.M.?"

"I don't know the exact time."

"Would this refresh your memory?" Carella asked, and started to hand her a computer printout.

"May I see that, please?" Alexander said, and took it from Carella's hand. Again, he looked at the document only perfunctorily, handed it to Cynthia, and asked, "Did you make this call?"

"Well, may I see it?" she said.

He handed her the printout. She read it silently and said, "Yes, I did."

"Is the time correct?" Carella asked.

"Well, that's the time listed here, so I guess that's the time it was."

"Ten-oh-seven."

"Yes."

"Did you tell the operator that you'd just come into your father's apartment and found him dead in bed?"

"Yes, I did."

"Did you ask her to send someone right away?"

"I did."

"Here's the call sheet from Adam Two," Carella said. "Their time of arrival ..."

"Adam Two?" Alexander asked.

"From the precinct here. One of the cars patrolling Adam Sector from eight A.M. to four P.M. today. Mr Hale's apartment is in Adam Sector. They list their time of arrival as ten-fifteen A.M. And this is my own Detective Division report, which lists the time of *our* arrival as ten-thirty-one. My partner and I. Detective Meyer and myself."

"All of which is intended to prove *what*, Detective?"

"Nothing at all, sir, except the sequence of events."

"Remarkable," Alexander said. "Not twenty-four minutes after Mrs Keating called 911, there were no fewer than four policemen at the scene! Wonderful! But before you ask any more questions, may I ask where all this is going?"

"I want Mrs Keating to tell me what she did *before* she called 911."

"She's already told you. She came into the apartment,

found her father dead in his own bed, and immediately called the police. *That's* what she did, Detective."

"I don't think so."

"What do *you* think she did?"

"I don't know. But I *do* know she was in that apartment for almost forty minutes before she called the emergency number."

"I see. And how do you know that?"

"The super told me he saw her going in at nine-thirty."

"Is that true, Cynthia?"

"No, it's not."

"In which, case, I'd like to suggest that we call off the questioning and go about our more productive endeavors. Detective Carella, Detective Meyer, it's been a distinct . . ."

"He's down the hall," Carella said. "In the lieutenant's office. Shall I ask him to come in?"

"*Who* is down the hall?"

"The super. Mr Zabriski. He remembers it was nine-thirty because that's when he puts out the garbage cans each morning. The truck comes by at nine-forty-five."

The room was silent for a moment.

"Assuming you *do* have this super . . ." Alexander said.

"Oh, I have him, all right."

"And assuming he *did* see Mrs Keating entering the building at nine-thirty . . ."

"That's what he told me."

"What exactly do you think happened in that apartment between then and ten-oh-seven, when she called the emergency number?"

"Well," Carella said, "assuming she herself didn't hang her father from that bathroom hook—"

"Goodbye, Mr Carella," Alexander said, and rose abruptly. "Cynthia," he said, "leave us hie yonder. Bob," he said to her husband, "it's a good thing you called me. Mr Carella here is fishing for a murder charge."

"Try Obstruction," Carella said.

"What?"

"Or Tampering with Evidence."

"What?"

"Or both. You want to know what I think happened, Mr Alexander? I think Mrs Keating found her father hanging from that hook . . ."

"Let's go, Cynthia."

". . . and took him down and carried him to the bed. I think she removed . . ."

"Time's up," Alexander said cheerfully. "Goodbye, Detec . . ."

". . . the belt from his neck, took off his shoes and socks, and pulled a blanket up over him. *Then* she called the police."

"For what purpose?" Alexander asked.

"Ask *her*, why don't you? All *I* know is that Obstructing Governmental Administration is a violation of Section 195.05 of the Penal Law. And Tampering with Evidence is a violation of Section 215.40. Obstructing is a mere A-Mis, but . . ."

"You have no evidence of *either* crime!" Alexander said.

"I know that body was *moved!*" Carella said. "And that's Tampering! And for *that* one, she can get four years in jail!"

Cynthia Keating suddenly burst into tears.

The way she tells it . . .

"Cynthia, I think I should advise you," her attorney keeps interrupting over and over again, but tell it she will, the way all of them—sooner or later—will tell it if they will.

"The way it happened," she says, and now there are *three* detectives listening to her, Carella and Meyer who caught the squeal, joined by Lieutenant Byrnes, because all of a sudden this is interesting enough to drag him out of his corner office and into the interrogation room. Byrnes is wearing a brown suit, a wheat colored button-down shirt, a darker brown tie with a neat Windsor knot. Even dressed as he is, he gives the impression of a flinty Irishman who's just come in off the bogs where he's been gathering peat. Maybe it's the haircut. His gray hair looks windblown, even though there isn't a breeze stirring in this windowless room. His eyes are a dangerous blue; he doesn't like anyone messing with the law, male *or* female.

"I stopped by to see him," Cynthia says, "because he really hadn't been feeling too good these days, and I was worried about him. I'd spoken to him the night before . . ."

"What time was that?" Carella asks.

"Around nine o'clock."

All three detectives are thinking he was still alive at nine last night. *Whatever* happened to him, it happened sometime after nine P.M.

Her father's apartment is a forty-minute subway ride from where she lives across the river in Calm's Point. Her husband usually leaves for work at seven-thirty. Their habit is to have breakfast together in their apartment overlooking the river. After he's gone, she gets ready for her own day. They have no children, but neither does she work, perhaps because she never really trained for anything, and at thirty-seven there's nothing productive she can really do. Besides—

She has never mentioned this to a soul before but she tells it now in the cramped confines of the interrogation room, three detectives sitting attentively stone-faced on one side of the table, her husband and her attorney sitting equally detached on the other. She doesn't know why she admits this to these men now, here in this confessional chamber, at this moment in time, but she tells them without hesitation that she never thought of herself as being particularly bright, just an average girl (she uses the word "girl") in every

way, not too pretty, not too smart, just, well … Cynthia.
And shrugs.

Cynthia is not one of the Ladies Who Lunch, but
she nonetheless busies herself mindlessly throughout the
day, shopping, going to galleries or museums, sometimes
catching an afternoon movie, generally killing the time
between seven-thirty A.M. when her husband leaves for
work and seven-thirty at night, when he gets home. "He's
in corporate law," she says, as if this completely explains his
twelve-hour day. She is grateful, in fact, for the opportunity
to visit her father. It gives her something to *do*.

She does not, in all truth, enjoy her father's company
very much. She confesses this, too, to the pickup jury of five
men who sit noncommittally around the long table scarred
with the cigarette burns of too many long interrogations over
too many long years. It is almost as if she has been wishing to
confess forever. She has not yet said a word about Tampering
or Obstructing, but she seems willing to confess to everything
else she has ever done or felt. It suddenly occurs to Carella
that she is a woman who has nobody to talk to. For the first
time in her life, Cynthia Keating has an audience. And the
audience is giving her its undivided attention.

"He's a bore," she tells them. "My father. He was a
bore when he was young, and now that he's old, he's an even
bigger bore. Well, he used to be a *nurse*, is that an occupation
for a man? Now that he's retired, all he can talk about is
this or that patient he remembers when he worked at 'The
Hospital.' I don't think he even remembers *which* hospital it
was. It's just 'The Hospital.' This or that happened at 'The
Hospital.' It's all he ever talks about."

The detectives notice that she is still referring to her
father in the present tense, but this is not uncommon, and
does not register as anything significant. They are patiently
waiting for her to get to Tampering and Obstruction. That is
why they are here. They want to know what happened in that

apartment between nine o'clock last night and ten-oh-seven this morning, when she dialed 911.

She has dressed for today's weather in a green tweed skirt and turtleneck sweater she bought at the Gap. Low-heeled walking shoes and pantyhose to match the skirt. She likes walking. The forecasters have promised rain for later today . . .

It is, in fact, still raining as she continues her recitation, but none of the people in the windowless room know or care about what's happening outside . . .

. . . and so she is carrying a folding umbrella in a tote bag slung over her shoulder. The subway station isn't far from her apartment. She boards the train at about twenty to nine, and is across the river and in the city forty minutes later. It is only a short walk to her father's building. She enters it at about nine-thirty. She remembers seeing the super putting out his garbage cans. Her father lives on the third floor. It is not an elevator building, he can't afford that sort of luxury. His wonderful days at "The Hospital" left him precious little when he retired. As she climbs the stairs, the cooking smells in the hallway make her feel a bit nauseous. She pauses for breath on the third-floor landing, and then walks to apartment 3A and knocks. There is no answer. She looks at her watch. Nine thirty-five. She knocks again.

The things he does often cause her to become impatient at best or exasperated at worst. He *knows* she is coming here this morning, she told him last *night* that she'd be here. Is it possible he forgot? Has he gone out somewhere for breakfast? Or is he simply in the shower? She has a key to the apartment, which he gave to her after the last heart attack, when he became truly frightened he might die alone and lie moldering for days before anyone discovered his corpse. She rarely uses the key, hardly knows what it looks like, but she fishes in her bag among the other detritus there, and at last finds it in a small black leather purse that also contains the key to his safe deposit box, further insurance against a surprise heart attack.

She slips the key into the keyway, turns it. In the silence of the morning hallway—most people off to work already, except the woman somewhere down the hall cooking something revoltingly vile-smelling—Cynthia hears the small oiled click of the tumblers falling. She turns the knob, and pushes the door open. Retrieving her key, she puts it back into the black leather purse, enters the apartment . . .

"Dad?"

. . . and closes the door behind her.

Silence.

"Dad?" she calls again.

There is not a sound in the apartment.

The quiet is an odd one. It is not the expectant stillness of an apartment temporarily vacant but awaiting imminent return. It is, instead, an almost reverential hush, a solemn silence attesting to permanency. There is something so complete to the stillness here, something so *absolute* that it is at once frightening and somehow exciting. Something dread lies in wait here. Something terrifying is in these rooms. The silence signals dire expectation and sends a prickling shiver of anticipation over her skin. She almost turns and leaves. She is on the edge of leaving.

"I wish I had," she says now.

Her father is hanging on the inside of the bathroom door. The door is opened into the bedroom, and his hanging figure is the first thing she sees when she enters the room. She does not scream. Instead, she backs away and collides with the wall, and then turns and starts to leave again, actually steps out of the bedroom and into the corridor beyond, but the mute figure hanging there calls her back, and she steps into the bedroom again, and moves across the room toward the figure hanging on the inside of the bathroom door, a step at a time, stopping before each step to catch her breath and recapture her courage, looking up at the man hanging there and then looking down again to take another step, watching her inching feet, moving closer and closer to the door and the grotesque figure hanging there.

There is something blue wrapped around his neck. His head is tilted to one side, as if it had dropped that way when he fell asleep. The hook is close to the top of the door, and the blue—scarf, is it? a tie?—is looped over the hook so that her father's toes are an inch or so off the floor. She notices that he is barefoot and that his feet are blue, a blue darker and more purplish than the fabric knotted around his throat. His hands are blue as well, the same dark purplish-blue that resembles an angry bruise all over the palms and the fingers and the backs of the hands, open as if in supplication. He is wearing a white shirt and gray flannel trousers. His tongue is protruding from his mouth. It appears almost black.

She steps up close to his body hanging there.

She looks up into his face.

"Dad?" she says, disbelievingly, expecting him to stick his tongue out farther, perhaps make a razzing sound, break into a grin, she doesn't know what, something, anything that will tell her he's playing a game, the way he used to play games with her when she was a little girl, before he got old ... and boring ... and *dead*. Dead, yes. He does not move. He is dead. He is really and truly dead and he will never grin at her again. She stares into his wide-open eyes, as green as her own, but flecked with pinpricks of blood, her own eyes squinched almost shut, her face contorted not in pain, she feels no pain, she doesn't even feel any sense of loss or abandonment, she has not known this man for too long a time now. She feels only horror and shock, and anger, yes, inexplicable *anger*, sudden and fierce, why did he *do* this, why didn't he *call* somebody, what the fuck is the *matter* with him?

"I *never* use such language," she tells the five men listening to her, and the room goes silent again.

The police, she thinks. I have to call the police. A man has hanged himself, my *father* has hanged himself, I have to notify the police. She looks around the room. The phone. Where's the phone? He should have a phone by the bed, he has a heart problem, a phone should always be within—

She spots the phone, not alongside the bed but across the room on the dresser, would it have cost him a fortune to install another jack? Her mind is whirling with things she will have to do now, unexpected tasks to perform. She will have to call her husband first, "Bob, honey, my father's dead," they will have to make funeral arrangements, buy a casket, notify all his friends, who the hell *are* his friends? Her mother, too, she'll have to call her, divorced five years, she'll say, "Good, I'm glad!" But first the police, she is sure the police have to be notified in a suicide, she has read someplace or seen someplace that you have to call the police when you find your father hanging from a hook with his tongue sticking out. She is suddenly laughing hysterically. She covers her mouth with her hand, and looks over it like a child, and listens wide-eyed, fearful that someone will come in and find her with a dead man.

She waits several moments, her heart beating wildly in her chest, and then she walks to the telephone and is about to dial 911 when something occurs to her. Something just pops into her mind unbidden. She remembers the key to the safe deposit box in the little black leather purse, and she remembers her father telling her that among other things like his silver high school track medal there is an insurance policy in that box. It isn't much, her father told her, but you and Bob are the beneficiaries, so don't forget it's there. She also remembers hearing somewhere, or reading somewhere, or seeing somewhere on television or in the movies—there is so *much* information out there today—but anyway *learning* somewhere that if somebody kills himself the insurance company won't pay on his life insurance policy.

She doesn't know if this is true or not, but suppose it is? Neither does she know how much he's insured himself for, it probably isn't a great deal, he never did have any real money to speak of. But say the policy's for a hundred thousand dollars, or even fifty or twenty or ten, who cares? Should the insurance company get to keep all those premiums he's paid over the years simply because something was troubling him so much—what the hell was troubling you, Dad?—that he had to hang himself? She does not think that is fair. She definitely does not think that is fair.

On the other hand . . .

Suppose . . .

Just suppose . . .

Just suppose he died in his sleep of a heart attack or something? Just suppose whoever it is who has to write a death certificate finds him dead in bed of natural causes? Then there'd be no problem with the insurance company, and she and Bob would be able to collect on however much the policy is for. She thinks about this for a moment. She is amazingly calm. She has grown used to the silence of the apartment, her father hanging there still and lifeless. She looks at her watch. It is a quarter to ten. Has she been in the apartment for only ten minutes or so? Has it been that short a time? It seems an eternity.

She is thinking she will have to take him down and carry him to the bed.

She moves up close to the body again. Looks into his dead green eyes, studies the pores on his face, the pinprick points of blood, the ugly protruding tongue, summoning the courage she needs to touch him, thinking if she can stand this close to death without vomiting or soiling herself, then surely she will be able to touch him, move him.

The fabric around his neck looks like the belt from a robe. She sees that her father knotted the ends so that it formed a loop and then slipped the loop over his head and around his neck. He must have used a stool or something to climb onto when he put the loop over the hook, and then he must have kicked the stool away in order to suspend himself. But where's the stool? Or did he use something else? She can't worry about that just now. *However* he did it, he *did* it, and unless she can take him down and carry him to the bed, she and her husband will lose out on the insurance, it's as simple as that.

She does not in these next few moments even once consider the fact that she is doing something that will later enable her to commit insurance fraud, she does not for an instant believe she is breaking the law. She is merely correcting an oversight, her father's stupidity in not realizing that committing suicide might negate the terms of the insurance policy, if what she heard is true. She's sure it must be true, otherwise how could she have heard about it?

Well, she thinks, let's do it.

The first touch of him—his face against hers as she hunches one shoulder under his arm and with her free hand hoists the belt off the hook—is cold and repulsive. She feels her flesh puckering, and almost drops him in that instant, but clings tight in a macabre dance, half-dragging, half-carrying him to the bed where she plunks him down at once, his back and buttocks on the bed, his legs and feet trailing. She backs away in revulsion. She is breathing hard. He was heavier than she expected he would be. The belt is still looped around his neck like a wide blue necklace that matches his grotesque blue hands and feet. She puts one hand behind his head, feels again the clammy coldness of his flesh, lifts the head, and pulls the belt free. She unfastens the knot, and then carries the belt to the easy chair across the room, over which the matching blue robe is draped. She debates pulling the belt through the loops on the robe, starts to do that, her hands trembling now, loses patience with the task, and simply drops it on the floor, alongside his shoes and socks.

She looks at her watch again.

It is almost ten o'clock.

Somewhere a church bell begins tolling the hour.

The sound brings back a poignant memory she can't quite recall. A Sunday sometime long ago? A picnic preparation? A little girl in a flowered sunsuit? She stands listening to the tolling of the bell. The sound almost causes her to weep. She continues standing stock still in the silent apartment, the church bell tolling in the distance. And at last the bell stops. She sighs heavily, and goes back to the bed again.

Her father is lying crosswise on it, just the way she dropped him, on his back, his legs bent at the knees and trailing to the floor. She goes to him and lifts the legs, turning the body so that he is lying properly now, his head on the pillow, his feet almost touching the footboard. She frees the blanket from beneath him, draws it down to the foot of the bed. She knows it will appear odd that he is in bed with his clothes on, knows a safer pretense would be to disrobe him before pulling the blanket up over his chest. But she has never seen her father naked in her lifetime, and the prospect of undressing him, the horrible thought of seeing his naked body cold and blue and shriveled and dead is so chilling that she takes an involuntary step backward, shaking her head, as if refusing even to consider such an act. The horror, she thinks. The horror. And pulls the blanket up over him, to just beneath his chin, hiding all but his face from view.

She goes to the phone then, and dials 911, and calmly tells the operator that she's just found her father dead in bed and asks her to please send someone.

*   *   *

"The girl was in shock," Alexander said. "She didn't know what she was doing."

"She just told us she was planning insurance fraud," Carella said.

"No, she didn't say that at all. She doesn't even know what the policy *says*. Is there really a suicide exclusion clause in that policy? Who knows? All she knows is that there's a policy in her father's safe deposit box. What kind of policy, in what amount, she doesn't know. So how can you say she was planning insurance fraud?"

"Well, gee, Counselor," Carella said, "when someone tries to make a suicide look like a natural death . . ."

"She didn't want the world to believe her father killed himself," Alexander said.

"Bullshit," Lieutenant Byrnes said.

One of the female officers had taken Cynthia Keating down the hall to the ladies' room. The three detectives were still sitting at the long table in the interrogation room. Alexander was standing now, facing them, pleading his case as if he were facing a jury. The detectives looked as if they might be playing poker, which perhaps they were. Carella had taken the lead here, questioning the Keating woman, eliciting from her what amounted to a confession to at least two crimes, and perhaps a third: Attempted Insurance Fraud. He looked a bit weary after almost twelve hours on the job. Meyer sat beside him like a man holding a royal flush in spades, wearing on his face a look of supreme confidence. The lady had told them all they needed to know. Alexander could do his little dance from here to Honduras, but he couldn't tap his way out of this one. Sitting with cards like these, Meyer knew the lieutenant would tell them to book her on all three counts.

"You really want to send that girl to jail?" Alexander asked.

Which was a good question.

Did they?

She may have been *contemplating* insurance fraud while committing certain criminal acts in order to establish a later claim, but until she actually submitted the claim, she hadn't actually committed the fraud, had she? So was what she'd done really too terribly harmful to society? Did they really want to send her to prison with ladies who had cut up their babies and dropped them down the sewer? Did they really want to send a nice Calm's Point housewife to a place where she'd be forced to perform sexual acts upon hardened female criminals who'd murdered liquor store owners or garage attendants? Was that what they *really* wanted?

It was a good question.

Until Carl Blaney called at eight-thirty that night to say he was just heading home after having completed the full autopsy on Andrew Henry Hale. He thought Carella might like to hear the results.

"I was running a routine toxicological analysis on his hair," Blaney said. "Washed, desiccated, and extracted hair samples with organic solvents. Injected the extracts into the spectrometer, and compared the results against known library samples."

"What'd you find?"

"Tetrahydrocannabinol."

"English, Doc."

"Marijuana. Did you find any in the apartment?"

"No."

"But that's not all the hair revealed."

"What else?"

"Rohypnol."

"*Row*-fin-all?" Carella asked.

"R-O-H-Y-P-N-O-L," Blaney said. "The brand name for a drug called flunitrazepam."

"I never heard of it."

"We don't see much of it in this city. No emergency-room episodes, no deaths resulting from its use. It's a benzodiazepine, pretty popular in the South and Southwest. Young people use it in combination with alcohol and other drugs."

"I thought you said this was asphyxia."

"It was. Bear with me. The hair results sent me back for another look at his blood. This time I was focusing on flunitrazepam and its 7-amino metabolites. I found only moderate levels of the parent drug—concentrations not significant enough to have contributed to the fatality. But enough to conclude that he'd definitely ingested at least two milligrams."

"Indicating?"

"Indicating he couldn't possibly have hanged himself. He'd have been unconscious. You're looking at a homicide here."

And so it began.

Chapter Two

It was raining relentlessly on the morning of October thirtieth, a Saturday, the day after the body of Andrew Henry Hale was found dead in his bed in an apartment on Currey and Twelfth. Carella and Meyer came running out of the precinct and into the parking lot behind it, drenched to the bone before they'd taken half a dozen steps. Rain banged on the roof of the car. Rain drilled Carella's head as he fumbled the key into the lock on the driver's side, rain smashed his eyes, rain soaked the shoulders of his coat and plastered his hair onto his forehead. Meyer stood patiently hunched and hulking on the passenger side of the car, eyes squinched, drowning in the merciless rain.

"Just take all the time in the world," he suggested.

Carella finally got the key into the lock, twisted it open, hurried inside, and reached across the seat to unlock the other door for Meyer.

"Whoosh!" Meyer said, and pulled the door shut behind him.

Both men sat breathless for a moment, enclosed now in a rattling cocoon, the windshield and windows melting with rain. Behind them, the precinct lights glowed yellow, offering comfort and warmth, odd solace for a place they rarely associated with either. Meyer shifted his weight, reached into his back pants pockets for a handkerchief, and dried his face and the top of his bald head. Carella took several Dunkin' Donuts paper napkins from the side pocket on the door and tried to blot water from his soaked hair. "Boy," he said, and grabbed more napkins from the door.

Together, the two men in their bulky overcoats crowded the front seat of the "company car," as they mockingly called it. They were partnered as often as not, the twin peculiarities of exigency and coincidence frequently determining more effectively than any duty chart exactly who might be in the squadroom when the phone rang. They had caught the Hale squeal together yesterday morning. The case was now theirs until either they made an arrest or retired it in the so-called Open File.

Carella started the car.

Meyer turned on the radio.

The insistent chatter of police calls scratched at the beating rain. It took a while for the ancient heater to throw any real warmth into the car, adding its clanking clatter to the steady drumming of the rain, the drone of the dispatcher's voice, the hissing swish of tires on black asphalt. Cops on the job listened with one ear all the time, waiting to hear the dispatcher specifically calling their car, particularly waiting for the urgent signal that would tell them an officer was down, in which case every car in the vicinity would respond. Meanwhile, as the rain fell and the heater hurled uncertain hot air onto their faces and their feet, they talked idly about Carella's birthday party earlier this month—a subject he'd rather have forgotten since he'd just turned forty—and the trouble Meyer was having with his brother-in-law, who never had liked Meyer and who kept trying to sell him additional life insurance because he was in such a dangerous occupation.

"You think our occupation is dangerous?" he asked.

"Dangerous, no," Carella said. "Hazardous."

"Enough to warrant what he calls *combat* insurance?"

"No, I don't think so."

"I rented a video last week," Meyer said, "Robin Williams is dead in it, he goes to heaven. One of the worst movies I ever saw in my entire life."

"I never go to movies where somebody dies and goes to heaven," Carella said.

"What you should never do is go to a movie with the word 'Dream' in the title," Meyer said. "Sarah likes these pictures where movie stars die and go walking around so mere mortals can't see them. So you never heard of it, huh?" Meyer said.

"Never," Carella said, and smiled. He was thinking if you worked with a man long enough, you began reading his mind.

"Your kids aren't teenagers yet," Meyer said. "Rophies? Roofies? Rope? R2? Those are all names the kids use for it."

"New one on me," Carella said.

"It used to come in one- and two-milligram tablets," Meyer said. "Hoffman-La Roche—that's the company that manufactures it—recently pulled the two-mill off the retail market in Germany. But it's still available here. That's another name for it, by the way. La Roche. Or even just Roach. How much did Blaney say the old man had dropped?"

"At least two mills."

"Would've knocked him out in half an hour. It's supposed to be ten times stronger than Valium, no taste, no odor. You really never heard of it?"

"Never," Carella said.

"It's also called the Date-Rape drug," Meyer said. "When it first got popular in Texas, kids were using it to boost a heroin high or cushion a cocaine crash. Then some cowboy discovered if he dropped a two-mill tab in a girl's beer, it had the same effect as if she drank a six-pack.

In ten, twenty minutes, she's feeling no pain. She loses all inhibitions, blacks out, and wakes up the next morning with no memory of what happened."

"Sounds like science-fiction," Carella said.

"Small white tablet," Meyer said, "you can either dissolve it in a drink or snort it. Ruffies is another name. The Forget Pill, too. Or Roofenol. Or Rib. Costs three, four bucks a tab."

"Thanks for the input," Carella said.

The men were on their way to Andrew Hale's bank.

They were now in possession of a court order authorizing them to open his safe deposit box. Inside that box, by Cynthia Keating's own admission, there was an insurance policy on her father's life. Her husband had also told them that his law firm was in possession of her father's will, which left to husband and wife all of the old man's earthly possessions— which did not amount to a hell of a lot. A passbook they'd found in the apartment showed a bank balance of $2,476.12. The old man had also owned a collection of 78 rpm's dating back to the thirties and forties, none of them rare, all of them swing hits of the day—Benny Goodman, Harry James, Glenn Miller—played and replayed over and over again until the shellac was scratched and the grooves worn. There were a few books in the apartment as well, most of them dog-eared paperbacks. There was an eight-piece setting of inexpensive silver plate.

True enough, in a city where a five-dollar bill in a tattered billfold was often cause enough for murder, these belongings alone might have provided motive. But not for two people as well off as the Keatings. Besides, this had not been a case of someone choosing a random victim on the street and then popping him, something that happened all the time. Someone had gone to a great deal of trouble here, first drugging the old man and next hanging him. The prize had to be worth the trouble.

Carella pulled the car into a No Parking zone in front of the bank. He flipped down his visor to show the pink police paper that normally warned off any cop on the beat, and then stepped out of the car and dashed through the rain toward the front of the bank, Meyer pounding along behind him.

Their court order opened the dead man's safe deposit box, and sure enough, they found an insurance policy for $25,000, with Andrew Hale's daughter and son-in-law listed as sole beneficiaries. The policy did, in fact, contain a suicide exclusion clause:

Section 1.5 SUICIDE

If the insured dies by suicide within one year from the Date of Issue, the amount payable by the Company will be limited to the premiums paid.

But the policy had been issued almost ten years ago.

Thursday night was the night in question.

According to what Cynthia Keating had told them, she'd spoken to her father at nine that night, and had found him hanging dead at nine-thirty or so the next morning. A check with the telephone company confirmed that she had indeed called his number at 9:07 the night before, and had spent two minutes on the phone with him. This did not preclude her later taking the subway across the river and into the trees, going up to his apartment, dropping a few pills in his wine or his beer or his bottled water, and then hanging him over a hook.

But—

Cynthia maintained that after having telephoned her father, she had gone to meet her girlfriend Josie at the movie theater a block from her apartment and together they had seen a movie that started around 9:15 and ended around

11:45, after which she and her friend Josie had gone for tea and scones at a little snack bar called Westmore's. She had returned home at around twelve-thirty, and had not left the apartment again until the next morning at around twenty to nine, at which time she had taken the subway across the river, and walked to her father's apartment, only to find Dad, poor Dad, hanging in the closet, and I'm feeling so bad. The movie she'd seen was part of a Kurosawa retrospective. It was titled *High and Low*, and it was based on a novel by an American who wrote cheap mysteries. A call to the theater confirmed the title of the film and the start and finish times. A call to her girlfriend Josie Gallitano confirmed that she had accompanied Cynthia to the movie and had later enjoyed a cup of tea and a chocolate-covered scone with her. Cynthia's husband, as was to be expected, confirmed that he had found her asleep in bed when he got home from a poker game at around one o'clock. She had not left the apartment again that night.

There had been six other men in that poker game. Keating claimed that the game had started at eight o'clock and ended at around a quarter past midnight. The six other men confirmed that he had been there during the times he'd stated. His wife, as was to be expected, confirmed that he'd come home at around one A.M., and had not left the apartment again that night.

It appeared to the detectives that their two prime suspects had airtight alibis and that whoever had dropped Rohypnol into Andrew Hale's drink and draped him over a closet hook was still out there boogying someplace.

At Hale's funeral on Sunday morning, they listened to a minister who had never met the man telling his sole remaining relatives what a fine and upstanding human being he'd been. Cynthia Keating and her husband Robert listened dry-eyed. It was still raining when the first shovelful of earth was dumped onto Hale's simple wooden casket.

It was as if he had never existed.

From home that Sunday night, Carella called Danny Gimp.

"Danny?" he said. "It's Steve."

"Hey, Steve," Danny said. "Whatta ya hear?"

This was a joke. Danny Gimp was an informer. *He*— and not Carella—was the one who heard things and passed them on. For money. The men didn't exchange any niceties. Carella got right down to business.

"Old guy named Andrew Hale ..."

"*How* old?" Danny asked.

"Sixty-eight."

"Ancient," Danny said.

"Got himself aced Thursday night."

"Where?"

"Apartment off Currey Yard."

"What time?"

"ME puts it around midnight. But you know how accurate PMI's are."

"How'd he catch it?"

"Hanged. But first he was doped with a drug called Rohypnol. Ever hear of it?"

"Sure."

"You have?"

"Sure," Danny said.

"Anyway," Carella said, "the only two people who had any reason to want him dead have alibis a mile long. We're wondering if maybe they knew somebody handy with a noose."

"Uh-huh."

"He's a lawyer ..."

"The dead man?"

"No. One of the suspects."

"A criminal lawyer?"

"No. But he *knows* criminal lawyers."

"That doesn't mean he knows hit men."

"It means there could've been access."

"Okay."

"Ask around, Danny. There's twenty-five grand in insurance money involved here."

"That ain't a lot."

"I know. But maybe it's enough."

"Well, let me go on the earie, see what's what."

"Get back to me, okay?"

"If I hear anything."

"Even if you don't."

"Okay," Danny said, and hung up.

He did not get back to Carella until the following Sunday night, the seventh of November. By that time, the case was stone cold dead.

Danny came limping into the place he himself had chosen for the meet, a pizzeria on Culver and Sixth. The collar of his threadbare coat was pulled high against the wind and the rain. A long, college-boy, striped muffler was wrapped around his neck, and he was wearing woolen gloves. He peered around the place as if he were a spy coming in with nuclear secrets. Carella signaled to him. A scowl crossed Danny's face.

"You shouldn't do that," he said, sliding into the booth. "Bad enough I'm meeting you in a public place."

Carella was willing to forgive Danny his occasional irritability. He had never forgotten that Danny had come to the hospital when he'd got shot for the first time in his professional life. It had not been an easy thing for Danny to do; police informers do not last long on the job once it is known they are police informers. Danny's eyes were darting all over the place now, checking the perimeter. He himself had chosen the venue, but he seemed disturbed by it now, perhaps because it was unexpectedly crowded at nine A.M. on a Monday morning. Who the hell expected people eating *pizza* for breakfast? But he couldn't go to the station house, and he didn't want Carella to come to his shitty little room over on the South Side because to tell the truth, it embarrassed him. Danny had known better times.

He was thinner than Carella had ever seen him, his eyes rheumy, his nose runny. He kept taking paper napkins from the holder on the table, blowing his nose, crumpling the napkins and stuffing them into the pockets of his coat, which he had not yet removed. He did not look healthy. But more than that, he looked unkempt, odd for a man who'd always prided himself on what he considered sartorial elegance. Danny needed a shave. Soiled shirt cuffs showed at the edges of his ragged coat sleeves. His face was dotted with blackheads, his fingernails edged with grime. Sensing Carella's scrutiny, he said in seeming explanation, "The leg's been bothering me."

"I'm sorry to hear that."

"Yeah, it still bothers me. From when I got shot that time."

"Uh-huh."

Actually, Danny had never been shot in his life. He limped because he'd had polio as a child. But pretending he'd been wounded in a big gang shoot-out gave him a certain street cred he considered essential to the gathering of incidental information. Carella was willing to forgive him the lie.

"You want some pizza?" he asked.

"Coffee might be better," Danny said, and started to rise.

"Sit," Carella said, "I'll get it. You want anything with it?"

"The pastry looks good," Danny said. "Bring me one of them chocolate things, okay?"

Carella went up to the counter and came back some five minutes later with two chocolate eclairs and two cups of coffee. Danny was blowing on his hands, trying to warm them. A constant flow of traffic through the entrance doors and past the counter kept bringing in the cold from outside. He picked up his coffee cup, warmed his hands on that for a while. Carella bit into his chocolate eclair. Danny bit into his. "Oh, Jesus," he said, "that is delicious," and took another bite. "Oh, Jesus," he said again.

"So what've you got?" Carella asked.

$25,000 was a big-enough prize in a city where you could buy anyone's dead ass for a subway token. If Robert Keating and his wife Cynthia had been otherwise engaged while her father was being hoisted and hanged, the possibility existed that they'd hired someone to do the job for them. In this city, you could get anything done to anybody for a price. You want somebody's eyeglasses smashed? You want his fingernails pulled out? His legs broken? You want him more seriously injured? You want him hurt so he's an invalid the rest of his life? You want him skinned, you want him burned, you want him—don't even mention it in a whisper—*killed*? It can be done. Let me talk to someone. It can be done.

"I've got quite a lot, actually," Danny said, seemingly more involved in his eclair than in doing business.

"Oh really?" Carella said.

On the phone last night, Danny had said only that he'd come up with something interesting. This morning, it seemed to be more than that. But perhaps this was just the prelude to negotiation.

Actually, Danny knew that what he had was very good stuff. So good, in fact, that it might be worth more money than Carella was used to paying. He hated negotiating with someone he considered an old friend, though he was never quite sure Carella shared the sentiment. At the same time, he didn't want to pass on information that could conceivably lead to a bust in a murder case, and then have Carella toss fifty bucks or so across the table. This was too good for that kind of chump change.

"I know who did it," he said, flat out.

Carella looked surprised.

"Yeah, I got lucky," Danny said, and grinned. His teeth looked bad, too. He was clearly not taking good care of himself.

"So let me hear it," Carella said.

"I think this is worth at least what the killer got," Danny said, lowering his voice.

"And how much is that?"

"Five grand," Danny said.

"You're joking, right?"

"You think so?" Danny said.

Carella did not think so.

"I'd have to clear that kind of money with the lieutenant," he said.

"Sure, clear it. But I don't think this guy's gonna hang around very long."

"What can I tell him?"

"Who?"

"My lieutenant."

Five thousand was a lot of money to hand over to an informer. The squadroom slush fund sometimes rose higher than that, depending on what contributions went into it in any given month. Nobody asked questions about a few bucks that disappeared during drug busts hither and yon, provided the money went into what was euphemistically called "The War Chest". But a big drug intercept on the docks downtown had slowed traffic in the precinct these past two months, and Carella wondered now if there was that much contingency cash lying around. He further wondered if the lieutenant would turn over that kind of money to a stoolie. Danny's information would have to be pure gold to justify such an outlay.

"Tell him I know who did it and I know where he is," he said. "If that ain't worth five grand, I'm in the wrong business."

"How'd you get this?" Carella asked.

"Fellow I know."

"How'd *he* get it?"

"Straight from the horse's mouth."

"Give me something I can run with."

"Sure," Danny said. "Your man was in a poker game."

"You talking about Robert Keating?" Carella said, surprised.

"No. Who's Robert Keating?"

"Then who do you mean?"

"The guy you're looking for," Danny said. "He was in a poker game this past Saturday night."

"Okay."

"Who's Robert Keating?" Danny asked again.

"Nobody," Carella said. "What about this game?"

"Your man was betting big."

"How big?"

"Thousand-dollar pots. Came in with a five-grand stake, worked it up to twenty before the night was through. Big winner."

"Is he a gambler?"

"No, he's a hit man who just *likes* to gamble."

"He from this city?"

"Houston, Texas. And heading back there."

"When?"

"Sometime this Wednesday. You want him, you better move fast. Funny about Houston, ain't it?"

Carella did not think there was anything funny about Houston.

"It must drive foreigners crazy," Danny said. "The way words are spelled the same, but pronounced different. In English, I mean."

"How does this *guy* spell his name?" Carella asked, fishing.

"Ho ho," Danny said. "There's a street in New York, you know, it's spelled exactly the same as the city in Texas, but it's pronounced *House*-ton Street. Instead, we say *Youse*-ton, Texas, after *Sam* Youse-ton, is the way he pronounced his name. Which is peculiar, don't you think?"

"How does this hit man pronounce his name?"

"Ho, ho, *ho*," Danny said, and shook his finger.

"Who hired him?" Carella said. "Can you tell me that?"

"I don't know who hired him."

"Why was the old man killed?"

"Somebody wanted what he had and he wouldn't turn it over. So they took him out of the picture."

"They?"

"Whoever."

"More than one person?"

"I don't know that for sure."

"You said 'they.'"

"Just an expression. All I know is the only way to get what they wanted was to have him dusted."

"The old man didn't have a pot to piss in, Danny."

"I'm telling you what I heard."

"From who?"

"My friend. Who got it straight from the hitter."

"He told your friend he *killed* somebody?"

"Of course not."

"I didn't think so."

"But he told him enough."

"Like what?"

"Drunk talk. Suppose this, suppose that."

"Suppose *what*, Danny?"

"Okay, *suppose* there's this old fart got something somebody else wants real bad and he won't part with it? And *suppose* this something is worth a lotta money? And *suppose* . . ."

"This is our man talking?"

"This is him. *Suppose* somebody's willing to pay a person five large to get rid of the old man and make it look like an accident? And *suppose* . . ."

"Did he use that word? Accident?"

"Yeah."

"And the price was five grand?"

"The same five he brought into the poker game."

"When did he tell your friend all this?"

"Saturday night. After the game. They went back to his hotel room, had a few drinks, smoked a few joints."

"Who supplied them?"

"The drinks?"

"The drinks, the pot."

"The hitter. It was his party. I gotta tell you something, Steve. When a guy makes a big score, and then he quadruples it in a card game, he wants to *talk* about it, you dig? He's *proud* of it. That's the way these guys' minds work. They want to tell you how great they are. My friend lost his shirt in that game Saturday night. Well, winners like to shit all over losers. So your hitter took pity on my friend, asked him to share a bottle and a couple of joints with him so he could tell him how fuckin terrific he is, gettin five grand to dust an old fart."

"But he didn't tell him that."

"The five grand, yes. The actual dusting, no."

"Then you've got nothing to sell."

"Oh, I've got plenty to sell. Remember what you told me on the phone? You asked did I hear anything on this old man got doped with R2 before somebody hung him in the closet. That ain't the kind of detail a person forgets, Steve. Well, before my friend left the hotel room—I think they had sex, by the way. My friend and the hitter. He's gay, my friend. Anyway, the hitter handed him a little present. A gift for the loser, you know? A consolation prize. Said it'd help his sex life. Grinning, right? It'll help your sex life, Harpo, give it a try. That's my friend's name, Harpo. So Harpo figured the guy was laying a Viagra cap on him. But instead, it was this." Danny reached into his coat pocket. He opened his hand. A blister-pack strip of white tablets was on the palm, the word *Roche* echoing over and again across its face. "Roach," Danny said. "Same as your hangman used."

"Who gave you that?"

"Harpo."

"Harpo what?"

"Marx," Danny said, and grinned like a barracuda.

"Let me get this straight."

"Sure."

"Poker game Saturday night ..."

"Right on Lewiston Avenue."

"Guy who killed Andrew Hale comes into the game with five grand, leaves it with twenty. Invites your friend Harpo up for a drink, some pot, a little sex, starts boasting about the hit, lays a strip of roach on him before they part company."

"You've got it."

"And you say the hitter's leaving town the day after tomorrow?"

"From what I understand."

"This isn't any high-pressured bullshit, is it, Danny?"

"Me? High-pressured?"

"I mean, he really *is* going back to Houston this Wednesday?"

"Is what Harpo told me."

"And he also told you the guy's name ..."

"He did."

"... and where he's staying."

"That's right."

"Out of the goodness of his heart."

"He's a friend. Also, I'll probably pass a little something on to him if your lieutenant comes through."

"I'll have to get back to you on this," Carella said.

"Sure, take your time," Danny said. "You got till Wednesday."

"I'll let you know," Carella said, and started to move out of the booth, suddenly remembering how cold it was outside on this eighth day of November. You got to be forty, and suddenly it was cold out there. He was sliding across the leatherette seat, swinging his legs out, starting to rise, Danny doing the same thing on the other side of the table, when the first shot pierced the din of the abnormally crowded room, silencing it in an instant. Even before the second shot sounded, people were diving under tables. It took a moment for Carella to spot the two gunmen advancing swiftly toward the booth, one black, one white, equal opportunity employment. It took another moment for him to realize Danny Gimp was their target.

His coat was already unbuttoned, he reached across his waist for a cross-body draw, the nine-millimeter Glock snapping out of its holster with a spring-assisted click. There were more shots. Someone screamed. Danny was scrambling across the floor on his hands and knees, trailing blood. A man running for the entrance doors knocked over one of the serving counters, and pizza toppings spilled all over the floor, tomato sauce running into anchovies and mushrooms and grated cheese and slippery slices of pepperoni. Carella upended a table, and ducked behind it. There was more screaming, two more shots very close by, footsteps pounding. He raised his head in time to see the gunmen running toward the front of the place, leaped to his feet, began chasing after them. There was still too much background for him to risk firing. He followed them out into the street, thought he had a clear shot, but they turned the corner in that instant and were gone.

Shit, he thought.

The last two shots Carella heard had been fired at close range into Danny's head. The shot near his cheek was fired with the muzzle of the gun almost touching the skin; there was a cluster of soot on the flesh but hardly any gunpowder around the wound itself. The shot closer to Danny's chin was fired from a few inches away; gunpowder particles were diffused over a two-inch diameter and the wound was encircled by a small area of soot. Danny was already dead when Carella knelt beside him.

A patrolman pounded into the pizzeria with his gun drawn, scaring the patrons even further, yelling "Stand back, everybody keep back," like an extra in an action-adventure movie. Tables and chairs had been overturned in the mad rush that virtually cleared the place of customers. But many of the patrons still lingered, either curious to see what a bleeding body looked like close up, or else hoping to wave to the television cameras if and when they got here. There was nothing jackasses liked better than to grin and wave at the camera while tragedy was unfolding in the foreground.

"I'm on the job," Carella told the patrolman. "Get an ambulance here."

A second patrolman entered the place now, his gun also drawn, his eyes wide, his face pale. He had never seen a dead body before except for that time in a funeral home when his uncle Pete died of sclerosis of the liver. The first patrolman, similarly inexperienced, was already on his mobile phone, telling Sergeant Murchison at the Eight-Seven that there'd been a shoot-out in the pizzeria on Culver and Sixth, Guido's, the place was called. "There's one person down, better send a meat wagon," he actually called it, causing Murchison to wince.

The television cameras arrived some five minutes before either the ambulance or a second car from adjoining Charlie Sector angled into the curb. A woman wearing a fake fur that *looked* fake told the roving reporter that all at once these two big guys came in and started shooting at the man lying on the floor over there, at which point the camera operator panned over to where Danny was lying in an ocean of slippery pizza toppings, blood and tomato sauce mingling to create an op-art camera op. The second patrolman told everybody to keep back; he was wondering if he should put up some of those yellow CRIME SCENE tapes he had in the trunk of the patrol car. Two teenagers wearing woolen watch caps, ski parkas, and baggy pants tried to position themselves behind the victim so they could grin and wave at the camera, but they were too late. The camera operator had already turned to the entrance door, where a pair of detectives from the Eight-Seven were walking in looking very official and busy, shields pinned to their overcoats, faces raw from the biting cold outside. Behind them, an ambulance was pulling in, which made for another good shot, the detectives with long strides and flapping overcoats, the flashing red lights on the ambulance, this was the camera operator's lucky day.

Arthur Brown, one of the responding detectives, would later tell everyone in the squadroom that even before Carella informed him, he knew the guy laying on the floor there was dead. The detective with Brown was Bert Kling. The minute he spotted Carella, he went over to him and asked, "What happened?"

"Two hitters nailed Danny Gimp," Carella said, and got to his feet, his coat sleeve stained with blood from Danny's wounds, the knees of his trousers soiled from all the pizza shit on the floor.

They all stood around while the stretchers came in.

The paramedics realized at once that there wasn't any urgency about getting Danny aboard.

Chapter Three

Since there were two homicides on the table this Tuesday morning—an unusual circumstance, even for the Eight-Seven—Lieutenant Byrnes told the detectives assembled in his office that he'd be skipping over all the usual shit and getting directly to the murders, if nobody had any objections. Andy Parker didn't think the murder of a two-bit stool pigeon should take priority over a drug bust he'd been trying to set up for the past two weeks, but he knew better than to challenge the lieutenant when he was wearing what Parker referred to privately as his "Irish Look."

Hal Willis wasn't too tickled to be passed over, either. He'd caught a burglary yesterday where the perp had left chocolate-covered donuts on his victim's pillow. This looked a lot like what the Cookie Boy used to do, but he'd jumped bail in August and was now only God knew where. So this guy was obviously a copycat, which similarity might have made for a little early morning amusement if the lieutenant hadn't pulled the chain. Like teenagers invited to a party and then requested not to dance, please, the two detectives slouched sourly against the wall, arms folded across their chests in unmistakable body language. They didn't even sniff at the bagels and coffee on the lieutenant's desk, a treat—or more accurately a bribe to encourage punctuality—paid for by the squadroom slush fund every Tuesday.

This was eight o'clock in the morning. A harsh, bright sunlight streamed through Byrnes's corner windows. All told, and including the lieutenant, there were eight detectives in the office. Artie Brown and Bert Kling had responded to the pizzeria shoot-out and were looking for anything they could get on the two shooters. Carella and Meyer wanted to explore the Hale case. The two detectives sulking against the wall didn't care to offer their thoughts on anything. They'd been shut out, and they were miffed, although Byrnes seemed blithely unaware of their annoyance. Cotton Hawes was neutral. His plate was clean at the moment. In fact, he'd been in court testifying all last week. Sitting in a leather easy chair opposite the lieutenant's desk, feeling curiously uninvolved, like a cop visiting from another city, he listened as the lieutenant summarized the two homicide cases, and then asked, "You think they're linked?"

"Maybe," Carella said.

"Meyer?" Byrnes asked.

"Only if they were trying to shut Danny up."

"You sure they weren't after Steve?"

"No, it was Danny," Kling said.

"Neither of them even fired a shot at me."

"Ten, twelve people saw them go straight for Danny," Brown said.

"They'd seen a lot of movies."

"Kept describing it as a gangland execution."

"In broad daylight?" Hawes asked, and shook his head skeptically. He was sitting in sunlight. It caught his red hair, setting it on fire. The single white streak over his left temple looked like a patch of melting snow.

"Nobody says your goons are brain surgeons."

"Black and white, huh?"

"And red all over."

"Could've been an old beef," Hawes suggested. "Finally caught up with him."

"Be a coincidence, the day he's meeting with Steve. But I buy coincidence," Byrnes said. "I've been a cop long enough."

"Coulda been they wanted him before he told Steve whatever it was he had to tell him," Brown said. He was straddling a wooden chair near the bookcases, a huge man with skin the color of a giant grizzly's coat. His shirt collar was open, and he was wearing over it a green sweater. His arms were resting on the chair's top rail.

"*Did* he tell you anything?" Kling asked. "Before they got him?"

"Not really. He wanted to get paid first."

"Gee, there's a surprise."

"How much was he looking for?" Hawes asked.

"Five grand."

Hawes whistled.

"What'd he promise?" Willis asked, giving in at last to his curiosity. He was the shortest man on the squad, wiry and intense, dark eyes reflecting the day's cold light. Parker turned to him with a sharp look, as if his best friend in the entire world had suddenly moved to Anniston, Alabama, to wallow in pig shit.

"He said he knew the name and address of the guy who did Hale," Carella said.

"Where'd he get *that*?" Willis asked, totally involved now. Parker stepped a little bit away from him.

"Pal of his was in a poker game with the hitter."

"Let me get this straight," Hawes said. "Danny was in a poker game with the hitter?"

"No, no," Meyer said. "A *friend* of Danny's was in the game."

"With the guy who hung Hale from the bathroom door?"

"Hanged him, yeah."

"Yeah, him?"

"The very."

"What is this, a movie?" Willis asked.

"I wish," Carella said.

"I'da paid him on the spot," Parker said suddenly, and then realized with a start that he'd broken his own sullen silence. Everyone turned to him, surprised by the vehemence in his voice, surprised, too, that he'd bothered to shave this morning. "That kind of information," he said, plunging ahead, "I'da asked him to wait while I went to rob a bank."

"I should've," Carella said.

"Who's this pal of his?" Kling asked. He was wearing this morning a brown leather jacket that looked like it had come from Oklahoma or Wyoming, but which he'd bought off a pushcart at a street fair this summer. Blond and hazel-eyed, with a complexion and lashes most women would kill for, he projected a country bumpkin air that worked well in Good Cop/Bad Cop scenarios. He was particularly well-paired with Brown, whose perpetual scowl could sometimes be intimidating. "Did Danny give you a clue?"

"Somebody named Harpo."

"It *is* a movie," Willis said.

"Harpo what?"

"Didn't say."

"He's gay," Meyer offered.

"White, black?"

"Didn't say."

"Where'd the card game take place?"

"Lewiston Av."

"The Eight-Eight."

"Yeah."

"Probably black," Parker said. "The Eight-Eight."

Brown looked at him.

"What?" Parker said. "Did I say something bothered you?"

"I don't know *what* you said."

"I said a card game in the Eight-Eight, you automatically figure black players," Parker said, and shrugged. "Anyway, fuck you, you're so sensitive."

"What'd I do, *look* at you?" Brown asked.

"You looked at me cockeyed."

"Break it up, okay?" Byrnes said.

"Just don't be so fuckin sensitive," Parker said. "Everybody in the world ain't out to shoot you a hundred and twelve times."

"Hey!" Byrnes said. "Did you hear me, or what?"

"I heard you. He's too fuckin sensitive."

"One more time, Andy," Brown said.

"*Hey!*" Byrnes shouted.

"All I'm sayin," Parker said, "is if this was a black card game, then Danny's friend Harpo, *and* the guy who hanged Hale, could *both* be black, is all I'm sayin."

"Point taken," Brown said.

"Boy," Parker said, and rolled his eyes.

"We finished here?" Byrnes asked.

"If we're finished," Parker said, "I'd like to talk about settin up a bust on a . . ."

"I meant are *you* two finished with this *bullshit* here?"

"What bullshit?" Parker asked.

"Let it go, Pete," Brown said.

Byrnes glared at both of them. The room was silent for several moments. Hawes cleared his throat.

"It's possible, you know," he said, "that one of the two shooters in the pizzeria was the guy who also did Hale."

"How do you mean?"

"He finds out Harpo told Danny about him, figures he'll take Danny off the board before he spreads the word. That's possible, too, you know."

"A hangman suddenly becomes a shooter?" Parker said.

"It's possible."

"There's a twenty-five grand policy, huh?" Willis said.

"Daughter and son-in-law the sole beneficiaries," Carella said.

"They know about it?"

"Oh yes."

"They're alibied to the hilt," Meyer said.

"So you're figuring a contract job."

"Is what Danny said it was. He said the killer got five grand to do the old man."

"Were those his exact words?" Byrnes asked.

"No, he said the old man had something somebody else wanted real bad and he wouldn't part with it. Something worth a lot of money."

"What'd he say about having him killed?"

"He said somebody was willing to pay five grand to kill the old man and make it look like an accident."

"But why?" Willis asked.

"What do you mean why?"

"You said the old man had something somebody else wanted ..."

"Right."

"So how's this somebody gonna *get* it if he has the old man killed?"

The detectives fell silent, thinking this over.

"Had to be the insurance money," Hawes said at last.

"Only thing anyone could get by having him killed."

"Which leads right back to the daughter and son-in-law."

"Unless there's something else," Carella said.

"Like what?"

"Was the guy tortured?" Hawes asked.

"No."

"Cause maybe the killer was *trying* to get whatever it was, and when he *couldn't* ..."

"No, he wasn't tortured," Meyer said. "The killer doped him and hanged him. Period."

"Smoked some pot with him, dropped roofers in his drink ..."

"Which is what the guy in the card game offered Harpo."

"Did these two guys know each other?" Parker asked.

"They met in the card game."

"Not *them* two. I'm talking about the old man and the guy who killed him."

Again, the room went silent. They were all looking at Parker now. Sometimes a great notion.

"I mean, were they buddies or something? Cause otherwise, how'd he get in the apartment? And how come they were smoking pot together and drinking together? They had to know each other, am I right?"

"I don't see how," Carella said. "Danny told me the killer was a hit man from Houston. Going back there tomorrow."

"Told you everything but what you wanted to know, right?"

"Did the old man ever go to Houston?" Byrnes asked.

"Well, I don't know."

"What *do* you know about him?"

"Not much. Not yet."

"Find out. And soon."

"Did he leave a will?" Hawes asked.

"Left everything he had to the kids."

"Which was what?"

"*Bupkes,*" Meyer said.

"What's that?" Parker asked.

"Rabbit shit."

"So then what's this *something* somebody wanted bad enough to kill for?"

"The MacGuffin," Hawes said.

"I told you," Willis said. "It's a fuckin movie."

"Movie, my ass," Byrnes said. "Get some composites made from the witnesses in that pizza joint. Let's at least find two guys who came in blazing in broad daylight, can we? And find out where that poker game took place. There has to be . . ."

"On Lewiston," Carella said. "Up in the . . ."

"*Where* on Lewiston? Our man's leaving *town* tomorrow."

The room went silent.

"I want you to treat this like a single case with Danny as the connecting link," Byrnes said. "One of the guys in that poker game *knew* Danny, and another one may have killed Hale. Let's find out who was *in* the damn game. And find out who that old man really *was*. He didn't exist in a vacuum. Nobody does. If he had something somebody wanted, find out what the hell it was. If it was just the insurance policy, then stay with the Keatings till you nail them. I want the four of you who caught the squeals to work this as a team. Split the legwork however you like. But *bring* me something."

Carella nodded.

"Meyer?"

"Yeah."

"Artie? Bert?"

"We hear you."

"Then do it," Byrnes said.

"What about my dope bust?" Parker asked.

"Stay," Byrnes said, as if he were talking to a pit bull.

There were several training exercises at the academy, each designed to illustrate the unreliability of eye witnesses. Each of them involved a variation on the same theme. During a class lecture, someone would come into the room, interrupting the class, and then go out again. The cops-in-training would later be asked to describe the person who'd entered and departed. In one exercise, the intruder was merely someone who went to one of the windows, opened it, and walked out again. In another, it was a woman who came in with a mop and a pail, quickly mopped a small patch of floor, and went out again just as quickly. In a more vivid exercise, a man came in firing a pistol, and then rushed out at once. In none of these exercises was the intruder accurately described afterward.

Brown, Kling, and the police artist interviewed fourteen people that Tuesday morning. Only one of them—Steve Carella—was a trained observer, but even he had difficulty describing the two shooters who'd marched into the pizzeria at ten minutes past nine the day before. Of all the witnesses who'd been there at the time, only two blacks and four whites remembered anything at all about the men. The white witnesses found it hard to say what the black shooter had looked like. If they'd been asked to tell the difference between Morgan Freeman, Denzel Washington, Eddie Murphy, and Mike Tyson, there'd have been no problem. Maybe. But when the police artist asked them to choose from representative eyes, noses, mouths, cheeks, chins, and foreheads, all at once all black men looked alike. Then again, they might have had similar difficulty describing an Asian suspect.

In the long run—like many other decisions in America—the result was premised on race. The blacks had better luck describing the black suspect, and the whites had better luck with the white one. The detectives were less than satisfied with what the artist finally delivered. They felt the composite sketches were ... well ... sketchy at best.

When Carella and Meyer walked in late that Tuesday

morning, Fat Ollie Weeks was sitting alone in a booth at the rear of the diner, totally absorbed in his breakfast. Acknowledging their presence with a brief nod, Ollie stabbed a sausage with his fork and hoisted it immediately to his mouth. A ribbon of egg yolk dribbled from the sausage onto Ollie's tie, where it joined a medley of other crusted and hardened remnants of breakfasts, lunches, and dinners devoured in haste. Ollie always ate as if expecting an imminent famine. He picked up his cup, swallowed a huge gulp of coffee, and then smiled in satisfaction and at last looked across the table at the two visiting cops. He did not offer his hand; cops rarely shook hands with each other, even during social encounters.

"So what brings you up here?" he asked.

"The murder yesterday," Carella said.

"What murder?" Ollie asked. Here in Zimbabwe West, as he often referred to his beloved Eighty-eighth Precinct, there were murders every day of the week, every minute of the day.

"An informer named Danny Gimp," Carella said.

"I know him," Ollie said.

"Two shooters marched into Guido's Pizzeria while we were having a conversation," Carella said.

"Maybe they were after you," Ollie suggested.

"No, I'm universally well-liked," Carella said. "They were after Danny, and they got him."

"Where's Guido's?"

"Culver and Sixth."

"That's *your* turf, man."

"Lewiston isn't."

"Okay, I'll bite."

"A pal of Danny's was in a poker game a week ago Saturday," Meyer said. "On Lewiston Avenue."

"Met a hitter from Houston who later treated him to a little booze, a little pot, some casual sex, and a strip of roofers."

"Uh-huh," Ollie said, and signaled to the waitress. "So what's that got to do with me?"

"Lewiston is up here in the Eight-Eight."

"So? I'm supposed to know every shitty little card game in the precinct?" Ollie said. "Give me another toasted onion bagel with cream cheese," he told the waitress. "You guys want anything?"

"Just coffee," Meyer said.

"The same," Carella said.

"You got that?" Ollie asked the waitress, who nodded and walked off toward the counter. "You think this card game's gonna lead you to the shooters?"

"No, we think it's gonna lead us to the hitter from Houston."

"World's just *full* of hitters these days, ain't it?" Ollie said philosophically. "You think your Houston hitter and the two pizzeria shooters are connected?"

"No."

"Then what are you . . . ?"

"Don't you work in the Eight-Three?" the waitress asked, and put down Ollie's bagel and the two coffees.

"I *used* to work in the Eight-Three," Ollie said. "I got transferred."

"You want more coffee?"

"Ah, yes, m'dear," Ollie said, doing his world-famous W. C. Fields imitation. "If it's not too much trouble, ah, yes."

"You like it here better than the Eight-Three?" the waitress asked, pouring.

"I like it better wherever *you* are, m'little chickadee."

"Sweet talker," she said, and smiled and walked off, shaking her considerable booty.

"People ask me that all the time," Ollie said. "Don't you work in the Eight-Three? As if I don't know where the fuck I work. As if I'm making a fuckin mistake about where I work.

The world's full of people playin *Gotcha!* They got nothin to do with their time but look for mistakes. Ain't your middle name Lloyd? Hell, no, it's Wendell. Oliver Wendell Weeks, I don't know my own fuckin middle name? If I told you once it was Lloyd or Frank or Ralph, I was lying, it was all part of my fuckin cover."

A faint effluvial odor seemed to rise from Ollie whenever he became agitated, as he was now. Ignoring his own bodily emanations, he picked up the bagel and bit into it, his gnashing teeth unleashing a gush of cream cheese that spilled onto the right lapel of his jacket.

"Has this guy got a name?" he asked. "The fag was in the card game with your hitter?"

"Harpo," Carella said.

"Works at the First Bap?" Ollie said.

Both detectives looked at him.

"Only Harpo I know up here," Ollie said. "I'm surprised he was in a card game, though. *If* it's the same guy."

"Harpo what?" Meyer asked.

"His square handle is Walter Hopwell, don't ask me how it got to be Harpo. I never knew he was queer till you guys mentioned it just now. Goes to show, don't it? Ain't you hungry?" he asked, and signaled to the waitress again. "Bring my friends here some more coffee," he said, "they're famous sleuths from a neighboring precinct. And I'll have one of them croissants there." He pronounced the word as if he were fluent in French, but it was only his stomach talking. "Thing I'm askin myself," he said, "is how come a white stoolie is pals with a Negro fag?"

Ollie liked using the word "Negro" every now and then because he believed it showed how tolerant he was, even though he realized it pissed off persons of color who preferred being called either blacks or African-Americans. But it had taken him long enough to learn how to say "Negro," so if they wanted to keep changing it on him all the time, they could go fuck themselves.

"Would he be at the church now?" Carella asked.

"Should be. They got a regular office setup on the top floor."

"Let's go," Meyer said.

"You wanna start a race riot?" Ollie asked, and grinned as if he relished the prospect. "The First Bap's listed as a sensitive location. I was you, I'd look up Mr Hopwell in the phone book, go see him when he gets home from work."

"Our man's leaving town tomorrow," Carella said.

"In that case, darlings, let me finish my breakfast," Ollie said. "Then we can all go to church."

Brown's mother used to call her "The Barber's Wife." This was another name for the neighborhood gossip. The theory was that a guy went to get a haircut or a shave, he was captive in the barber's chair for an hour or so, he told the barber everything on his mind. The barber went home that night, and over supper told his wife everything he'd heard from all his customers all day long. The Barber's Wife knew more about what was happening in any neighborhood than any cop on the beat. What Brown and Kling wanted to do now was find The Barber's Wife in Andrew Hale's building.

There were six stories in the building, three tenants to each floor. When they got there that morning at a little past ten, most of the tenants were off to work. They knocked on six doors before they got an answer, and then another two before they found the woman they were looking for. Her apartment was on the same floor as Andrew Hale's. She lived at the far end of the hall, in apartment 3C. When she asked them to come in, please, they hesitated on the door sill because she was cooking something that smelled unspeakably vile.

The stench was coming from a big aluminum pot on the kitchen stove. When she lifted the lid to stir whatever was inside the pot, noxious clouds filled the air, and Kling caught sight of a bubbling liquid that appeared viscous and black. He wondered whether there was eye of newt in the pot. He wanted to go outside in the hall again, to throw up. But the woman invited them into a small living room where, mercifully, there was an open window that rendered the stink less offensive. They sat on a sofa with lace doilies on the arms and back. The woman had false teeth, but she smiled a lot nonetheless. Smiling, she told them her name was Katherine Kipp, and that she had been a neighbor of Mr Hale's for the past seven years. They guessed she was in her sixties, but they didn't ask because they were both gentlemen, sure. She told them her husband had worked in the railroad yards up in Riverhead till he had an accident one day that killed him. She did not elaborate on what the accident might have been, and they did not ask. Kling wondered if the late Mr Kipp had possibly sampled some of the black brew boiling on the kitchen stove.

They asked her first about the night of October twenty-eighth, because this was the night someone had been in Hale's apartment boozing it up and smoking dope and everything, and incidentally hanging Hale from a hook on the bathroom door. Had Mrs Kipp seen anything? Heard anything?

"No," she said.

"How about anytime *before* that night?" Brown asked. "See anybody going in or out of his apartment?"

"How do you mean?" Mrs Kipp asked.

"Anyone who might've visited Mr Hale. A friend, an acquaintance . . . a relative?"

"Well, his daughter used to stop by every now and then. Cynthia. She visited him every so often."

"You didn't see her on the night of the twenty-eighth, did you?" Kling asked.

64

"No, I did not."

"How about anyone else?"

"That night, do you mean?"

"That night, or any other time. Someone he might have felt comfortable enough to sit with, talk to, have a drink or two, like that."

"He didn't have many visitors," Mrs Kipp said.

"Never saw anyone going in or out, hm?" Brown said.

"Well, yes. But not on a regular basis."

"I'm not sure I understand you, Mrs Kipp."

"Well, you said a friend or an acquaintance . . ."

"That's right, but . . ."

"I'm assuming you meant someone who came to see Mr Hale on a regular basis. A friend. You know. An acquaintance."

"We meant *anyone*," Kling said. "Anyone who came here to see Mr Hale. However many times."

"Well, yes," Mrs Kipp said. "There was someone who came to see him."

"How often?" Brown asked.

"Three times."

"When?"

"In September."

It began raining again just as Carella swung the sedan into the curb in front of the First Baptist Church. They waited for five or six minutes, hoping the rain might let up. When it appeared hopeless, they piled out of the car, and ran for the front doors of the church. Ollie pushed a doorbell button to the right of the jamb.

The church was housed in a white clapboard structure wedged between a pair of six-story tenements whose red-brick facades had been recently sandblasted. There were sections of Diamondback that long ago had been sucked into the quagmire of hopeless poverty, where any thoughts of gentrification were mere pipe dreams. But St Sebastian Avenue, here in the Double-Eight between Seventeenth and Twenty-first, was the hub of a thriving mini-community not unlike a self-contained small town. Along this stretch of avenue, you could find good restaurants, markets brimming with prime cuts of meat and fresh produce, clothing stores selling designer labels, repair shops for shoes, bicycles, or umbrellas, a new movie complex with six screens, even a fitness center.

Ollie rang the doorbell again. Lightning flashed behind the low buildings across the avenue. Thunder boomed. The middle of the three doors opened. The man standing there, peering out at the detectives and the rain, was some six feet, two or three inches tall, Carella guessed, with the wide shoulders and broad chest of a heavyweight boxer, which in fact the Reverend Gabriel Foster once had been. His eyebrows were still ridged with scars, the result of too much stubborn resistance against superior opponents when he was club-fighting all over the country. At forty-eight, he still looked mean and dangerous. Wearing a moss-green corduroy suit over a black turtleneck sweater, black loafers and black socks, a massive gold ring on the pinky of his left hand, he stood just inside the arched middle door to his church while the detectives stood in the rain outside.

"You brought the rain," he said.

According to police files, Foster's birth name was Gabriel Foster Jones, but he'd changed it to Rhino Jones when he started boxing, and then to Gabriel Foster when he began preaching. Foster considered himself a civil rights activist. The police considered him a rabble-rouser, an opportunistic self-promoter, and a race racketeer. Which was why his church was listed in the files as a sensitive location. "Sensitive location" was departmental code for anyplace where the uninvited presence of the police might cause a race riot. In Carella's experience, most of these locations were churches.

The detectives kept standing in the teeming rain on the wide front steps of the church, waiting for the preacher to invite them in. He showed no sign of offering any such hospitality.

"Detective Carella," Carella said, "Eighty-seventh Squad. We're looking for a man named Walter Hopwell, we understand he works here."

"He does indeed," Foster said.

The rain kept battering them.

"Apparently he knew a man named Daniel Nelson, who was killed yesterday morning," Meyer said.

"Yes, I saw the news."

"Is Mr Hopwell here now?" Carella asked.

"Why do you want to see him?"

"We think he may have information pertaining to a case we're investigating."

"You're the man who shot and killed Sonny Cole, aren't you?" Foster said.

Carella looked at him.

"What's that got to do with the price of fish?" Ollie asked.

"Everything," Foster said. "The officer here shot and killed a brother in cold blood."

A brother, Ollie thought.

"The officer here shot the individual who killed his father," Ollie said. "Which has nothing to do with Walter Hopwell."

Rain was running down his cheekbones and over his jaw. He stood sopping wet in the rain, looking in at the dry comfort of the preacher inside, hating the son of a bitch for being dry and being black and looking so fucking smug.

"You're not welcome here," Foster said.

"Well, gee, then here's what we'll have to do," Ollie said.

"Let it go, Ollie," Carella said.

"Oh no way," Ollie said, and turned back to Foster again. "We'll ask the D.A. to subpoena Hopwell as a witness in a murder investigation. We'll come back with a grand-jury subpoena for Walter Hopwell, alias Harpo Hopwell, and we'll stand in the rain here outside your pretty little church here and ask anyone who comes out, 'Are you Walter Hopwell, sir?' If the answer is yes, or if the answer is *no* answer at all, we'll hand him the subpoena to appear before the grand jury at nine-thirty tomorrow morning. Now if he goes before a grand jury, it might take them all day to ask him the same questions *we* could ask in half an hour if you let us in out of the rain. What do you say, Rhino? It's your call."

Foster looked at Ollie as if deciding whether to punch him in the gut or drop him instead with an uppercut to the jaw. Ollie didn't give blacks too much credit for profound thinking, but if *he* was Foster, he'd be figuring Carella here had indeed slain a no-good murderer who merely happened to be of the same color as the reverend himself—but was this a good enough reason to take a substantial position at this juncture in time? This past August was already ancient history. Was the slain brother, who'd incidentally been *stalking* Carella with a nine-millimeter pistol, reason enough to precipitate a major confrontation at this late date? Ollie was no mind reader, but he guessed maybe Rhino here was thinking along those lines.

"Come in," Foster said at last.

She had heard them arguing.

"The walls are paper thin in this building," she said. "You can hear everything. Well, just listen," she said. "Let's not talk for a minute or so, you'll understand what I mean. Let's just be still, shall we?"

The detectives did not wish to be still, not when Mrs Kipp had just told them that the normally reclusive Andrew Hale had been visited by someone three times during the month of September. But they fell silent nonetheless, listening intently. Someone flushed a toilet. A telephone rang. They could hear, faintly, what sounded like voices on a television soap opera.

"Do you see what I mean?" she asked.

Hear what you mean, Kling thought, but did not say.

"Was this a man or a woman?" Brown asked. "This person who visited Mr Hale."

"A man."

"Did you *see* him?"

"Oh yes. But only once. The first time he was here. I knocked on Mr Hale's door to ask if he needed anything at the grocery store. I was going down to the grocery store, you see . . ."

The way Katherine Kipp remembers it, she first hears the visitor shouting as she comes out into the hallway and is locking her door. The voice is a trained voice, an actor's voice, an opera singer's voice, a radio announcer's voice, something of that sort, thundering through the closed door to Mr Hale's apartment and roaring down the hallway.

She can make out words as she approaches the door to 3A. Mr Hale's visitor is shouting something about the chance of a lifetime. He is telling Mr Hale that only a fool would pass up this opportunity, this is something that is coming his way by sheer coincidence, he should thank his lucky stars. You can make *millions*, the man shouts. You're being a goddamn jackass!

She is standing just outside Mr Hale's door now.

She is almost afraid of knocking, the man sounds so violent. At the same time, she is afraid *not* to knock. Suppose he does something to Mr Hale? He sounds apoplectic. Suppose he *hurts* Mr Hale?

The voice stops abruptly the moment she knocks on the door.

"Yes?"

"Mr Hale? It's me. Katherine Kipp."

"Just a second, Mrs Kipp."

The door opens. Mr Hale is wearing a cardigan sweater over an open-throat shirt and corduroy trousers. The man sitting at the kitchen table is drinking a cup of coffee.

"Do you know Mr Hale's son-in-law?" Kling asked.

"Yes, I do."

"Was that who the man was?"

"Oh no."

"Do you *know* who the man was?"

"No. Well, I'd recognize him if I saw him again. But no, I don't know him."

"Mr Hale didn't introduce him or anything?"

"No."

"What'd he look like?" Kling asked.

Walter Hopwell worked with at least a dozen other people on the top floor of the church. These people had nothing to do with church hierarchy. Up here, there were no deacons, no trustees, no pastor's aides, no church secretaries or announcement clerks. Instead, these men and women were all employees hired by Foster to generate the personal publicity, promotion, and propaganda that had kept him in the public eye and the political arena for the past ten years. Except for three young white men and a white woman, all of them were black.

Here in Hopwell's small private office, a room hung with photographs of Malcolm X, Martin Luther King, and Nelson Mandela, its windows dripping rainsnakes, Carella and Meyer talked to Hopwell while Fat Ollie stood by with a somewhat supercilious smirk on his face, as if certain that the man they were questioning was an ax murderer at best or a serial killer at worst. Hopwell looked like neither. A slender man with finely sculpted features and a head shaved as bald as Meyer's, he wore black jeans, a black turtleneck sweater, and a fringed suede vest. A small gold earring pierced his left ear lobe. Ollie figured this was some kind of signal to other faggots. Or was that the right ear?

"Danny Nelson was killed yesterday morning, did you know that?" Carella asked.

"Yes, I saw it on television," Hopwell said.

"How'd you happen to know him?" Meyer asked.

"He did some work for me."

"Oh?"

"What kind of work?" Carella asked.

"Research," Hopwell said.

Ollie rolled his eyes.

"What sort of research?" Meyer asked.

"Information on people who've been critical of Reverend Foster."

A fuckin snitch researcher, Ollie thought.

"How long was he doing this for you?"

"Six months or so."

"You knew him for six months?"

"Yes."

"Came here to the church, did he?"

"Yes. With his reports."

"What'd you do with these reports?"

"I used them to combat false rumors and specious innuendoes."

"How?"

"In our printed material. And in the reverend's radio addresses."

"When I met with Danny yesterday morning," Carella said, "he mentioned a card game you'd been in . . ."

"Yes."

"... with a man from Houston."

"Yes."

"Who won a lot of money."

"Yes, he did."

"Did you have a conversation with this man afterward?"

"We had a drink together, yes. And shared some conversation."

"Did he mention having killed someone?"

Gee, that's subtle, Ollie thought.

"No, he didn't say he'd killed anyone."

"What did he say?"

"Am I getting involved in something here?" Hopwell asked.

"We're trying to locate this man," Meyer said.

"I don't see how I can help you do that."

"We understand you know where he is."

"No, I don't."

"Danny said you know this man's name ..."

"Yes, I do."

"... and where he's staying."

"Well, I know where he was on Saturday night. I don't know if he's there now. I haven't seen him since last Saturday night."

"What's his name?" Carella asked.

"John Bridges was what he told me."

"Where was he staying? Where'd you go that night?"

"The President Hotel. Downtown. On Jefferson."

"What'd he look like? Describe him."

"A tall man, six two or three, with curly black hair and pale, blue-green eyes. Wide shoulders, narrow waist, a lovely grin," Hopwell said, and grinned a lovely grin himself.

"White or black?"

"A very light-skinned Jamaican," Hopwell said. "With that charming lilt they have, you know? In their speech?"

✳   ✳   ✳

"He was white," Mrs Kipp said. "About forty-five, I would say, with dark hair and blue eyes. Big. A big man."

"How big?" Brown asked.

"Very big. About your size," she said, appraising him.

Brown was six feet two inches tall and weighed in at a buck ninety-five. Some people thought he looked like a cargo ship. For sure, he was not a ballet dancer.

"Any scars, tattoos, other identifying marks?" he asked.

"None that I noticed."

"You said you only saw him the first time he was here. How do you know it was the same man the next two times?"

"His voice. I recognized his voice. He had a very distinctive voice. Whenever he got agitated, the voice just *boomed* out of him."

"Was he agitated the next two times as well?"

"Oh dear yes."

"Shouting again?"

"Yes."

"About what?"

"Well, the same thing again, it seemed to me. He kept yelling that Mr Hale was a goddamn fool, or words to that effect. Told him he was offering real money here, and there'd be more to come down the line . . ."

"More money to come?"

"Yes. Down the line."

"More money later on?"

"Yes. Year after year, he said."

"What was it he wanted?" Brown asked.

"I have no idea."

"But you got the impression . . ."

"Yes."

". . . that Mr Hale had something this man wanted."

"Oh yes. Very definitely."

"That this man had come to see Mr Hale three times in a row ..."

"Well, not in a row. He came once at the beginning of September, again around the fifteenth, and the third time about a week later."

"To make an offer for whatever it was Mr Hale had."

"Yes."

"Three times."

"Yes. Was my impression from what I heard."

"And Mr Hale kept refusing to give him whatever this was."

"Told the man to stop bothering him."

"How did the man react to this?"

"He threatened Mr Hale."

"When was this?"

"The last time he was here."

"Which was when? Can you give us some idea of the date?"

"I know it was a holiday."

Brown was already looking at his calendar.

"Not Labor Day," he said.

"No, no, much later."

"Only other holiday in September was Yom Kippur."

"Then that's when it was," Mrs Kipp said.

"September twentieth."

"That's the last time he came here."

The room went silent. Again, as Mrs Kipp had promised, they could hear all the noises of the building, unseen, secret, almost furtive. In the silence, they became aware again of the baneful stink from the pot boiling on the kitchen stove.

"And you say he threatened Mr Hale?" Brown asked.

"Told him he'd be sorry, yes. Said they'd get what they wanted one way or another."

"'They'? Was that the word he used? *They*?"

"Pardon?"

"'*They'd*' get what they wanted?"

"Yes. I'm pretty sure he said 'they.'"

"What was it he wanted?" Brown said again.

"Well, I'm sure I don't know," Mrs Kipp said, and got up to go stir her pot again.

"Danny told me this man was boasting about having received five grand," Carella said.

"Oh, I think he was making all that up," Hopwell said.

"Making what up?"

"The five thousand dollars."

"Why would he do that?"

"To impress me."

"Told you somebody had given him five thousand dollars . . ."

"Well, yes, but he was making it up."

"Five thousand dollars to kill somebody."

"No, he didn't say that."

"What did he say?"

"I hardly remember. We were drinking a lot."

"Did he tell you there was an old man . . ."

"Yes."

"Who had something somebody else wanted . . ."

"Well, yes, but that was all make-believe."

"The old man was make-believe?"

"Oh, I think so."

"Someone wanting him dead was make-believe?"

"John had an active imagination."

"Someone willing to pay five thousand dollars to kill this old man and make it look like an accident . . ."

"I didn't believe a word of it."

"But it's what he told you, isn't it?"

"Yes, to impress me."

"I see. To impress you. Did he give you a strip of roofers when you left the hotel?"

"As a matter of fact, he did. But roofers aren't a controlled substance."

"Mr Hopwell, if I told you that an old man was drugged with Rohypnol and later hanged to make it look like a suicide, would you *still* believe John Bridges was trying to impress you when he told you he'd been paid five thousand . . ."

"He didn't say exactly that. You're putting words in my mouth."

What'd *he* put in your mouth? Ollie wondered.

"What *did* he say, exactly?" Meyer asked.

"He was telling a story. He was saying *suppose* a person had been offered a certain amount of money . . ."

"Five thousand dollars."

"Yes, he mentioned that sum. But it was all supposition. He was making up a story."

"A story about someone who was offered five grand to kill someone . . ."

"He never used that word. He never said the word 'kill.' I'd have been out of there in a minute. He was just bragging. To impress me."

"What word *did* he use?"

"I don't know, but it wasn't the word 'kill,' he never said anything about killing anyone. Listen, who remembers *what* he said? We were drinking a lot."

"And smoking a lot of pot, too, is that right?"

"Well, a little."

"Which *is* a controlled substance."

"Haven't you ever smoked pot, Detective?"

"Did he mention any names?" Meyer asked.

"No."

"Didn't say *which* old man he'd been hired to . . ."

"It was just a story."

"Didn't say *who* had hired him to kill this old man?"

"A good story, that was all."

"Didn't say *who* had given him the five grand he later used as his stake in the poker game . . ."

"He was just a terrific storyteller," Hopwell said.

"You didn't think you should call the police after you heard this terrific story, huh?" Carella said.

"No, I didn't."

"Don't you read the papers, Mr Hopwell?"

"Only for items about the reverend."

"How about television? Don't you watch television?"

"Again, only to . . ."

"So when John Bridges told you he'd been paid five thousand dollars to kill an old man and make it look like . . ."

"He never used the word 'kill.' I told you that."

"*Whatever* word or words he used, you never made a connection between what he was saying and a man named Andrew Hale, who'd been all over television that week?"

"Never. I *still* don't make any connection. I don't know anything about this old man you say was killed. Look, I told you John's name, I told you where he was staying. If he did something wrong, you'll have to take that up with him."

"What else can you tell us about him?"

"He had a scar down the left-hand side of his face."

"What kind of scar?"

"It looked like a knife scar."

"You're just remembering a *knife* scar?" Ollie said. "Guy has a fuckin *knife* scar on his *face*, and it's the last thing you mention about him?"

"I try not to notice deformities or infirmities," Hopwell said.

"Do you remember any *other* deformities or infirmities?"

"No."

"How about identifying marks or tattoos? Like a mole, for example, or a birth ..."

"Well, yes, a tattoo," Hopwell said, and hesitated. "A blue star on the head of his penis."

There was no one named John Bridges registered at the President Hotel. Nor had there been anyone registered under that name on the night of November sixth. When they gave the manager the description Hopwell had given them, he said he couldn't recall anyone who'd looked or sounded Jamaican, but this was a big hotel with thousands of guests weekly, and it was possible there'd been any number of Jamaicans registered on the night in question.

They checked the register for anyone from Houston, Texas. There'd been a guest from Fort Worth who'd checked in on the fourth and out the next night, and another from Austin, who was here with his wife and two kids; they did not bother him. Their computer showed no outstanding warrants for anyone named John Bridges. Neither was anyone listed under that name in the Houston telephone directory.

Carella called Houston Central and talked to a man who identified himself as Detective Jack Walman. He told Carella he'd been a cop for almost twelve years now and knew most of the people doing mischief in this town, but he'd never run across one had a knife scar down the left-hand side of his face and a blue star tattooed on his pecker.

"That does beat all," he said. "What's the star stand for? The lone star state?"

"Could be," Carella said.

"What I'll do," he said, "I'll run it through the computer. But that's an unusual combination, ain't it, and I'd sure remember something peculiar like that if I'd ever seen it. Unless, what coulda happened, he mighta got the knife scar *before* he got the tattoo. Lots of these guys get jailhouse tattoos, you know. In which case, there wouldn't be *both* of them on the computer, you follow? We get plenty knife scars down here. Is your man Chicano?"

"No. A Jamaican named John Bridges."

"Well, we got something like two thousand Jamaicans here, too, so who knows? What'd he do, this dude?"

"Maybe killed two people."

"Bad, huh?"

"Bad, yes."

"Musta hurt, don't you think?" Walman said. "Gettin tattooed that way?"

He called back an hour later to say he'd searched the system—city *and* state—for any felon named John Bridges and had come up blank. As he'd mentioned earlier, there were plenty facial scars in the state of Texas, and if Carella wanted him to fax printouts on each and every felon who had one, he'd be happy to oblige. But none of the facial scars came joined to tattooed dongs. One of the old-timers here at the station, though, remembered a guy one time had a little American flag tattooed on *his* wiener, if that was any help, it waved in the breeze whenever he got an erection. But he thought the guy was doing time at Angola, over Louisiana way. Aside from that, Walman was sorry he couldn't be of greater assistance. Carella asked him to please fax the facial-scar printouts, and thanked him for his time.

They were right back where they'd been on the morning of October twenty-ninth, when they'd first caught the squeal.

Chapter Four

There were three airports servicing the metropolitan area. The largest of them, out on Sands Spit, flew three direct flights and six connecting flights to Houston on most weekdays. The airport closest to the city flew nine direct flights and eleven connecting flights. Across the river, in the adjoining state, direct flights went out virtually every hour, starting at 6:20 A.M. Twenty-one non-stop and connecting flights left from that airport alone. Altogether, a total of fifty flights flew to Houston almost every day of the week. It was a big busy city, that Houston, Texas.

Starting early Wednesday morning, the tenth day of November, twelve detectives began surveillance of the check-in counters at Continental, Delta, US Airways, American, Northwest, and United Airlines, looking for a Jamaican with a knife scar who might be headed for either Houston-Intercontinental or Houston-Hobby on a direct flight, or on any one of the flights connecting through Charlotte, Dallas/Fort Worth, New Orleans, Detroit, Chicago, Memphis, Atlanta, Cleveland, Pittsburgh, or Philadelphia. None of the men boarding any of the flights even remotely fit the description Harpo Hopwell had given them.

There were still a lot more flights going out that day.

✳   ✳   ✳

"Who's in charge here?" the assistant medical examiner wanted to know.

Ollie merely gave him a look: he was the only person here with a gold and blue-enameled detective's shield pinned to his jacket lapel, so who the hell did the man *think* was in charge? The only other cops at the scene were a pair of blues, both of them standing around looking bewildered, their thumbs up their asses. Did the man think *uniforms* were now handling homicide investigations?

Or maybe the man had forgotten that he and Ollie had worked together before. Ollie could not imagine this; he did not consider himself an eminently forgettable human being. Did the man work with detectives as fat as Ollie every day of the week? The man *had* to know that the fat detective in the loud sports jacket was the one in charge here. Or was he pretending not to know Ollie because he didn't want Ollie to think the only *reason* he remembered him was *because* he was fat? If so, that was stupid. Ollie *knew* he was fat. He also knew that behind his back people called him Fat Ollie. He considered it a measure of respect that nobody ever called him this to his face.

"Oh, hello, Weeks," the ME said, as if noticing him for the first time, which was tantamount to suddenly noticing a hippopotamus at the dinner table. "What've we got?"

"Dead black girl in the kitchen," Ollie said.

The ME's name was Frederick Kurtz, a Nazi bastard if Ollie had ever met one. Even had a little Hitler mustache under his nose. Little black satchel like some mad doctor at Buchenwald. Wearing a rumpled suit looked as if he'd slept in it all this past week. Had a bad cold, too. Kept taking a soiled handkerchief from his back pocket and blowing fresh snot into it, the fuckin Nazi. Ollie followed him into the kitchen.

The girl lay on her back in front of the sink counter,

the knife still in her. This was going to be a real tough call. It would take a fuckin Nazi rocket scientist to diagnose this one as a fatal stabbing. Nobody had yet taken the knife out of her because rule number one was you didn't touch anything till the ME officially pronounced the vic dead. Ollie waited while Kurtz circled the body like a vulture, trying to find a comfortable position from which to examine the dead girl. He put his satchel down on the floor beside her, and leaned over close to her mouth, as if hoping to catch a shimmer of breath from her lips. Ollie was thinking if the girl was still breathing, she'd be sanctified before nightfall. Be the first black saint from this city. Kurtz placed his forefinger and middle finger on the side of her neck, feeling for a pulse in the carotid artery. Fat Chance Department, Ollie thought.

"Reckon she's dead?" he asked, trying to sound like John Wayne, but succeeding only in sounding like W. C. Fields. Ollie sometimes tried to do Tom Hanks, Robin Williams, and Robert De Niro, but somehow all his imitations came out sounding like W. C. Fields. He didn't realize this. He actually considered his imitations right on the money, and often thought of himself as the man with the golden ear. Kurtz knew sarcasm when he heard it, however, even when it came from a fat dick who neither looked nor sounded like a cowboy. He didn't answer Ollie. Instead, he put his stethoscope to the girl's chest, already knowing she was dead as a doornail, to coin a medical phrase, and went about his examination pretending Ollie wasn't there, something difficult to do under any circumstances. A voice from the bedroom doorway startled Kurtz, echoing as it did his own earlier question,

"Who's in charge here?" Monoghan asked.

Same stupid question from another jackass who should know better, Ollie thought. In this city, the detective catching the squeal was the cop officially investigating the case from that moment on. Detective Monoghan, his partner Detective

Monroe, and various other detectives from the Homicide Division were sent to the scene of any murder in their bailiwick, to serve in a so-called advisory and supervisory capacity. The reason for their existence was that this city was a bureaucratic monolith that cost more to run than the entire nation of Zaire.

In this city, ten people were necessary to do the job of one person. What this city did was hire high school dropouts, put them in suits, and then teach them how to greet the public with blank stares on their faces. In this city, if you needed a copy of, say, your birth certificate or your driver's license, you stood on line for an hour and a half while some nitwit pretended to be operating a computer. When he or she finally located what you were there for, you had to go over to the post office and stand on line for another hour and a half to purchase a money order to pay for it. That was because in this city, municipal employees weren't allowed to accept cash, personal checks, or credit cards. This was because the city fathers knew the caliber of the people who were featherbedding throughout the entire system, knew that cash would disappear in a wink, knew that credit cards would be cloned, knew that personal checks would somehow end up in private bank accounts hither and yon. That's why all those people behind municipal counters gave you such hostile stares. They were angry at the system because they couldn't steal from it. Or maybe they were pissed off because they couldn't qualify for more lucrative jobs like security officers at any of the city's jails, where an ambitious man could earn a goodly amount of unreportable cash by smuggling in dope to the inmates.

Monoghan and Monroe were necessary to such a system.

Without two jackasses here to tell an experienced detective like Ollie how to do his job, the system would fall apart in a minute and a half. The Homicide dicks knew damn well who was in charge here. Oliver Wendell Weeks was in charge here. It bothered them, too, that in days of yore, the Homicide Division in this city had merited the measure of respect it now enjoyed only on television. Nowadays, Homicide's proud tradition was vestigial at best. All that remained of its elegant past were the black suits Homicide cops still wore, the color of death, the color of murder itself.

Both Monoghan and Monroe were wearing black on this dismal November afternoon. They looked as if they were on their way to a funeral home to tell some Irish mick like themselves how sorry they were that Paddy O'Toole had kicked the bucket, poor drunken soul. The consistent thing about Ollie Weeks was that he hated everyone, regardless of race, creed, or color. Ollie was a consummate bigot. Without even knowing it.

"These two Irishmen walk out of a bar?" he said.

"Yeah?" Monoghan said.

"It could happen," Ollie said, and shrugged.

Neither Monoghan nor Monroe laughed.

Kurtz, the fuckin Nazi, laughed, but he tried to hide it by blowing his nose again, because to tell the truth these two big Irish cops scared hell out of him. He guessed Ollie was of English descent, or he wouldn't have told such a joke to two Irishmen dressed like morticians and looking somewhat red in the face to begin with.

"What is that, some kind of ethnic slur?" Monoghan asked.

"Some kind of stereotypical innuendo?" Monroe asked.

"Is she dead or not?" Ollie asked the ME, changing the subject because these two Irish jackasses seemed to be getting touchy about their drunken cronies.

"Yes, she's dead," Kurtz said.

"Would you wish to venture a guess as to the cause?" Ollie said, this time trying to sound like a sarcastic British barrister, but it still came out as W. C. Fields.

"Coroner's Office'll send you a report," Kurtz said, thinking he could ace the Big O, but Ollie merely smiled.

"I can't blame you for being so cautious," he said, "knife stickin out of her chest and all."

Fuck you, Fat Boy, the ME thought, but he blew his nose instead and walked out.

The Homicide dicks wandered around the apartment looking grouchy. Ollie guessed they were still smarting over his Irish joke, which he thought was a pretty good one, hey, if you can't take a joke, go fuck yourself. There were enough personal items around the place—an engagement calendar, an address book, bras and panties in the dresser— to convince Ollie that the girl lived here and wasn't just visiting whoever had juked her. The super of the building confirmed this a few minutes later when he came upstairs to see how the investigation was coming along. One thing Ollie hated—among other things he hated—was amateur detectives sticking their noses in police work. He asked the super what the girl's name was, and the super told him she was Althea Cleary, and that she'd been living here since May sometime. He thought she was from Ohio or someplace like that. Idaho maybe. Iowa. Someplace like that. Ollie thanked him for the valuable information and his citizenly concern and ushered him out of the apartment. One of the responding blues told him the lady who'd phoned the police was in the hall outside waiting to talk to him, was it okay to let her in?

"What makes you think it wouldn't be okay?" Ollie asked.

"Well, it being a crime scene and all."

"That's very good thinking," Ollie said, and smiled enigmatically. "Show her in."

The woman was in her late fifties, Ollie guessed, wearing a green cardigan sweater and a brown woolen skirt. She told Ollie that she and Althea were friends, and that she'd knocked on her door around two o'clock to see if she wanted to go down for a cappuccino.

"I work at home," the woman said. "And Althea was home a lot, too. So sometimes, we walked over to Starbucks for cappuccino."

"What is it you do?" Ollie asked. "At home, I mean."

"Well, I teach piano," she said.

"I always wanted to play piano," Ollie said. "Could you teach me five songs?"

"I'm sorry?"

"I want to learn five songs. I want to play five songs like a pro. Then when I go to a party, I can sit down and play the five songs and everybody'll think I know how to play piano."

"Well, if you can play five songs, then actually you *are* playing the piano, aren't you?"

Ollie hated smart-ass women, even if they knew how to play piano.

"Sure," he said, "but I mean they'll think I know *more* than just the five songs."

"I suppose I could teach you five songs," the woman said.

"Have you got a card or anything?"

"Don't you want to know about Althea?"

"Sure, I do. Have you got a card? I'll give you a call, you can teach me five songs sometime. Do you know 'Night and Day'?"

"Yes, I do. You should understand, however ... I normally teach classical piano. To children, mostly."

"That's okay, all I want is five songs."

"Well," the woman said, and sighed, and opened her handbag. She fished in it for a card, found one, and handed it to Ollie. The name on the card was Helen Hobson.

"How much do you charge?" he asked.

"We can discuss that," she said.

"Maybe you can give me a flat rate for just the five songs," he said. "Did she work nights or what?"

His change of direction was so abrupt that Helen actually blinked.

"You said she was home a lot," Ollie said.

"Oh, yes. She worked nights. At the telephone company."

Ollie hated the telephone company. He could easily imagine some irritated subscriber stabbing Althea Cleary in the chest half a dozen times.

"I liked her a lot," Helen said. "She was a very nice person."

"Who you used to have cappuccino with every now and then."

"Almost every day."

"But today when you went down, you found her dead."

"The door was open," Helen said, nodding.

"Standing wide open, you mean?"

"No, just a crack. I thought this was odd. I called Althea's name, and when I got no answer, I walked in. She was in the kitchen. On the floor there."

"What'd you do then?"

"I went up to my own apartment and called the police."

"What time was this, Miss Hobson?"

"A little after two. My lesson ended at two, I don't have another one till four. So I came down to see if Althea wanted to come with me to Starbucks."

"How'd you come down?"

"By the stairs. I'm only one flight up."

"See anybody on the way down?"

"No one."

"Anybody outside her apartment?"

"No."

"When did you notice the door was open?"

"Immediately."

"Before you knocked or anything?"

"I didn't knock at all. I saw the door standing open maybe an inch or two, so I called her name, and went in."

"Thanks, Miss Hobson, we appreciate your help," he said. "I'll call you about the lessons. All I want to learn is five songs."

"Yes, I understand."

"'Night and Day,' and four others. So I can impress people."

"I'm sure they'll be very impressed."

"Hey, tell me about it," Ollie said.

"You got this under control here?" Monoghan asked.

"Soon as the technicians get here," Ollie said. "What's holding up traffic? Is the Pope in town or something?"

"You gonna tell a Pope joke now?"

"I only know one Pope joke," Ollie said.

"Maybe this lady here can teach you four more," Monroe said. "Then you can really impress people. You can play five songs on the piano, tell five Pope jokes, and maybe five Irish jokes if there are any Irishmen in the crowd."

"Sounds like a good idea," Ollie said. "You know four Pope jokes, Miss Hobson?"

"I don't know any Pope jokes at all," she said.

"I need four more Pope jokes," Ollie said. "I'll have to get them someplace else, I guess."

"Can I leave now?" she asked.

"You want some advice?" Monroe said.

"Sure, what's that?" Ollie said.

"There are lots of Irishmen on the job. I wouldn't go telling any more Irish jokes, I was you."

"Gee, is that your advice?"

"That's our advice," Monroe said.

"You think telling Irish jokes might be politically incorrect, huh?"

"It might be downright dangerous," Monroe said.

"Gee, I hope that's not a threat," Ollie said.

"It ain't a threat, but you can take it as one if you wish."

"Can I leave now?" Helen said again.

"Cause you know," Ollie said, "I don't give a rat's ass about what's politically correct or what ain't. All I want to do is learn my five songs and my five Pope jokes, is all I want to do, and maybe in my spare time find out who stabbed this little girl. So if you got no further advice to dispense here . . ."

"Is it all right if I go?" Helen asked.

"Go already, lady," Monoghan said.

"Thank you, Officers," she said, and hurried out of the apartment.

"What if I told you I myself was Irish?" Ollie asked.

"I wouldn't believe you," Monroe said.

"Why? Cause I ain't drunk?"

"That's the kind of remark can get you in trouble," Monoghan said, wagging his finger under Ollie's nose.

"I once bit off a guy's finger, was doing that," Ollie said, and grinned like a shark.

"Bite *this* a while," Monoghan said.

"Good thing the piano teacher's already gone," Ollie said, shaking his head in dismay.

"Who's in charge here?" one of the technicians asked from the doorway.

"Well look who's here!" Ollie said.

"Keep us advised," Monoghan said.

You fat bastard, he thought, but did not say.

That Wednesday morning, at a few minutes past eleven, Arthur Brown knocked on the door to Cynthia Keating's apartment.

"Yes, who is it?" she asked.

"Police," Brown said.

"Oh," she said. There was a long silence. "Just a minute," she said. They heard a latch turning, tumblers falling. The door opened a crack, held by a security chain. Cynthia peered out at them.

"I don't know you," she said.

Brown held up his shield.

"Detective Brown," he said. "Eighty-seventh Squad."

"I already spoke to the others," she said.

"We have a few more questions, ma'am."

"Is this legal?"

"May we come in, please?"

"Just a second," she said, and closed the door to take off the chain. She opened it again, said, "Come in," and preceded them into the apartment. "This better be legal," she said.

"Ma'am," Kling said, "do you know a man named John Bridges?"

"No. Let me see *your* badge, too," she said.

Kling fished out a small leather holder, and flashed the gold and blue-enameled shield.

"Excuse me," she said, and went directly to the telephone on the kitchen wall. She dialed a number, waited, listening, and then said, "Mr Alexander, please. Cynthia Keating." She waited again. "Todd," she said, "the police are here. What's your advice?" She listened again, nodded, kept listening, finally said, "Thanks, Todd, talk to you," and hung up. "Gentlemen," she said, "unless you have a warrant for my arrest, my attorney suggests you take a walk."

There was something very comforting about being alone at last in the dead girl's apartment. First of all, the silence. This city, the one thing you could never find anyplace was peace and quiet. There were always sirens going, day and night, police or ambulance, and there were car horns honking, mostly taxicabs, foreigners from India or Pakistan leaning on their horns day and night because they were remembering how fast their camels used to race across the desert sands where there were no traffic lights. Noisiest damn city in the entire universe, this city. Ollie much preferred the silence here in the dead girl's apartment.

He sometimes felt if he hung around a dead person's apartment long enough, he would pick up the vibrations of the killer. Get into his or her skin somehow. He had read a story once—he hated reading—where the theory was the image of a person's murderer would be left on the person's eyeballs, the retina, whatever. Total bullshit. But the silence in a victim's apartment was almost palpable, and he gave real credence to the notion that if he stood there long enough, in the silence, the vibrations of the killer would seep into his bones, though to tell the truth this had never happened to him. Nonetheless, he stood stock still at the foot of the dead girl's bed now, imagining her as he'd first seen her on the kitchen floor, knife in her chest, trying to feel what the killer had felt while he was stabbing her, trying to get into his skin. Nothing happened. Ollie sighed, farted, and began his solitary search of Althea Cleary's apartment.

What he hoped he definitely would not find was her parents' names. He did not want to have to call them personally and tell them their daughter was dead. He wasn't good at such stuff. To Ollie, when a person was dead he was dead, and you didn't go around wringing your hands or tearing out your hair. He couldn't think of a single dead person he missed, including his own mother and father. He guessed if his sister Isabelle died, he would miss her a little, but not enough to be the one who got up and said some kind words about her at the funeral service because to tell the truth he couldn't think of a single kind thing he might care to say about her, dead *or* alive. Like most living people,

Isabelle Weeks was a pain in the ass. She once told him he was a bigot. He told her to go fuck herself, girlfriend.

He had already looked through the dead girl's address book and appointment calendar, but he hadn't found any listings for anybody named Cleary. There were a few names for people in Montana, which wasn't either Ohio or Idaho or Iowa as the super had guessed, but these weren't Clearys, and he didn't plan on calling somebody in Montana just to find out if they were related to a dead black girl he didn't want to tell them about in the first place. Her appointment calendar wasn't much help, either. She probably was new here in the city, which maybe explained why she had cappuccino all the time with the lady upstairs who taught piano. Ollie would have to give her a call. *Night and Day*, he thought. And maybe *Satisfaction*, which was one of his favorite songs, too.

He went to the girl's dresser now, and opened the top drawer, looking for he didn't know what, anything that would tell him something about either her or whoever had been with her on the night she died. There were cops who went by the book, canvassed the neighborhood first, asked Leroy and Luis, Carmen and Clarisse did they see anybody going in or out of the apartment, but up here in Zimbabwe West, nobody ever saw nothing if you were a cop. Anyway, he preferred getting to know the vic first, and *then* getting to know whoever knew her. Besides, Ollie liked dead people much better than he did most living ones. Dead people didn't give you any trouble. You went into a dead person's apartment, you didn't have to worry about farting or belching. Also, if the vic was a girl, you could handle her panties or panty hose— like he was doing now—without anybody thinking you were some kind of pervert. Ollie sniffed the crotch of a pair of red panties, which was actually good police work because it would tell him was the girl a clean person or somebody who just dropped panties she had worn right back in the drawer without rinsing them out. They smelled fresh and clean.

Being in her apartment, sniffing her panties, going through the rest of her underwear, and her sweaters and her blouses and her high-heeled shoes in the closet, and her coats and dresses, one of them a blue Monica Lewinsky dress, going through all her personal belongings, trying to find something, wondering what kind of person could have stabbed the girl it looked like half a dozen times and then left a fuckin bread knife sticking out of her chest, opening her handbag and rummaging through the personal girl things in it, he felt both privileged and inviolate, like an invisible burglar.

Carl Blaney was weighing a liver when Ollie got downtown at four o'clock that Wednesday afternoon. It was still raining, though not as hard as it had been earlier. The morgue and the rain outside both had the same stainless steel hue. He watched as Blaney transferred the liver from the scale to a stainless steel pan. Personally, Ollie found body parts disgusting.

"Is that hers?" he asked.

"Whose?" Blaney said.

"The vic's."

"That's all we've *got* here is vics."

"Althea Cleary. The little colored girl got stabbed."

"Oh, that one."

"What do you do here, you just go from one liver to another?"

"Yep, that's all we do here," Blaney said dryly.

"So what've you got for me?" Ollie asked.

✳   ✳   ✳

There was nothing Meyer liked better than to irritate Fat Ollie Weeks. The man was calling to talk to Carella, but Carella was down the hall. Meyer could not resist the temptation.

"Do you plan to sue this guy?" he asked.

"What guy is that?" Ollie asked.

He had never sued anybody in his entire life. He figured the lawyers of the world were rich enough.

"This guy who wrote this book with a lot of police stuff in it."

"What guy?" Ollie asked again.

"This Irishman who wrote a book. You're famous now, Ollie."

"The fuck is *that* supposed to mean?" Ollie said.

"On the other hand, it *does* say in the front of the book that the names, characters, places, and incidents are either products of the author's imagination, or are used fictitiously."

"Wonderful," Ollie said. "Tell Steve I called, okay? I got to see him about something."

"'Any resemblance to actual events or locales or persons is entirely coincidental,'" Meyer quoted. "Is what it says. So I guess it *is* just a coincidence."

"*What* is just a coincidence?" Ollie asked.

"His name being so similar to yours and all," Meyer explained.

"Whose name?"

"This guy."

"*What* guy?" Ollie asked for the third fuckin time.

"This guy in this police novel written by this Irish journalist."

"Okay, I'll bite," Ollie said.

"Fat Ollie Watts," Meyer said, drawing the name out grandly. "Not that anyone ever calls *you* Fat Ollie," he added at once.

"They better *not*," Ollie said. "What do you mean, Fat Ollie Watts?"

"Is the name of a character in this book."

"A *character*? Fat Ollie *Watts*?"

"Yeah. But he's just a minor character."

"A *minor* character?"

"Yeah, some kind of cheap thief."

"Some kind of cheap *thief*?"

"Yeah."

"Called Fat Ollie *Watts*?"

"Yeah. Pretty close, don't you think?"

"*Close?* It's right on the fuckin *nose!*"

"Well, no. Watts isn't Weeks."

"It ain't, huh?"

"It's even spelled differently."

"Oh, is that right?"

"I wouldn't worry about it."

"On your block, Fat Ollie *Watts* ain't Fat Ollie *Weeks*, huh? Then what is it?"

"It's Watts."

"Who the fuck *is* this guy?"

"Fat Ollie Watts," Meyer said. "I just told you."

"Not *him!* The guy who wrote the fuckin *book!* Don't he even know I exist?"

"Gee, I guess not."

"He's writing a book about *cops* and he never heard of *me*? A real *person*? He never heard of Oliver Wendell *Weeks*?"

"Oh, come on, Ollie, relax. This is just another Thomas Harris ripoff serial-killer novel. I wouldn't worry about it."

"Does this fuckin guy live on *Mars*, he never heard of *me*?"

"He lives in Ireland, I told you."

"*Where* in Ireland? In some booth in a pub? In some stone hut by the side of the road? In some fuckin smelly *bog*?"

"Gee, I'm sorry I even mentioned it."

"What's this guy's name?"

"I told you. Fat Ollie . . ."

"Not *him*," Ollie said. "The writer. The fuckin *writer!*"

"I'll tell you the truth," Meyer said, grinning, "I've already forgotten it."

And hung up.

The two men met in a bar at five that afternoon. Both were officially off duty. Carella ordered a beer. Ollie ordered a Harvey Wallbanger.

"So what's this about?" Carella asked.

"I told you on the phone."

"Some girl got stabbed . . ."

"Black girl named Althea Cleary. Eight times, according to the ME. Knife was still in her chest. Weapon of convenience. Matches the set in her kitchen. Thing that made me think of you was Blaney telling me . . ."

"Which Blaney?"

"I don't know. How many Blaneys are there?"

"Two. I think."

"Well, this was one of them," Ollie said. "He told me the girl had maybe been doped. With guess what?"

Carella looked at him.

"Yeah," Ollie said.

"Rohypnol?"

"Rohypnol. Hey, bartender!" he yelled. "Excuse me, but did you put any *vodka* in this fuckin drink?"

"I put vodka in it," the bartender said.

"Cause what I can do, I can take it down the police lab, we'll run some toxicological tests on it, see if there's any alcohol in it at all."

"Everything's in it *supposed* to be in it," the bartender said. "That's a good strong drink you got there."

"Then whyn't you make me another one just like it, on the house this time, it's so fuckin good."

"Why on the house?" the bartender asked.

"Cause your toilet's leakin and your bathroom window's painted shut," Ollie said. "Those are both violations."

Which they weren't.

"You're sure she was doped?" Carella said.

"According to Blaney."

"And he's sure it was roofers?"

"Positive."

"What you're suggesting is a link to my case."

"By George, I think you've got it."

"You're saying because they were both doped . . ."

"Yep."

". . . and later murdered, there's a link."

"Which don't seem like too extravagant a surmise."

"I think it's a very far reach, Ollie."

"Here's your Wallbanger," the bartender said, and banged it down on the bar.

Ollie shoved his chair away from the table and walked over to pick it up. Watching him, Carella thought he moved surprisingly fast for a fat man. Ollie lifted the glass, sipped at it, smacked his lips, said, "Excellent, my good fellow, truly superior," and came back to the table. "It ain't a far reach at all," he told Carella.

"No? You're saying the same person who *hanged* my guy may have *stabbed* your girl."

"I'm saying there's a pattern here. In police work, we call it an M.O."

"Gee, thanks."

"Happy to inform," Ollie said, and raised his glass in a silent toast, and drank. "There ain't no vodka in this one, either," he said and looked into the glass.

Carella was thinking.

"Questions," he said.

"Shoot."

"Do you have any evidence at *all* that Allison Cleary . . . ?"

"Althea."

". . . knew John Bridges?"

"None at all. But they could have met."

"How?"

"Guy's up from Houston, right? Out on the town, from what it appears, am I right? With a little help from his friends, he does a hanging, then goes out to play some cards on the weekend. Meets our little faggot friend Harpo, introduces *him* to his friends, too, here, pal, take these with you, they'll help your sex life, tee hee. Meaning, if Harpo is ever bisexually inclined, he can drop a few tabs in a young lady's drink, induce her to slobber the Johnson. Which is exactly what Bridges or *whoever* he is done two nights later to little Althea Cleary."

"Where do you think they met?"

"Lady lives upstairs from her has cappuccino with her every now and then. Tells me the girl works nights for the telephone company. Okay, I'm prowling her pad, I find a social security card in her handbag. You want to know where she worked?"

"You just told me. The telephone company."

"Yeah, but not AT&T. What I done, I checked the ID number on her social security card with Soc Sec Admin. Employer contributions on her behalf were made for the past six months to a go-go joint called The Telephone Company on The Stem downtown. Wanna go dancin, Steve-a-rino?"

The last plane to Houston that Wednesday night, a non-stop Delta flight scheduled to arrive at Houston-Intercontinental at 9:01 P.M., closed its doors at 6:00 P.M. sharp.

There were no Jamaicans on it.

*　　　*　　　*

A dive called The Telephone Company, Carella didn't know what to expect. Maybe something on the style of the Kit Kat Klub of *Cabaret* fame, telephones on all the tables, numbered placards indicating which table was which, girls phoning from table to table, "This is table twenty-seven, calling table forty-nine. Sitting all alone like that . . ." and so on.

But when they got there at ten o'clock that night, the only telephones in sight were the house phone sitting behind the bar and a pay phone on the wall to the right of the entrance door. The joint was located on Lower Stemmler, all the way downtown, where The Stem became a narrower passage lined with meatpacking houses, the occasional restaurant, and an assortment of clubs featuring masturbaters in drafty dungeons; cross-dressers wearing smeared lipstick, high heels, and crude tattoos; raving teeny boppers in spangles and pinkish-green hair; pneumatic West Coast starlets thrilling to the big bad city or—as was the case here in The Telephone Company—an assortment of topless girls wearing thong panties and gyrating on a crescent-shaped stage.

The detectives roamed around like casual customers. Smoke drifted in bluish-gray layers in the beam of follow spots illuminating half a dozen girls slithering restlessly across the stage, eyes slitted, tongues wetting glossy lips, imitation sex oozing from every pore with each insinuating spike-heeled step they took. If a man signaled from one of the tables below the stage, a wink of the eye or a flick of the tongue acknowledged that the girl would join him on the dance break, to negotiate whatever suited his fancy behind the plastic palms in a back room called The Party Line. One peek into that room told the detectives exactly what was going on back there. A bouncer gave them a look, but said nothing to them.

A dozen or so men sat at tables below the stage, drinking, chatting among themselves, trying to look bored by the exhibition of all that flesh up there because demeaning these women was part of the joy of participation. Even the men who would never dream of taking one of these girls into the back room for actual sex knew that just sitting here while the girls displayed themselves was a way of telling them they could be had for a price—*were*, in fact, being had for a price, witness the ten-dollar bills tucked into G-string bands. The girls, on the other hand, perhaps to convince themselves they hadn't already been broken by this city or the men in this city, told themselves that only a jackass would part with ten bucks to watch a girl bouncing her tits or bending over to spread the cheeks on her ass.

Here in the spotlight-pierced gloom stinking of stale cigarette smoke and sour sweat, over the deafening roar of music blaring from speakers on pillars and posts, the detectives introduced themselves to the man behind the bar, who told them he was Mac Gordon, owner of the club. Gordon looked to be some six feet, three inches tall. His eyes appeared blue, but who could tell in the near-darkness? One thing for sure, he had a red handlebar mustache.

"Did a girl named Althea Cleary work here?" Carella asked.

"Still does. Should be in any minute now."

"Don't count on it," Ollie said.

"What do you mean?"

"She was murdered last night."

"Holy smokes. And here I thought this was about some kind of violation."

"What kind of violation did you have in mind?" Ollie asked.

"Well, gee, how would I know?"

Carella wasn't here to throw a scare into the owner; all he wanted was information. Ollie, on the other hand, couldn't resist being a fucking cop.

"You're not thinkin of the hand jobs in the back room, are you?" he asked.

"I don't know what that's supposed to mean, sir."

"Fifty bucks a throw."

"Not here, sir."

"A hundred for a blow job where the jungle gets thicker?"

"I don't know what jungle you mean, sir."

"Back there at the very *back* of the back room," Ollie said. "All them fake trees dripping moss and shit."

"You must be thinking of some other place," Gordon said.

"Yeah, maybe. You didn't see Althea taking some kind of Jamaican back there last night, did you?"

"I sure didn't," Gordon said.

"Guy with a knife scar on his face?"

"Nossir."

"Who *did* you see with her?"

"I believe she was talking to various gentlemen at various times during the night."

"Gentlemen, huh?"

"Yes, sir."

"Talking to them, huh?"

"Yes, sir. And sharing an occasional drink."

"Sharing a drink, I see. Did she happen to *leave* here with one of these gentlemen?"

"That is strictly against the rules, sir."

"Oh, there are rules."

"Yes, sir, very strict rules. None of the performers here ..."

"Performers, I see."

"... is allowed to leave the club with any of the customers. Or even to make arrangements to *meet* any of the customers outside the club."

"How many girls you got working here?" Ollie asked.

"A dozen or so. Fourteen. Sixteen. It varies on different nights."

"How many were here last night?"

"I would say ten or twelve."

"Which?"

"Ten. Eleven."

"Are they all here tonight? All ten or eleven of these girls?"

"I believe so, yes. I would have to check the time cards."

"Oh, you have time cards, do you?"

"Yes, sir, this is a business establishment."

"I'm sure it is. Find out which girls were here last night, okay? We want to talk to them. You got a nice quiet place where we can visit?"

"I suppose you could use my office," Gordon said. "If you don't mind the clutter."

"Gee, that's very kind of you, thanks," Ollie said.

Carella wanted to kick him in his fat ass.

The girls ranged in age from nineteen to thirty-four. That was because Gordon knew better than to hire anyone under eighteen. The mayor's vigorous anti-vice campaign notwithstanding, Gordon was running a virtual whore house here, lacking only genital penetration to qualify for full statehood. Five of the *eleven* girls, it turned out to be, were white. The remaining six were black. Some of them were experienced, some of them were straight off the train from Oaken Bucket, Minnesota. Nine of the girls were single. Two of them were married. Even some of the single girls had children. Three of the girls had worked in massage parlors ...

"Where it can sometimes get rough," a girl named Sherry told them. "Because doin massage, you *alone* with the dude, you dig? It ain't like here, where they's a whole *buncha* shit goin on."

When she laughed, she exposed a gap in her mouth where two front teeth were missing.

"Which is great for givin derby, hm?" she said, and laughed again, and covered her mouth with a hand on which there was a fake emerald ring as big as all Hong Kong.

None of the girls seemed nervous talking to two detectives. Carella and Ollie both figured Gordon was spreading some heavy bread among the neighborhood law enforcement types. Carella abhorred the widespread practice. Ollie considered it all part of the game, ah yes.

Two of the girls had worked the hostess circuit.

"This's much better," one of them said. "You never knows what you goan walk into when you take a hos'ess call."

Her name was Ruby Sass.

"Mah whole name's Ruby Sassafras Martin," she said, "but I think Ruby Sass got *pinch* to it, don't you?"

She was a black girl with bleached blond hair, wearing a bra top and G-string covered with sequins the color of her name. Silicone breasts virtually spilled out of her top, but she paid them no mind. Instead, she puffed on her cigarette and sipped at the drink the detectives had purchased for her. She told them she was studying drama and dance during the day, which they believed was as authentic as her blond hair. She also told them she'd seen Althea go in the back room with three different guys last night.

"Finely went home at two A.M.," she said. "Approximate."

"Alone?"

"Meaning?"

"Meaning was she with anyone? What else does alone mean?"

"Depends on whether you're president of the United States."

"I'm not," Ollie said.

"Didn't think so."

"Was she alone or wasn't she?"

"Let me tell you something about this business, okay?" Ruby said. "Guys who come here, they don't want all the hassle of arrangements or commitments, you comprehend? They make they business deal, whatever it's for, and that's whut it is. So Mac tellin us don't meet no men outside, don't take no men home with you, that happens ony like once in a blue moon, anyway. Like some college kid with pimples all over his face falls in love with one of the girls up there dancin, he keeps stuffin bills in her gadget, axes her to go the back room with him. Kid like that, he keeps comin back for more, you play him like a fish till he finely works up the courage to ax could he go home with you. Then you tell him sure, but that's gonna *coss* you, honey. By then, he'll go along with whatever you say, cause he is yours, darlin, he is completely yours. You play it right he'll become yo own personal muff diver and pay you for the pleasure besides."

"Does that mean Althea was alone?" Carella asked.

"It means far as I could see, Althea left the club alone. Whether somebody was waitin outside for her is another matter. But let me tell you suppin else bout this business ..."

"We're all ears," Ollie said.

"Most guys I know—and this prolly includes you—they have sex with a woman, the next thing they want is to go home and go to sleep. Especially sex a guy pays for. You ever pay for sex?"

"Never in my life," Ollie said.

"Didn't think you had to, handsome fella like you," Ruby said dryly, and sucked on her cigarette. "But even with a freebie, your average guy today, he don't want to wake up the next morning with some beast in bed, am I right? Or even some beauty, for that matter."

"I don't mind wakin up with beauties in my bed," Ollie said.

"Then you're different from the average guy we get in here. The guys who come here don't want *commitment*, you comprehend? It's as simple as that. They come here, they get they pleasure, and that's it. So are you tellin me that here's a guy who *pays* for sex in a whore house—is what this is here, you know—and then *still* wants more an hour later? What is this, Chinese food?"

"You're saying he *won't* want more."

"Is what I'm saying. If he goes in the back room with a girl, that's usually enough to satisfy him."

"What if he *doesn't* go in the back room?" Carella asked.

"Then he'd be too fuckin timid to ask a girl to meet him on the outside. Besides, why would she?"

"Why wouldn't she?"

"Cause first of all, we exhausted when we leave here two-thirty, three in the morning. We're on that stage shakin our asses all night long, hopin to snare as many ten-dollar bills as we can, but what does that come to? A hundred bucks maybe? The back room is where the money is. If we catch a wink from one of the tables, we go sit with the guy for twenty minutes while he tells us the story of his life and all we're thinkin is do I buy a ticket or not, you want a hand job, a blow job, what is it you want, mister? Without being able to say none of this out loud cause he might be a fuckin cop, excuse me."

"You said Althea bought three half-hour tickets last night," Carella said.

"Thass right. An' if that's all the time she bought, then whut the boys wanted was hand jobs. Tickets woulda cost her twenty for the half-hour, she probably charged fifty, sixty to milk 'em. When we're doin more *serious* work, ahem, we usually buy an hour ticket for fifty bucks, charge the john a full C for it. What Mac does is rent *space* to us, you comprehend? The back room is *space*, that's all. He lets us use his stage to advertise our goodies only cause his customers drink while they watchin us."

"So if a guy went in the back room with Althea last night ..."

"Yeah, it woulda been a hand job. That's what we buy a half-hour ticket for."

"Anybody follow her out? When she left last night?"

"Not that I seen."

"Where were you when you saw her leaving?"

"Onstage. It was the last dance. The last dance starts at two. The place closes at two-thirty, three."

"So she left before the last dance, is that it?"

"Guess she'd made money enough by then," Ruby said, and shrugged again.

"How? You said a hundred is tops for G-string change ..."

"Well, a hundred, a hun'twenty ..."

"Okay, and if she got fifty for each trip to the back room ..."

"Sixty be more like it."

"Okay, that netted her forty on each trip. That's a hun'twenty plus the G-string money comes to two-forty. What time do you girls start?"

"Nine."

"If she left at two, that was five hours," Ollie said. "Divide two-forty by five, you come up with forty-eight bucks an hour. She coulda made more workin at McDonald's."

"Not hardly."

"You consider forty-eight an hour good wages?"

"Most nights we do better."

"If two-forty was all she'd earned last night, why'd she leave half an hour before closing?"

"Maybe she was tired."

"Or maybe she'd arranged for somebody to meet her outside and take her home," Carella said. "Is that possible?"

"Anything's possible," Ruby said.

"What'd these guys look like?" Ollie asked. "The ones who went back with her."

"Who *knows* what any of these creeps look like?"

"Any of them look Jamaican?"

"Whut's a Jamaican look like?"

"This one was light-skinned, with blue-green eyes and curly black hair. Around six-two or -three, broad shoulders, narrow waist, a lovely grin, and a charming lilt to his speech."

"If I'd seen anybody like that aroun here," Ruby said. "I'da axed him to marry me."

That Wednesday night, the airwaves were full of stories about Danny Gimp and his two murderers. Slain stool pigeons do not normally attract too much attention. Unless they're killed in a place as public as a pizzeria, in broad daylight, during a week when television was panting for something sensational to captivate the imagination of the ever-salivating American viewing audience. The hanging death of a nondescript old man in a shabby little apartment in a meager section of the city was nothing as compared to two bald-faced gunmen striding into a pizzeria during the breakfast hour and blazing away like Butch and Sundance, albeit one had been black.

In a city divided by race, even the racial symmetry was reason for jubilance. For here, if nowhere else, a black man and a white man seemed to have worked in harmonious accord to rid the earth of that vilest of all human beings, the informer. Danny Gimp, unremarkable and unregarded while alive, became in death something of an inverted martyr, a man made suddenly famous by his extinction. In a world where wars were given mini-series titles, Danny and his two bold slayers stepped out of reality into the realm of truth made to *seem* fictitious, achieving in the space of several days a notoriety reserved for mythical bad guys and their destroyers. Killers though they were, The White Guy and The Black Guy had slain The Rat. One would have thought, from the interest generated on television, that once the salt-and-pepper assassins were apprehended, they'd be awarded medals and a ticker tape parade down Hall Avenue.

That Wednesday night, all five networks featured stories about Danny Gimp, the black and white shooters, and the similarly hued pair of detectives—Brown and Kling—who had responded to the call. The talking heads on the cable channels, babbling away on shows joining in their titles the words "pizza," "shootout," "terror," "confrontation," and "ambush" in various unimaginative combinations, endlessly debated whether a police informer was truly a "rat" as the term was commonly understood, why illegal guns seemed to proliferate at such an alarming rate in American cities, and whether it was politic or merely politics to have a black-and-white detective team investigating a case involving a black and a white shooter.

Thursday came and Thursday went.

So did Friday and Saturday.

And Sunday.

And all at once it was a new week.

In days of yore, the police department used to run a lineup every Monday to Thursday morning. Detectives from squads all over the city would gather in the gymnasium at headquarters downtown, where the Chief of Detectives paraded any felony offender arrested the night before. This was done solely to acquaint the people in law enforcement with the people doing mischief in their town, the premise being that the bad guys would continue being bad all their lives and it was a good thing to be able to recognize them on the street.

Nowadays, lineups were held only for purposes of identification, the suspected perp standing on a lighted stage with five innocent people, two of whom were usually squadroom detectives, the victim sitting behind a one-way mirror hoping to pick out a winner. But there was also another type of lineup, and it took place on television news programs whenever the tapes from hidden surveillance cameras were shown. On the five o'clock news that Monday night, the surveillance tapes from the pizzeria cameras were run for the first time, revealing in all their glory the two bold gunmen who had sprinted into the place and sprayed it with bullets. Danny Nelson's assailants were identifiable chiefly by race, but otherwise blurry to anyone who didn't really know them. In any event, no one came forward.

In a brilliant public-relations move, however, Restaurant Affiliates, Inc.—the company that owned the Guido's Pizzeria chain—now posted a $50,000 reward for any information leading to the capture and conviction of the two gunmen who'd shot up their fine establishment on Culver Avenue. That RA, Inc. seemed more interested in the damage done to their place of business than to the untimely demise of Danny Nelson went unnoticed by television viewers and newspaper readers alike. Informers were admittedly the scum of the earth, the campaign suggested, but public places should not be submitted to wanton violence. Linking pizza to after-school sports and public prayer, the TV commercials and newspaper ads called for swift apprehension of the culprits and stricter gun control everywhere in this wild and woolly nation. In conjunction with the police, an 800 line was set up and strict confidence was guaranteed any caller. A newspaper columnist wryly commented that Charlton

Heston had stopped eating pizza in favor of a Japanese dish called Shogun Sushi, a weak pun on "shotgun," but this was the afternoon paper. The column caused no end of amusement among the executive types up at RA, Inc.

Still no one came forward.

In a bit more than three weeks' time, the Danny Gimp case passed from intense media scrutiny to total oblivion.

Thanksgiving Day seemed almost an afterthought.

Chapter Five

He had drunk too much, and had argued with his uncle Dominick too loudly about whichever war was current wherever in the world. His uncle's attitude was always and ever "Let's bomb the shit out of them!" Carella had heard these words from him ever since he was old enough to understand, and his mother had always warned, "Dom, the children," but that hadn't stopped Uncle Dominick who looked like an enforcer for the mob, and who—for all Carella knew, but never asked—might very well have been one in his younger days.

They had got back home to Riverhead at about nine that night and the twins had reminded them, as if they needed reminding, that there was no school tomorrow, so they'd allowed them to stay up for a Thanksgiving special on NBC. Carella was still grumbling about his thick-headed uncle and Teddy was signing that maybe he should take a nice hot shower before he went to bed because tomorrow was another day, and *he* wasn't off from school, and there would always be another war to fight in this sorry world of ours and more people out of whom to bomb the S-H-I-T, which word she spelled out letter by letter with her fingers lest Carella miss the point that he was beginning to *annoy* her. He came out of the shower looking wet and contrite and in need of a haircut, which she hadn't noticed before.

He didn't say anything to her until she herself was in her nightgown—a long flannel granny because even with the temperature set at seventy-two, the old house was drafty and cold on this dank November night—her dark hair loose about her face, wearing a moisturizing cream she claimed was non-greasy but which he swore was made from goose grease, pulling back the covers, and jumping in quickly, and then reaching over to turn out the light—but his flying fingers caught her attention.

"I'm sorry," he said aloud, signing simultaneously.

She was half-turned away from him, she missed what he was saying. He said it again.

"I'm sorry."

And signed it.

Only baby boomers in their late forties believed that love meant never having to say you're sorry. Everyone else knew that if you truly loved someone and had hurt her, you *had* to say you were sorry—but you only had to say it once. You didn't have to get down on your hands and knees and beg forgiveness over and over again for the rest of your life, not if the person believed you. You just said it once. "I'm sorry." Unless you had a wife who could not hear your voice because she'd been born without hearing, and could not see your hands because her back was partially turned, in which case you said it again. "I'm sorry." And she heard you this time, and nodded, and took one of your hands between both hers, and nodded again.

They left the light on.

She moved into his arms, on his pillow, and he kissed the top of her head and held her close and told her it hadn't been his jackass uncle Dom who'd caused him to drink too much at his mother's house this cold Thanksgiving Day, but instead it was the dead old guy hanging from a bathroom hook and Danny Gimp getting shot in that pizzeria and the girl stabbed uptown in Fat Ollie's precinct that made him feel so goddamn worthless. It was suddenly as if all the cases he'd ever closed out had burst open again, exploding into a triple fireworks display trailing white-hot sparks on the night, a single brutal case where everything seemed linked but perhaps nothing was. And on top of that, his jackass uncle Dom probably *had* been a muscle man for a neighborhood smalltime hood named Vinnie Pineapples, a fat slob with bigger tits than most women had.

Teddy listened to everything he had to say, her eyes performing their magic trick of watching his moving fingers and his moving lips at one and the same time, and then she told him how she herself always felt so worthless at the beginning of the holidays because there were so many gifts to buy, but especially this year when they were short of cash because of the payments on the new car. She didn't want to take a job stuffing grocery bags at the supermarket, but at the same time not very many prospective employers wanted someone around the office who was handicapped, even though she could take steno and type eighty words a minute and was proficient in Word and Quicken and was very well-organized, go ask the twins. So he had to forgive her if sometimes she moped around the house, it was just that she often felt she wasn't doing enough for him or the children, wasn't doing enough for *herself*. And Vinnie Pineapples probably *did* have bigger tits than hers.

In the dead of night, in the dark, with the children sleeping soundly in their separate bedrooms down the hall, and the house as still as her own silent world, they comforted each other.

In a little while, Teddy fell asleep.

Carella lay awake for most of the night.

* * *

A lapsed Catholic—the last time he'd been to church was when he'd investigated the murder of a priest slain during vespers—Carella should have felt some vestiges of religious fervor during the Yuletide season, but instead he felt only guilt. Thanksgiving Day marked a full month since Andrew Hale was murdered. The beginning of the Christmas shopping season on the following day should have signaled the beginning of a month-long celebration that would not end until the last carol was sung and the last nog drunk on Boxing Day. Instead, it served as a reminder that the case was still unresolved. Carella wondered if Fat Ollie Weeks, a mile or so uptown, was experiencing the same feelings of helplessness and remorse. He almost called him. Instead, he slogged through a caseload that seemed to grow more mountainous day by day, taking small solace from the fact that the children seemed to be finding more joy in the holiday season than he did.

Meyer was similarly depressed.

A Jew in a Christian nation, he always felt oddly dispossessed at Christmas time. Never mind the euphemistic Chanukah bush he and Sarah had put up for the kids when they were small and still believed in Santa Claus. Never mind the gifts and the greetings exchanged. Try as he might to convince himself that the season had less to do with religion than with people being kind to each other, he could never shake the knowledge that this was not *his* holiday. He had once invited Carella and his family to a seder, and Carella had later confessed that he'd felt oddly out of place, even though Meyer had himself conducted the traditional ceremony, in English. Carella would hide Meyer in his basement in a minute and fight a thousand Nazis who tried to break down the door. Carella would break the head of anyone who made the slightest derogatory remark to Meyer. Carella would defend Meyer with his honor and his very life. But he had felt strange celebrating Passover with him. A measure of their friendship was that he'd been able to admit this.

In much the same way, Meyer had once asked Carella if *all* his Christmas cards read "Seasons Greetings" or "Happy Holidays" or "Yuletide Joy" or the like, or were these just the cards he sent to Meyer and other Jewish friends each year? Did Carella send other cards that read "Merry Christmas"? And if so, was it to spare Meyer's feelings that he sent the generic card? Carella told him *all* his cards were similarly antiseptic because what he was celebrating each December was not the birth of Christ, but instead the peace he hoped would prevail at Christmas time—a view he was sure would provoke a flood of letters from people he didn't know. Meyer said, "In fact, *I'll* write you a letter, you heathen!"

Thus encouraged, Carella went on to wonder aloud why he sent Christmas cards at *all* since he knew in his heart of hearts that Christmas—in America, at least—was simply a commercial holiday designed by merchants eager to recoup losses they'd sustained during the rest of the year. Meyer asked him if he was using the word "merchants" in an anti-Semitic way, and Carella said, "Vot minns anti-Semitic?" and Meyer said, "In that case, I wish to remind you that 'White Christmas' was written by a Jew." Carella said, "Giuseppe Verdi was a Jew?" Thus encouraged, Meyer said, "'A Rose in Spanish Harlem,' too." All amazed, both men went out to drink fervent toasts to Mohammed and Buddha.

That was too many Christmases ago.

This year, they shared a guilt that had something to do with what each considered a solemn duty to protect and preserve. A lonely old man had been befriended by someone who'd later drugged him and hanged him. A nineteen-year-old black quasi-hooker had been drugged in the same manner and then stabbed to death, most possibly by the same person who'd slain the old man. That person was either still here in this city, or else in Houston, Texas, or else only God knew where. For all they knew, he himself might be dead by now, killed in a bar fight or a motorcycle crash, murdered by a stiffed hooker or a miffed lover. Until they knew for certain, both cases sat in the Open File, neither resolved nor any longer under investigation, exactly like the Danny Nelson assassination.

But then, on the last day of November, Carella opened the morning paper.

The article was headlined "Jenny Redux."

Norman Zimmer, whose "Tea Time" is still running after 730 performances, has announced the acquisition of all rights to "Jenny's Room," a musical he plans to revive here next fall.

"Auditions will start this week," he said, "with rehearsals planned for the spring. We're looking for an L.A. tryout in late June, early July." Mr Zimmer added that negotiations were already under way with a top female star whose name he refused to divulge.

For those with long memories, "Jenny's Room" was first produced in 1927, as a vehicle for Jenny Corbin, a popular musical comedy performer of the day. It did not fare well with the critics and closed within a month. Mr Zimmer is certain this will not be its fate this time around. "I've worked too hard acquiring the rights," he said. "The original copyright holders have all passed on, and it was a matter of tracking down whoever had succeeded to their ownership. We found one of them in London, another in Tel Aviv, a third in Los Angeles."

The quest ended happily five days ago when

the last of the successors, a woman named
Cynthia Keating, signed on the dotted line,
right here in the big bad . . .

Carella spit out a mouthful of coffee.

He found a listing for a Zimmer Theatrical downtown on
The Stem and called the office shortly after nine A.M. A
woman told him Mr Zimmer would be at auditions all
day today, and when Carella told her he was a detective
investigating a homicide—the magic word—she gave him
an address for Octagon Theater Spaces and told him the
auditions were being held down there, she didn't know in
which studio. "They don't like to be bothered, though," she
added gratuitously.

Octagon Theater Spaces was a six-story building in a section
of the city called King's Road after the one in London, but
bearing scant resemblance to it. The actual name of the
street was Kenney Road, a heavily trafficked thoroughfare
lined with furniture warehouses, electrical supply stores, auto
repair shops, a garage for the city's Department of Sanitation
trucks, and an occasional restored and renovated factory like
the Octagon and its virtual twin down the street, Theater
Five, an eight-story structure divided into large rehearsal
spaces. A receptionist told them there were six studios on
each floor. In some of them, rehearsals were in progress; in
others, auditions were being held. The *Jenny's Room* auditions
were in studio four, on the second floor.

A lumbering elevator dating back to the building's
factory days took them to the second floor, where they
stepped out into a large entrance hall, one wall of which
was hung with pay phones. The pleasant hum of busy chatter

hung on the air. Good-looking men and women—this was their profession, after all—greeted each other familiarly, all of them seeming to know each other. Actors holding scripts, dancers in tights and leg warmers roamed from telephones to rehearsal halls, elevators to corridors, rest rooms to audition rooms. They glanced only cursorily at Carella and Brown, knowing at once that they weren't actors, but unable to peg their occupations.

Brown hadn't expected to be in the field today. He was wearing blue jeans, a ski sweater with a reindeer pattern, a green ski parka over it, and a blue woolen watch cap pulled down over his ears. He looked as square as a tuba. Carella could have passed for some guy here to read the gas meter. He was wearing a heavy mackinaw over a maroon sweater and gray corduroy trousers. No hat, although his mother constantly told him if his head got cold, he'd be cold all over. Both men were wearing wool-lined pull-on Bean boots. As they came down the corridor looking for studio four, a young girl in jeans and a leotard top chirped, "Hi," smiled, and flitted on by.

A door with a frosted-glass upper panel was lettered with the words STUDIO FOUR. It opened onto a small waiting room lined with folding chairs upon which sat young men and women in street clothes, all of them intently studying pages Carella assumed had been photocopied from a master script. A feverish-looking young man wearing glasses and a V-necked vest sweater over an apple green shirt asked Carella if he was here for Jenny. Carella showed him his shield and said he was here to see Mr Norman Zimmer. The young man didn't seem to get it at first.

"Will you need sides?" he asked.

Carella didn't know what sides were.

"I'm a police detective," he said. "I'm here to see Mr Zimmer. Is he here?"

"Just a second, please, I'll see," the young man said, and

opened a door beyond which Carella glimpsed a very large room lined with windows on one side. The door closed again. Brown shrugged. The man was back a moment later. He said auditions would be starting at ten, but Mr Zimmer could spare them a few minutes before then. "Please go right in," he said.

Carella looked at his watch.

It was a quarter to ten.

At the far end of the room, Zimmer—or a man they assumed was Zimmer—stood alone behind a row of folding chairs behind a bank of long tables. The moment they stepped into the room, he said, "What's this about, gentlemen?"

Brown blinked.

His voice. I recognized his voice. He had a very distinctive voice. Whenever he got agitated, the voice just boomed out of him.

Mrs Kipp's words. Describing the voice of the man who'd visited Andrew Hale three times during the month of September, arguing with him each time, threatening him.

The voice was a trained voice, an actor's voice, an opera singer's voice, a radio announcer's voice, something of that sort.

Carella—remembering the description from the report Kling and Brown had filed—was himself suddenly paying very close attention to the man who now came around the end of the row of tables, walking toward them.

"Mr Zimmer?" he asked.

"Yes?" His voice sounded as if it were coming over a bullhorn.

"Detective Carella. My partner, Detective Brown."

"How do you do?" Zimmer said, and extended his hand. His grip was like a moray eel's. "I haven't much time," he said. "What is it?"

Like Andrew Hale's visitor, Zimmer had dark hair and blue eyes. He was about Brown's size, a tank of a man with a barrel chest, and a belly that overhung the waistband of dark blue trousers. A blue jacket matching the pants was draped over the back of the chair he'd been sitting in. He wore a white shirt with the sleeves rolled up and the collar unbuttoned. The knot of his tie was pulled down. The tie sported alternating stripes, yellow to match his suspenders, navy blue to complement them and to pick up the color of his suit. *A big man*, Mrs Kipp had said. *Very big.*

"Sorry to bother you," Carella said. "We know you're busy."

"I am."

"Yes, sir, we realize that. But if you can spare a moment ..."

"Barely."

"... there are some questions we'd like to ask."

"What about?"

He was scowling now. Carella wondered what had put him so immediately on the defensive. Brown was wondering the same thing.

"Did you know a man named Andrew Hale?" he asked.

"Yes. I also know he was murdered. Is that what this is about?"

"Yes, sir, it is."

"In which case ..."

"Did you ever have occasion to visit Mr Hale?" Carella asked.

"I met with him on three occasions," Zimmer said.

"What for?"

"We had business to discuss."

"What kind of business?"

"*That* is none of your business."

"Get into any arguments on those occasions?" Brown asked.

"We had some lively discussions, but I wouldn't call them arguments."

"Lively discussions about what?"

The door from the waiting room opened, and a tall, thin woman wearing a mink coat and matching hat stepped into the room, hesitated, said, "Oops, am I interrupting something?," and seemed ready to back out again.

"No, come on in," Zimmer said, and turned immediately to the detectives again. "I'm sorry," he said, "but why are two police detectives asking me . . . ?"

"Won't you introduce me, Norm?" the woman said, and took off the mink and tossed it casually over the back of one of the chairs.

"Forgive me, this is Connie Lindstrom," Zimmer said. "Detectives Carella and Brown."

She was a woman in her mid-thirties, Carella guessed, wearing the mink hat at a rakish tilt that gave her a somewhat saucy look. Dark hair showed around the edges of the silky brown hat. Darker eyes flashed at Carella for a moment. "Nice to meet you," she said, and turned away.

"Mr Zimmer," Carella said, "do you know a woman named Cynthia Keating?"

"I do."

"Do you know she's Andrew Hale's daughter?"

"I do."

"Did she recently sign some papers for you?"

"Yes, she did."

"Assigning some rights to you?"

"Why should a business deal we made with Cynthia Keating . . . ?"

"*We?*" Brown asked.

"Yes. Connie and I are co-producing *Jenny's Room*."

"I see."

Threatened him how?

Told Mr Hale he'd be sorry. Said they'd get what they wanted one way or another.

They? Was that the word he used? They?

123

Pardon?

They'd get what they wanted?

Yes. I'm pretty sure he said they.

So now we've got *two* producers, Brown thought, and *they* are doing this show here. The rights to which they finally got from a woman whose dear old dad got killed a month ago. My, my, what a tiny little world we live in.

"The newspaper said you worked very hard acquiring the rights to this show," he said.

"Yes, we did."

"Original copyright holders all dead . . ."

"I'm sorry, but this is *really* none of your . . ."

"Had to track down whoever'd succeeded to ownership, isn't that correct?"

"Wow, it is fucking *cold* out there!" a voice from the door said, and a short, dark man wearing ear muffs, a camel-hair coat, and blue jeans stuffed into the tops of unbuckled galoshes—though it wasn't snowing outside— burst into the room like a rocket. "Sorry I'm late," he said, "there's construction on Farrell Avenue."

"There's *always* construction on Farrell Avenue," Connie said, and opened her handbag. Removing a package of cigarettes from it, she lighted one, blew out a stream of smoke, and said, "Excuse me, Norm, but there are some things we ought to discuss before . . ."

"This won't take a minute more," Zimmer said.

"One of the owners in London," Brown said. "Another in Tel Aviv."

"Is that some kind of code?" the man in the camel-hair coat asked. He swung a tote bag off his shoulder, took off the ear muffs, carefully folded them into their own spring mechanism, unzipped the tote, and dropped them inside it. Tossing his coat carelessly over Connie's mink, he said, "Are we reading truck drivers today?"

Brown guessed he and Carella were the truck drivers in

question. "Mr Zimmer," he said, "when did you learn that Andrew Hale's daughter owned these rights you needed?"

"Why should our business affairs be of any interest to you?" Connie asked suddenly and quite sharply.

"Ma'am?" Brown said.

"Don't 'ma'am' *me*, mister," she snapped. "I'm young enough to be your daughter." She turned abruptly to Carella, effectively dismissing Brown. Puzzled, he gave her a closer look. He figured her to be thirty-two, thirty-three, what the hell did she mean, old enough to be her father? Or did she find it difficult to judge a black man's age? Was he dealing with a closet racist here?

"If your visit has anything at all to do with our show," she told Carella, "perhaps our lawyers ..."

"You won't be needing lawyers just yet, Miss Lindstrom," he said.

"Is that some sort of threat?" Zimmer asked.

"Sir?"

"The 'just yet'? Are you indicating we *might* be needing lawyers sometimes in the future?"

"Anytime you want one, that's your legal right, sir," Carella said.

"Oh, look, the new police politeness," the man in the unbuckled galoshes said, and rolled his eyes.

"You are?" Brown asked.

"Rowland Chapp. I'm supposed to be *directing* this show. If ever I get a chance to *cast* the damn thing."

"Mr Zimmer," Carella said, "these rights you bought from Cynthia Keating. Did she inherit them from her father?"

"If you need information regarding the acquisition of rights, you'll have to talk to my attorney. Meanwhile, you've wasted enough of my time. Goodbye."

"Does that answer your question?" Chapp said, and nodded. "Good, we have work to do here, so do curtsy and go home." He sat abruptly on one of the folding chairs, took off the galoshes, removed from his tote bag a pair of soft leather loafers, and slipped into them. "Where's Naomi?" he asked. Rising abruptly—he was a man of swift, decisive movements, Brown noticed—he clapped his hands like a schoolmarm calling together an unruly class, said, "Ten after ten, kiddies, no more questions!"

Ignoring him, Brown asked, "Is that why you went to see Hale? To talk about the rights to *Jenny's Room?*"

"Yes," Zimmer said.

"Where the hell is *Naomi?*" Chapp shouted.

The door opened. A blond, blue-eyed woman wearing a black parka, a black cowboy hat, and black jeans came in and walked swiftly toward the tables.

"Right on cue," Chapp said.

Naomi—if that was her name—smiled quizzically at the detectives, pulled a face that asked Who the hell *are* these people, unzipped the parka, and said, "Sorry I'm late."

"Construction on Farrell," Connie said.

"Got it," Naomi said, aiming a finger at her and pulling an imaginary trigger. Under the parka, she was wearing a long black sweater pulled low over the jeans. She did not take off the black hat.

"Are you a cattle rustler?" Chapp asked her.

"Yes, Ro," she said.

Connie was lighting another cigarette from the stub of the first one.

"You don't plan to *smoke* while people are *singing* in here, do you?" Naomi asked, appalled.

"Sorry," Connie said, and stubbed it out at once.

The door to the waiting room burst open. The bespectacled young man who'd earlier asked Carella if he'd need sides popped his head in.

"The piano player's here," he said.

"Good," Chapp said. "What's that in the corner there, Charlie?"

"A piano?" Charlie said cautiously.

"Good. Introduce it to the piano player. Who's our ten o'clock?"

"Girl named Stephanie Beers."

"Send her right in."

"You heard him," Zimmer told the detectives.

"Just one more question," Carella said.

"Just."

"How'd *Hale* acquire those rights?"

"I have no time to go into that just now."

"When *will* you have time?" Carella asked.

"You said just *one* more question," Chapp reminded him.

The door opened again.

"Morning, morning!"

A man wearing a short overcoat, a long muffler, and bright red woolen gloves walked directly to the upright piano angled into the corner, took off his overcoat and gloves, hurled them on top of the piano, yanked out the bench, and sat. A tall, redheaded woman walked in almost immediately behind him.

"Good morning, everyone," she said. "I'm Stephanie Beers."

"Hi," Chapp said. "I'm Rowland Chapp, director of *Jenny's ...*"

"I *love* your work, Mr Chapp."

"Thank you. Naomi Janus, our choreographer. And our two producers, Connie Lindstrom and ... Norm? Sorry, but we really *must ...*"

"Coming."

"We'll be back," Carella said.

"What are you going to sing for us?" Chapp asked, smiling.

*   *   *

A call to the Hack Bureau had revealed no pickups outside The Telephone Company at two A.M. or thereabouts on November 10. So you think, a black hooker, who gives a shit? Then you think some guy dropped roofers in her beer or gingerale and *stabbed* her? That ain't fair, is what you think. So you start wondering how the girl got home that night if she didn't take a taxi. Did somebody drive her home in his own car, which was the worst of all possibilities? Or did she take the subway or a bus? Not many girls wanted to risk the subway at two in the morning, even though it was faster than surface transportation. After midnight, a bus driver had to let you out anywhere along the route, and not just at designated stops, a peculiarly civilized option in a city often cited for barbarism. So Ollie figured maybe the girl *did* take a bus home the night she was killed. In which case it was possible she'd met whoever later killed her either *on* the bus or after she got *off* the bus, both magnificent speculations but better than nothing when all you had was nothing. If you went this route, you were thinking the two crimes were unrelated. The roofers in each crime were then just a coincidence, which Ollie did not rule out. No working cop ever ruled out coincidence. Only in Sweden did learned scholars scoff at coincidence.

Ollie checked his bus schedules and discovered there was a bus that stopped on the corner of Stemmler and Lowell at 2:05 each weekday morning, which bus Althea probably couldn't have caught since the stop was three blocks from the club, which Ruby said she'd left at 2:00 A.M. approximate. There was another bus twenty-one minutes later at 2:26 A.M. which she could have caught easily enough. So Ollie went downtown three weeks after the murder of Althea Cleary, and stood in the bitter cold on the corner of Stemmler and Lowell, waiting for the 2:26 A.M. bus. There was one other person at the bus stop, a man carrying a black lunch pail. Ollie figured him at once for a regular. Guy carrying a lunch pail at two-thirty in the morning, was he going to a baseball game? No, he was going to work. And if he was going to work at this hour on a Tuesday night, chances are he was also going to work on a Tuesday night three weeks ago. Ollie waited till the bus arrived and they'd both boarded it before he struck up a conversation with the man.

"My name is Oliver Wendell Weeks," he said. "I'm a detective," and showed his shield.

The man said nothing.

Looked at the shield.

Nodded.

Said nothing.

"You ride this bus every night at this time?" Ollie asked.

"Mornings, actually," the man said. "This time of night, it's morning already."

"On my block," Ollie said, "if it's still dark, it's nighttime."

"Who can argue with that?" the man said. "My name's Jimmy Palumbo, I'm a short-order cook in a deli in Riverhead. We start serving at six, I have to be there at four-thirty to set up. I'm afraid to ride the subways, so I take a bus to work. Takes me two hours to get there from where I live. But at least I get there alive, am I right?"

Who asked you? Ollie wondered.

"Were you on this bus, at this time, three weeks ago?" he said.

"On a Tuesday, you mean?

"Yes. Three weeks ago tonight."

"I'm on this bus *every* Tuesday at this time. I'm prompt and punctual. I also make the best hash browns in the business. You want to know the secret of making great hash browns?"

"No," Ollie said. "I want to know do you remember

seeing this girl on this bus three weeks ago at this time."
He took from his jacket pocket a black-and-white print
the Photo Unit had made from a picture recovered in
Althea's apartment. "Black girl," he said, "nineteen years
old, five-seven or eight, weighed about a hun'fifteen. Recall
seeing her that Tuesday?"

"No," Palumbo said. "Why? What'd she do?"

"Did you *ever* see her on this bus? At *any* time?"

"Not that I recall. Usually the bus is empty till it hits
the stop near the Sands Spit Bridge. Lots of people connect
there. They come over the bridge, make the connection. Of
course, when I say empty, I don't mean *literally* empty. I mean
just a handful of people. Most people prefer the subway, but
I value my life too highly. Two hours later, I'd risk it. But
two-thirty in the morning? No way."

Who asked you? Ollie thought again.

"Where would she have got off, this girl?" Palumbo
asked.

"What difference does it make where she got *off*," Ollie
asked, "if she didn't get *on* in the first place?"

"Cause maybe I noticed her getting off, but not on,"
Palumbo said. "Lots of times, people don't notice things
till later."

"She woulda got off at Hanson Street. Or maybe
she signaled the driver to let her off between Slade and
Hanson."

"I don't even know where that is. Hanson Street."

"It's up in Diamondback."

"That where you work?"

"Yes."

"What's that precinct up there?"

"The Eight-Eight."

"Oh yeah, right."

"You know it?"

"No."

Ollie figured there was no use talking to this jackass. He changed his seat and watched the silent city passing by outside. This was the time of day he liked best, the empty hours between midnight and dawn, a time when the sleepless city lay coiled with menace and surprise. If he were not a cop, he would never venture outdoors at this time of night, however safe the Mayor said it was. Let the Mayor take a little stroll out there where blurred figures clustered under street lamps and cars cruised slowly past on the night. Let him.

Through his own image reflected darkly in the window, he could see the city beyond, changing from white to Latino in the wink of an eye, and then Latino to black as the bus lumbered farther uptown through forsaken streets where steam drifted up from sewer lids and rats scurried in packs from sidewalk to sidewalk. Let the Mayor take his stroll, the fuck.

He signaled for a stop where he supposed Althea would have if she'd taken the bus home that night. It was close to three-thirty. The short-order cook was dozing as Ollie made his way to the front of the bus. The door opened. The driver asked, "You be all right up here, man?"

"I'm a cop," Ollie said, and stepped out into the night.

There was an arrogance in his girth and his waddle, an insolence in his gaze that advertised his profession a mile away. If you didn't know this man was a cop, you had no right being out on the street at this hour. And if you recognized him as such, you'd be a damn fool to mess with him. Ollie knew the shield wasn't much protection these days; in some instances it would as easily encourage a slug as dissuade one. But the demeanor that said he was a cop also warned that there was a nine-millimeter semi-automatic in a holster under his jacket. He walked the empty hours of the night with not-quite immunity, but with something as close to it as anyone deserved.

At three-thirty in the morning, Althea Cleary's street was a lot livelier than Ollie expected it would be. An all-night Korean grocery store stood ablaze with light on one corner. An all-night diner, equally incandescent, occupied the corner opposite. In a way, these two bustling places of business were good news. They widened the field of possible suspects beyond the invisible John Bridges; Althea could have left the club alone, got on and off the bus alone, and—in either the diner *or* the grocery store—met the man who'd later killed her. On the other hand, did Ollie really *need* or *want* a wider field? Why not expand the number of suspects to include the entire city, the entire state, the entire nation? Why not work this fucking case for the rest of his life?

He almost went home to bed.

This was, after all, just a little black hooker here.

Instead, he went into the grocery store, and sauntered over to the cash register with his coat open and his belly and the butt of the nine showing, hoping the smiling idiot behind the counter would think he was about to hold up the joint, heh heh. Inject a little humor here, right? Throw a minor scare into these slopes here, while never forgetting the magnitude of the mission, ah yes.

"Let me talk to the manager," he said.

The manager or the owner or whoever he was came over grinning nervously.

"You know this girl?" Ollie asked.

The man looked at the picture.

"She live aroun corner," he said.

"Right. Ever see her?"

"She killed," he said.

"When's the last time you saw her?" Ollie asked.

"Before kill."

"When before?"

"Night before. She come in, buy milk."

"What time was that?"

"Same now."

"Three-thirty, around then?"

"T'ree-t'irty, yes."

"Was she alone?"

"Alone, yes."

"Say anything to you?"

"Say hello, goodbye."

"Did you thank her for buying the milk?"

"What?"

"Forget it. How long was she in here?"

"Fi' minute. Go across street diner."

"Thanks," Ollie said, and winked. "English word," he explained, and walked out.

The diner at this hour was packed with what Ollie called "denizens," which in his dictionary—but no one else's—was the antonym of "citizens." Here were the predators, the occupiers of the night, the people who woke up at midnight and began stalking the city like the wild animals they were. White, black, Latino, they all talked too loud and looked too tough till you shoved a nine in their face. The minute Ollie walked in, they knew he was a cop. To make the point clearer, he tossed open his coat and jacket, flashing the nine again. He didn't want to sit on a stool with his back to the door. He took a booth in the corner instead, where he could watch the counter as well as anyone coming in or going out. He lifted a menu from where it was nesting between the napkin holder and the salt and pepper shakers, studied it briefly, and signaled to the waitress. She was thirty-three or -four, Ollie guessed, not a beautiful woman, but there was something very sexy about her weariness.

"Bring me two burgers and a large order of fries," he told her.

"We only got one size order of fries," she told him.

"What size is that?"

"It don't have a designation. It's just the fries we serve as a side order."

"Okay, bring me two of them."

"They're just the normal size of the side order."

"Good, bring me two of the normal size."

"I mean, that's not their *designation* or anything, they don't *have* a designation. That's just the size they are."

"That's fine," Ollie said. "Two orders. Whatever size they are."

"Two burgers, two sides of fries," the waitress said, and walked off to place the order. When she came back some five minutes later, Ollie's shield was sitting on the table. He pointed to it, winked, and said, "When it quiets down a little, I want to talk to you."

The waitress looked at the shield.

"Sure," she said. "I have a break at four. I'll bring myself a cup of coffee."

"What would you say if I told you I know how to play piano?" he asked.

"Do you?"

"I'm gonna learn."

"Good for you," she said. "I'll see you later."

She came back again at a few minutes past four. She offered him a cigarette, lighted one for herself when he refused, and then sipped at the coffee she'd carried with her to the table. Stretching her legs, she said, "So who killed who?"

"How'd you guess?"

"You look like Homicide."

"Bite your tongue," Ollie said.

"I used to date a Homicide cop."

"Did he wear black underwear?"

"No. Black everything else though."

"What's your name?" Ollie asked.

"Hildy. What's yours?"

"Ollie Weeks. I work out of the Eight-Eight."

"Okay."

"Hildy, you prob'ly know a girl was killed around the corner here last month. Girl named Althea Cleary."

"Yeah."

"You know her?"

"Yeah. She used to come in here all the time. I think she was a dancer or something. Either that or a hooker. She'd come in here two, three in the morning almost every night."

"Was she in here the night she got killed?"

"I don't even know when that was."

"November ninth."

"You're still lookin for whoever done it, huh?"

"Still lookin."

"November ninth," she said, thinking.

"Would've been a Tuesday night."

"I can't say for sure."

"Do you remember *any* night this month when she might've come in here with a guy? Some kind of Jamaican, tall, easy grin. Would've had a knife scar down the left-hand side of his face."

"Oh yeah," she said, nodding.

"You remember him?"

"Mean-looking son of a bitch. Light complexion, kind of bluish-green eyes, lots of white back there someplace. But Althea didn't come *in* with him. He was here already."

"Tell me what happened."

"He walked in, it must've been two-thirty or so," Hildy said. "First thing I noticed was the scar. Well, hell, you couldn't miss it. You see lots of knife scars up here, but this one was a beaut. What you *don't* see much of up here is Jamaicans, though. You get all colors of the rainbow up here, but this ain't what you'd call a Jamaican neighborhood.

That's further uptown, near the ballpark, you know? Minute he asked for a cup of coffee, I caught the Jamaican speech. You know how they sound. Cop of coffee ond a scrombled egg son'wich," she said, trying to sound Jamaican but failing miserably; Ollie knew because he had such a finely tuned ear. "Anyway, Althea didn't come in till sometime later."

"You knew her by name?"

"Oh sure. She was a regular."

"How about the Jamaican? Did *he* give you a name?"

"Nope."

"Who made the first move?"

"You mean him or Althea? Actually, it was him. She took a seat in one of the booths, ordered whatever it was, I forget. He wandered over, introduced himself, sat down."

"You didn't hear a *name* when he introduced himself, did you?"

"Nope."

"John Bridges?"

"Nope. Took off his hat, though."

"Polite."

"Oh yes."

"Curly black hair, right?"

"Well, I didn't notice if it was curly, but it was black, all right."

"He seem gay to you?"

"Gay? Hell, no."

"So what happened with the two of them?"

"*Was* she a hooker?" Hildy asked.

"Not officially. She worked in a topless joint down-town."

"Cause she got real friendly with him, is what I mean."

"Did they leave here together?"

"Yeah."

"What time?"

136

"Around three-thirty."

"Arm in arm, or what?"

"Well ... friendly. Like I said."

"Think she was heading home with him?"

"Saw them turning the corner together. Through the window there," Hildy said, and nodded toward it.

"Then it was a possibility."

"A likelihood. So when do you start?"

"Start what?"

"Piano lessons."

"Oh. Soon."

"You'll have to play for me sometime," she said.

"What's your favorite song? I'll learn it."

"Gee, that's hard to say. Without dating myself."

"That's not always true. You got songs they call standards, you didn't have to be a teenager at the time to know them."

"Like what?"

"Like 'Stardust,' for example. Everybody knows 'Stardust.'"

"I don't."

"You don't?"

"Nope."

"How about 'Night and Day'?"

"Is that a song?"

"You never heard of 'Night and Day'?"

"Never."

"Sinatra? You heard of Frank Sinatra?"

"Of *course* I heard of Frank Sinatra."

"That was one of his big songs, 'Night and Day.'"

"I don't know it."

"What Sinatra songs *do* you know?"

"'Mack the Knife.'"

"That was Bobby *Darrin's* big hit."

"It was not."

"Of *course* it was. You know any other Sinatra songs?"

"Sure."

"Which ones?"

"'Strangers When We Meet'?"

"That was a *book*."

"No, it was a *song*."

"'Strangers in the *Night*' was the song."

"Oh yeah, right."

"Do you know any Beatles' songs?"

"Sure, I do."

"Which ones?"

"The one about diamonds?"

"'Lucy in the Sky with Diamonds'?"

"Right, that's it."

"Any others?"

"Sure, but I can't remember their names offhand."

"What songs *do* you remember?"

"Well, there's 'Back 2 Good' by Matchbox 20?"

"Uh-huh."

"And 'Bad.' By U2. You know that one?"

"Uh-huh. What else?"

"How about 'Uninvited'?"

"Uh-huh."

"Alanis Morrisette? You ever hear of her?"

"Uh-huh."

"'Criminal'? You oughta know that one, a cop. Fiona Apple?"

"Uh-huh," Ollie said. "Well, I guess I could learn some of those songs for you." He'd already forgotten the titles. "How about 'Satisfaction'?" he asked. "You know 'Satisfaction'?"

"Sure," Hildy said. "The Rolling Stones."

Bingo, Ollie thought.

*   *   *

The special 800 line was officially called the Police Information Network, or PIN for short. The team of twelve police officers manning the line called themselves "The Rat Fink Squad." The female officer who answered one of the phones that Tuesday afternoon said, "Police Information Network, good morning."

A woman's voice said, "I saw the Guido's Pizzeria commercial."

"Yes, ma'am?" the officer said.

"Is this call being recorded?" the woman asked.

"Yes, ma'am, it is," the officer said.

"Do you have caller ID there?"

"Yes, ma'am, we do."

The officer had been instructed to tell the truth in answer to any caller's questions. She thought this was stupid, but that was what they'd told her.

"Then it's a good thing I called from work, huh?"

"Either way, ma'am, whatever you tell us will remain strictly confidential."

"I don't want to say anything to anyone but a detective," the woman said.

"Shall I ask a detective to call you back?" the officer asked.

"Please," the woman said.

Bert Kling spoke to her shortly after three P.M. and went to see her at home later that evening. She lived in a five-story walkup outside the Eight-Seven, on Coral Street farther downtown, near the old Regency Theater building. Betty Young turned out to be white and thirtyish, a good-looking, dark-haired, blue-eyed woman who told him she'd just got home twenty minutes ago. When he arrived, she was still wearing the suit and jacket he assumed she'd worn to work that morning, standing at the kitchen counter, eating a

Twinkie and drinking a glass of milk. She asked him if he'd care for anything, and when he declined, she invited him into the living room of the one-bedroom apartment where she sat on the sofa and he sat on an easy chair facing her. Through the row of windows behind her, Kling could see the tall smokestack of a building several doors away, dominating the skyline.

She told him she worked as a receptionist for the accounting firm he'd called, and she'd been able to make ends meet until her mother in Orlando, Florida, suffered a stroke this past August. Which was why she could sure use the fifty thousand bucks Guido's was offering, what with all the additional medical expenses and all.

"But what I want to make sure of," she said, "is that I'll be protected in this thing. We're talking about murder here, you know."

"Yes, Miss, I know."

"So what kind of protection would I be getting if I tell you what I know?"

Kling explained that her name would be kept confidential, that she would not be called as a witness in any criminal proceeding ...

"I'm not a witness, anyway," she said. "I didn't actually *see* anybody kill anybody."

"But you do have information that would lead us to the person or persons responsible?"

"Yes, I do. The point is, how can I be *sure* my name won't be made public?"

"Well, there would be no need to do that."

"Suppose some television reporter gets nosy, how do I know the cops won't tell him my name? Or the Guido's people? How can I be sure?"

"You can't," Kling said. "You'd just have to trust us."

She gave him a look that said *Trust* you? In this city, he was used to such looks.

"And how do I know I'll get my money?" she asked.

"Same thing," he said. "Trust."

"Uh-huh."

"Or maybe ... I know *we* wouldn't do this if it was a *police* reward ... but maybe the company'd be willing to put half the money in escrow to begin with and then pay the rest after arrest and conviction."

"Arrest and *conviction*?" she said.

"Yes, that's the ..."

"Oh, no, wait a minute," she said. "Suppose you arrest the guy who did the shooting and then your D.A. screws up? Why should I be responsible for a conviction?"

"Well, those are the terms of the Restaurant Affiliates offer. Arrest and ..."

"The *who* offer?"

"Restaurant Affiliates. That's the corporation that owns the Guido's chain. Arrest and conviction is what they stipulated."

"Then it's not really a genuine offer, is it?"

"I think it's genuine, Miss."

"How? If some inept D.A. lets him walk, I don't get the reward. How's that genuine?"

"Well, the D.A.'s Office wouldn't bring it to trial if they didn't think they had a strong case."

"But they *lose* cases all the time, don't they?"

"Well ... no. Not all the time. I would say they win many more cases than they lose."

"Still, where's my guarantee? I stick my neck out ..."

"Win or lose, your safety would be protected. If you identified this person for us ... I'm assuming you know only *one* of the shooters, am I right?"

Betty looked surprised.

"What gives you *that* idea?" she asked.

"Well, you referred to 'the *guy* who did the shooting' and just now you said something about the D.A. letting *him* walk. Him. Singular. So I'm assuming you know only one of them."

"Gee, an actual detective," she said, a remark which in this city didn't surprise Kling. In fact, nothing in this city surprised Kling. He plunged ahead regardless. "In any case," he said, "I don't want to ask you any questions until you're ready to answer them. So . . ."

"I won't be ready to answer them till Guido's assures me I'll get the fifty thousand if what I tell you leads to *charges*, never mind conviction. If there's a catch to this, they can just forget the whole thing."

"I can't speak for them, of course, but I don't think there's a catch. I think they genuinely want to apprehend these guys. Or even *one* of them, if that's all the information you have."

She said nothing.

He looked at her.

"You could feel perfectly safe," he said.

She still said nothing.

"Let me take this back to my lieutenant," Kling said. "He'll want to make some calls. If we can tell Restaurant Affiliates we've actually got someone who's willing to come forward with information . . ."

"I am."

"I understand that."

"But only if they drop the conviction part of it. I want my money the minute he's charged with the crime. I mean, suppose I'd seen O.J. stabbing his wife and I gave the police information that led to *his* arrest? And then he walked. Do you see what I mean?"

"But you said you *didn't* witness the actual shooting . . ."

"That's right, I didn't witness the shooting itself. But I know one of the men who did it."

"Why'd you decide to come forward at this time, Miss Young?"

"My conscience was bothering me."

She paused a moment, and then said, "Also, I broke up with him last week."

The deputy chief in charge of PIN was informed by Lieutenant Byrnes of the Eighty-seventh Squad somewhere away the hell uptown that one of his detectives had interviewed a young woman who claimed to know one of the shooters in the pizzeria rumble, but would not divulge any information about him until she was assured she'd get the reward money the moment criminal charges were brought—all of this in a somewhat breathless rush from Byrnes who was, to tell the truth, a bit excited by what Kling had brought home.

"The fuck she think she is?" the deputy chief asked.

"You might want to discuss this with the Guido's people," Byrnes suggested.

"They'll say no," the deputy chief said.

He was wrong.

The executives up at Restaurant Affiliates, recognizing another brilliant public relations coup when they saw one, immediately pounced upon it. On television that night— with commercial spots going for hundreds of thousands of dollars a minute—all five major networks and most of the cable channels gave at least two minutes of free broadcast time to the news that RA, Inc., ever mindful of the uncertainties of the criminal justice system, were revising their reward offer. If anyone provided information leading to the arrest and *indictment* of the shooters, the $50,000 was theirs for the asking.

RA Inc.'s advertising people might have been forgiven for linking the singular "anyone" with the plural "theirs" because they were selling a product and they didn't want to offend any feminist who might object to the proper but politically incorrect "his." Too clumsy to say "his or hers for the asking." Much easier to say "theirs" and play it ungrammatically safe, as if anyone cared. But the journalists reporting the revised offer should have known better. Instead, they read it verbatim from the ad agency's press release, compounding the felony. Further aiding and abetting, most of them closed their reports with the slogan RA, Inc. had paid millions to popularize over the years: "So come on over to Guido's for a *nicer* pizza!"

There was enough bitterness and bile in Betty Young to corrode the hull of a battleship. Divorced at the age of thirty-two, after eleven years of seemingly blissful marriage to a stockbroker who ran off to the Pacific with a Hawaiian woman visiting the city—

"An easy lei," Betty mentioned.

—she'd finally met the man she thought she could unreservedly love again. This happened just this past March, when Maxwell Corey Blaine, a good ole thirty-seven-year-old white boy from Grits, Georgia, walked into the accounting firm for which she worked and asked for some help filling out his income tax return. Ole Maxie, it seemed, worked for a pool hall up in Hightown, a largely Dominican section of the city, but this did not seem at all ominous to Betty at the time, she being the most tolerant of human beings except when it came to cheating sons of bitches, "May they *both* drop dead," she also mentioned.

Maxie's title at the pool parlor was "table organizer," an occupation he found difficult to describe to Betty with any precision, but apparently a job requiring skills enough to warrant a salary of three thousand dollars a week. His employer, a man named Enrique Ramirez, was dutiful in supplying a W-2 as tax time rolled around, but that wasn't the problem. Apparently, the state of Georgia wanted Maxie to file a return for the *previous* year, during which time not only had he been unemployed, he had also been in jail. Maxie wondered if the meager wages he'd earned in the prison laundry washing other inmates' uniforms was taxable income. Betty passed him on to one of the firm's junior accountants, who straightened out the entire mess—but that was another story.

To tell the truth, Betty found Maxie's imprisonment somewhat exciting. He had been sent to the state prison in Reedsville on what they called in Georgia "aggravated assault," a felony that carried with it a sentence of one to twenty. He'd been paroled in January and had left the state to come straight north, in itself a violation, but the hell with Georgia, he'd found his own sweet little peach right here.

"He called me his sweet little peach," Betty said.

She moved in with him on April 16 of this year, the day after the firm filed his tax returns. He told her fairly early on that the reason he'd been sent to prison was that he'd broken the back of a person who owed money to a gambler in Atlanta, for whom Maxie was working at the time. The person was now paralyzed from the waist down, but that wasn't Maxie's fault, since all he'd planned to do was encourage the man to pay up, not cripple him for life, a story the Fulton County District Attorney had not bought.

There was something frightening, Betty admitted—but also exciting—about Maxie's size. She guessed he was about six feet, four inches tall, and had to weigh something like two hundred and ten, with muscles everywhere and jail house tattoos on his shoulders and arms. It was perhaps his size that caused him to seek employment similar to what he'd had in Atlanta. "Table organizer," it turned out, was a euphemism for "enforcer," Maxie's job being to bring to task any miscreant drug dealer who failed to pay Ramirez any moneys owed to him. Ramirez dealt cocaine—and "a lot of designer drugs," according to Betty—and was connected to the Colombian cartel in a strutting bantam cock sort of way, several steps higher than the snotnosed sellers proliferating like cockroaches in the streets uptown, but nowhere close to the invisible, untouchable upper echelons of Dopeland.

In October sometime, it was brought to Maxie's attention that a stoolie and sometime courier named Danny Gimp had done grievous harm to Ramirez. Apparently, a dealer in Majesta had agreed to pay *El Jefe*—as Ramirez was familiarly called—$42,000 for two kilos of coke. Ramirez turned the packaged snow over to Danny for delivery, but it never found its way to Majesta. The way *El Jefe* looked at it, he was out not only the coke but also the profit he would have made on the coke. It was one thing to owe money to him but quite another to steal from him. This was an unpardonable offense. This did not call for mere physical retribution. This called for extinction.

On the morning of November 8, after a night of somewhat torrid lovemaking, Maxie showered and dressed and told Betty he was going out to meet a friend of his for pizza.

"He grinned when he said this," Betty mentioned.

On the following Monday night, Betty saw the video tape on television and thought she recognized Maxie as the white gunman shooting up Guido's.

"They ought to get better cameras," she said. "I have to tell you the truth, if I didn't *know* Maxie, I never would have recognized him from the tape."

The closest she came to telling Maxie that she'd seen him on the tape, and suspected he was one of the men who'd killed the rat everyone was talking about, was at breakfast a week or so later when she casually remarked, "By the way, how did you enjoy your pizza that morning?"

"What the fuck you talkin about?" Maxie said.

Four days later he moved in with an eighteen-year-old bitch whose sole claim to fame, according to Maxie, was that she knew how to do The Moroccan Sip. Whatever that was. As if Betty *cared* what it was.

All she wanted was for the cops to arrest him and send him to the electric chair. Was that a lot to ask for a lousy fifty thousand bucks?

She told them all this on Wednesday morning, the first day of December.

At a quarter past one the next morning, five detectives from the Eight-Seven drove all the way downtown to kick in Maxwell Corey Blaine's front door.

Only one of them got shot.

Chapter Six

They went in with a No-Knock arrest warrant and Kevlar vests because from what Betty Young had told them, the dude in here was no cookie-cutter.

The trouble with most tenement buildings in many parts of this city was that they hadn't been designed for close police work. Maxwell Corey Blaine did not live on a ranch in Beaucoup Acres, Louisiana, where the sheriff's folk could drive up a tree-lined, moss-covered driveway and then storm the front door with a battering ram, five cops on either side of it—my how all dee cattles was afeard. Maxwell—or Maxie, as he was familiarly called by his once and former rat fink girlfriend—lived in a six-story walkup on a narrow street in Calm's Point, part of a section that had once been beautiful and civilized, had since become ugly and barbarous, and was currently targeted for gentrification in the next ten years, a cycle that was doomed to repeat itself though no one on the city council had a clue.

The building was constructed of red brick dimmed by the soot of centuries. The stairways were steep and the hallways narrow. There were four apartments on each floor, and at this hour of the morning—they had assembled outside at a quarter to two—the sounds of deep slumber rumbled from behind double-locked doors. They felt clumsy in the heavy-duty vests. They were dressed for winter as well, wearing layered clothing under the vests, gloveless now that they were inside the building, all of them carrying AR-15 assault rifles. No room for a battering ram in these turn-of-the-century hallways, stairs winding back on themselves until the men reached the fifth-floor landing and regrouped.

These men were colleagues and friends. There were no petty quarrels to settle here, no one was trying to trick anyone else into "taking the door," which defined the ten most dangerous seconds in any policeman's life. Kling simply told the others *he* would take the door. It was him and Brown, he said, who'd initially caught the pizzeria squeal, so this was their case and officially their bust, *if* they made a bust here tonight, so he'd take the door, with Brown and Carella as flankers, and Willis and Meyer as backups. It was very cold on that fifth-floor landing. His breath feathered from his mouth as he whispered all this to the others.

He was holding the heavy Colt carbine in both hands. Inside the apartment here, there was a man who'd maybe committed murder, a man the judge had felt was sufficiently dangerous to merit a No-Knock. The team was a good one. These men had worked together before, and they knew exactly what was coming down here tonight, exactly what they were supposed to do. Carella and Brown would flank the door. Kling would kick it in. The moment the lock was history, all three would rush the room, with Willis and Meyer fanning in behind them. If they were lucky, it would all be over in two, three minutes.

Kling put his ear to the wood, listening.

He heard nothing.

He kept listening a moment longer, backed off the door, and ascertained with little head nods that the others were ready. He took a deep breath, brought up his right knee, the left arm extended for balance, his right hand grasping the pistol grip of the rifle. The force of his kick, combined with his forward momentum and the weight of his body, smashed the wood gripping the lock's bolt to the striker plate and jamb. He followed the splintered door inward, Carella and Brown peeling off from either side of the doorway and rushing after him into the apartment, Meyer and Willis not a heartbeat behind.

"Police!" Kling shouted and behind him the voices of the others echoed the word, "Police! Police!" as the men fanned into the apartment, eyes darting. Willis hit a wall switch and a ceiling light snapped on. They were in a small, shabby living room crowded with overstuffed furniture. To their left was a tiny walk-in kitchen. On the right wall, there were three closed doors. They guessed the one nearest the entrance opened on a closet. The bathroom was probably behind the middle door, the bedroom behind the last door on the wall, where it would have windows facing the street. No one commented aloud on any of this. They had been in many similar apartments and they knew tenement layouts. They simply moved behind Kling toward the last door on the wall, no hinges showing on this side of the door, it would open inward. He grabbed the knob, twisted it, again shouted "Police!," and hurled the door open, the assault rifle leading him into the room.

Kicking in the door, rushing the room, zeroing in on what they expected was the bedroom had maybe taken all of thirty seconds. In that same amount of time, the man who'd presumably been in bed when they arrived had already crossed the room to the dresser, opened the top drawer in it, yanked out what looked like a nine-millimeter pistol, and now turned to point it at Kling.

"*Gun!*" Kling shouted and hurled himself flat on the floor, rolling away from the shooter as Brown and Carella started into the room. The bedroom was dark. In the faint spill of light from the living room, they didn't see the girl in bed until she screamed, and she didn't scream until the giant standing at the dresser in white Jockey shorts and a white tank-top shirt fired two shots in rapid succession, not at Kling, but at the doorway, now filled with Brown's considerable bulk. Brown hurled himself to the left just as the shots exploded. The first slug missed him, missed Carella as well, who was coming through the door behind him. The second slug buried itself in the door jamb.

"There's a gun!" Meyer shouted back to Willis, and ran through the doorway, firing in the direction of the muzzle flashes. The girl was screaming hysterically now. The guy in his underwear was blasting away at anything that came through that door, hitting nothing but the door and the doorjamb until Willis, the smallest of the targets, came in like a dancer and took a hit in his thigh where there was no vest to protect it. The slug spun him around. His leg slid out from under him.

The guy at the dresser suddenly realized there were five guys with heavy assault weapons here, and only one of them was down. He could keep firing away for the rest of the night, with that crazy bitch on the bed screaming and screaming, or he could call some kind of truce here before somebody riddled him like a polka dot pie.

"Cool it, boys," he said, and threw down the gun.

Brown swatted him with an open hand that felt like a ten-pound hammer.

On the floor, Willis was trying to stanch the flow of blood from his thigh.

The one thing that could take all the joy out of police work was the sudden realization that it wasn't all fun and games. The graveyard shift had relieved at a quarter to midnight. The assault team had arrived a half hour later, to begin gearing up in the locker room. Now, at a little past four A.M., almost every detective on the squad came to the building on Grover Avenue, wanting to know what the hell had happened. Men not due to relieve until eight that morning came in because they'd "heard" something. Men who were supposed to be on vacation or out sick came drifting back to the squadroom, wanting to know all the details.

Sergeant Murchison told them Hal Willis had got shot, something all of them already knew or they wouldn't have flocked back here. What they wanted was *details*, man, but the only people who *had* the details were the four other cops who'd been along on the bust. Two of them, Kling and Brown, were locked in with the lieutenant and Maxie Blaine. The other two, Carella and Meyer, were at St Mary's Hospital with Willis. There was no one accessible who seemed to have any hard information, and so the gathered detectives settled for speculation instead.

All they knew was that something had gone terribly wrong in that apartment. And since Bert Kling had been leading the assault, the musing cops began thinking perhaps he was the one who'd done something wrong and was therefore somehow responsible for Willis being in the hospital. On the other hand, some of the detectives began thinking that maybe Willis himself had been responsible for his "accident," and this led to the further consideration that possibly he was a hard-luck cop. Because either he wasn't doing his job right—and this was merely whispered—or else he was jinxed. Either way, he was not a man to be partnered with. Police work was dangerous. You did not want to be riding with a hoodoo jinx of a cop who raised the odds. Or so some of the detectives on the squad began thinking, and a few actually began saying, on that bleak December morning. Loyalty among policemen was somewhat like loyalty among soldiers. When the shit was flying, it was all for one and one for all. But that didn't mean you had to go out drinking together after the battle was fought and won. Or lost, as seemed to be the case tonight, despite the fact that an arrest had been made. All in all, Willis getting shot cast a pall over the squadroom that made business as usual seem not as musketeerlike as it appeared on television.

In the squadroom that early morning, there was the usual collection of miscreants dragged in the night before: your snatch of hookers, your stealth of burglars, your clutch of muggers, your dime bag of pushers. Hookers were normally treated with jolly forbearance, the cops copping an occasional feel when opportunity allowed, the girls engaging in mock barter for leniency though they knew from experience that none was in the offing. This morning, it was different. The girls rounded up the night before were brusquely herded into the wagons that would take them downtown to Central Booking, no Sally-and-Sue banter this morning; they were whores, and a cop had been shot, and there was no time for jovial bullshit.

Burglars—unless they were junkie burglars—were usually treated with some measure of respect. For reasons understood only by cops, a burglar was mysteriously considered to be some kind of gentleman, even though he invaded a person's home, violated his privacy, and ran off with his personal goods. Professional burglars were very rarely violent. Cops appreciated this. They would kick a *junkie* burglar's ass six times around the block, but they would treat a *pro* like an equal who merely happened to be on the opposite side of the law. Not this morning. This morning, a cop had been shot, and there was no Hello-George-When-Did-You-Get-Out familiarity. This morning, everybody was a fucking criminal and everybody was guilty.

This morning, the victimizers suffered most.

Assault was never a very popular crime, but this morning if you'd beaten up an old lady in the park and stolen her purse, you were in for it, man. A minor assault wasn't the same as shooting somebody, but to the cops of the Eighty-seventh Precinct, it came damn close on this morning when one of their own had been assaulted with a deadly weapon. But if you had to be detained at the Eight-Seven this morning, the *worst* thing to be was a narcotics peddler. Too many police officers had been shot and killed by men selling dope to school kids, and whereas such criminals were never made to feel welcome in any precinct in the city, this morning the association of narcotics to murder and especially the murder of policemen was very keenly felt here at the Eight-Seven—especially when word had it that the perp being interrogated by Kling and Brown was an enforcer for the Colombian cartel.

Even aware of recent screaming headlines and protests and marches to City Hall, even cognizant of a public scrutiny that could escalate minor incidents into federal cases, the cops of the Eight-Seven were a mite careless this morning, if not downright reckless, shoving shackled prisoners into holding cells or vans when a mere invitation might have sufficed, using abusive and derisive language, acting-out all their personal fears, rages, and hatreds, treating criminals of any color or stripe exactly like the scumbags, shitheads, and evil sons of bitches they were, while at the same time themselves behaving like the brutal, detestable pricks the citizens of this city always *knew* they were.

Crime did not pay on this particular Thursday morning.

Not with a cop in St Mary's Hospital.

She had known Kling was leading a No-Knock arrest early this morning and when she'd first answered the phone and was informed that there was a cop down and he'd been taken to St Mary's with what was first reported as a stomach wound, she thought it might be Kling. She was relieved to learn that he hadn't been the victim, but any cop shot was a problem for Sharyn Cooke because she was a deputy chief surgeon in the police department and her job was to make sure any cop injured on her watch received the best treatment this city had to offer.

The unfortunate spelling of Sharyn's first name was due to the fact that her then thirteen-year-old, unwed mother didn't know how to spell Sharon. This same mother later put her through college and then medical school on money earned scrubbing floors in white men's offices after dark. Sharyn Cooke was black, the first woman of color ever appointed to the job she now held. Actually, her skin was the color of burnt almond, her eyes the color of loam. Off the job, she often wore smoky blue eye shadow and lipstick the color of burgundy wine. To work, she wore no makeup at all. High cheekbones, a generous mouth, and black hair worn in a modified Afro gave her the look of a proud Masai woman. At five-nine, she always felt cramped in the compact automobile she drove and was constantly adjusting the front seat to accommodate her long legs. It took her forty minutes to drive from her apartment at the farther reaches of Calm's Point to St Mary's Hospital in the depths of lower Isola, close by the apartment building in which Maxie Blaine had been captured. St Mary's was perhaps the second-worst hospital in the city, but that was small consolation.

A visit to Willis in the ER assured Sharyn that this wasn't the stomach wound she'd been dreading, but some two to three percent of all fatal bullet wounds occurred in the lower extremities and the bullet was still lodged in his thigh, close to the femoral artery. She did not want some jackass fresh out of medical school in the Grenadines to be poking around in there and possibly causing severe hemorrhaging. She went immediately to the head of the hospital, a nonpracticing physician named Howard Langdon. Langdon was wearing a gray flannel suit with wide lapels that had gone out of style ten years ago. He was wearing a pink shirt and a knit tie a shade darker than the suit. He had white hair and a white goatee. He looked as if his picture should have been on a fried chicken carton.

Langdon had once been a very good surgeon, but that didn't excuse the way he now ran St Mary's. Sharyn herself was a board-certified surgeon—which meant she'd gone through four years of medical school, and then five years as a resident surgeon in a hospital, after which she'd been approved for board certification by the American College of Surgeons. She still had her own private practice, but as a uniformed one-star chief she worked fifteen to eighteen hours a week in the Chief Surgeon's Office for an annual salary of $68,000. In this city, some twenty to thirty police officers were shot every year. Sharyn wasn't about to let one of them languish here at St Mary's.

As politely as she could, she told Langdon she wanted Detective Willis ambed over to Hoch Memorial, half a mile uptown—and three hundred light years away in terms of service and skill, which she did not mention. Langdon looked her dead in the eye and asked, "Why?"

"I'd like him to be there," she said.

Again, Langdon asked, "Why?"

"Because that's where I feel he'll receive the sort of care I want him to have."

"He'll receive excellent care here as well," Langdon said.

"Doctor," Sharyn said, "I really don't want to argue this. The detective needs immediate surgery. I want him ambed over to Hoch Memorial right this minute."

"I'm afraid I can't discharge him," Langdon said.

"It's not your call to make," Sharyn said.

"I run this hospital."

"You don't run the police department," she said. "Either

you have an ambulance at the ER door in three minutes flat, or I'll have him nine-elevened out of here. *Say*, Doctor."

"I can't let you do this," Langdon said.

"Doctor, I'm in charge here," Sharyn said. "This is my job and my mandate. That detective is moving out of here *now*."

"They'll think it's because St Mary's isn't a good hospital."

"Who are you talking about, Doctor?"

"The media," Langdon said. "They'll think that's why you moved him."

"That *is* why I'm moving him," Sharyn said coldly and cruelly and mercilessly. "I'm calling Hoch," she said, and turned on her heel, walked to the nurses' station, and snapped her fingers at a telephone. The nurse behind the counter handed it to her at once. Langdon was still floating in the background, looking angry and defeated and sad and somehow pitiable. Dialing, Sharyn told the nurse, "Get an ambulance around to the back door, and wheel the detective out. I'm moving him." Into the phone she said, "Dr Gerardi, please," and waited. "Jim," she said, "this is Sharyn Cooke. I've got a cop with a thigh wound, he's being transferred right this minute from St Mary's." She listened, said, "Tangential," listened again, said, "Nonperforating. It's still in there, Jim, can you prepare an OR and a surgical team, we'll be there in five minutes. See you," she said, and hung up, and looked at the nurse who was standing there motionless. "Is there a problem, Nurse?" she asked.

"It's just . . .," the nurse said, and looked helplessly across the counter to where Langdon was standing. "Dr Langdon?" she asked. "Is it all right to order an ambulance?"

Langdon said nothing for several moments.

Then he said, "Order it," and walked away swiftly, down the long polished tile corridor, not looking back, turning a corner, out of sight.

Sharyn went to Willis where he lay on a wheeled table behind ER curtains, an oxygen tube in his nose, an IV in his arm.

"I'm getting you out of here," she said.

He nodded.

"You'll be uptown in five minutes."

He nodded again.

"I'll be with you. Do you need anything?"

He shook his head.

Then, quite unexpectedly, he said, "It wasn't Bert's fault."

Section 125.27 of the Penal Law stated that a person was guilty of murder in the first degree when he caused the death of a police officer engaged in the course of performing his official duties. Maxie Blaine hadn't killed anyone, but he'd opened fire indiscriminately on a roomful of cops armed with an arrest warrant. This meant they had him cold on five counts of attempted murder one, a Class A-1 felony punishable by fifteen to life as a minimum on each count. In this city, you didn't shoot a cop and walk. No self-respecting D.A. would even *consider* a plea when he had four other police officers ready to testify that ole Maxie Blaine here had repeatedly pulled the trigger of the gun that downed a fellow police officer. If they needed civilian corroboration, they were sure they could get that from the eighteen-year-old girl who'd been screaming in Maxie's bed, and whose lawyer had advised her to remain silent until he saw which way the wind was blowing here.

The girl's lawyer—whose name was Rudy Ehrlich—didn't yet know the wind was blowing toward lethal injection, the penalty for first-degree murder in this state. So far, all Ehrlich knew was that his client's "friend" had wounded a police detective, and that she'd been a possible witness to the shooting. In such cases, Ehrlich's motto was "Speech is silver, silence is golden." As a matter of fact, this was Ehrlich's motto in *any* criminal case. He got a lot of money for this advice, which was only common knowledge to any schoolyard kid who'd ever been frisked for a firearm.

Maxie Blaine knew instinctively and through bitter experience on his meteoric rise through Georgia's criminal justice system that "Silence Is Golden" was really and truly a terrific rule to follow whenever you were dealing with law enforcement types. He also knew that he had just now popped a cop, and he knew in his secret heart of hearts that a month or so ago he had killed a man the media had later identified as a police informer, so long, Ratso. He suspected the reason the cops had come a-rappin on his door at two in the morning was they needed desperately to know had he really *done* that little rat bastard. Which he wasn't ready to admit since he wasn't pining just yet for a massive dose of Valium.

In an instance such as this, where they already had him on inadvertently plugging a cop in a moment of panic, the damn girl shrieking like a banshee and all, Blaine shrewdly calculated that maybe there was a deal to be made if he played his cards right. So whereas he asked for a lawyer— no experienced felon ever did *not* ask for a lawyer when he was in custody—he nonetheless figured he'd answer their questions until he saw where they were going. The minute he figured out what they really *had* here—he didn't see how they could possibly tie him to the pizzeria shooting—why that was when he could maybe squirm his way out of this, maybe talk the D.A. into covering everything he'd done including the Guido's thing for a plea that might grant him parole in twenty years, maybe even fifteen. In other words, he thought the way many criminals think: he thought he could outsmart two experienced detectives, a lieutenant who'd seen it all and heard it all, and even his own attorney, a man named Pierce

Reynolds, a transplanted good ole boy from Tennessee, who naturally urged silence.

The interrogation started in the lieutenant's office at six o'clock on that morning of December 2, by which time Blaine's attorney had arrived and consulted with him, and Blaine had been read his rights and verified that he understood them. To protect his own ass in any subsequent client-lawyer law suit, Reynolds went on record as having advised Blaine to remain silent and Blaine went on record as having been so advised. All the bullshit out of the way, the questioning proper began at six-fifteen A.M. with Detective-Lieutenant Peter Byrnes himself eliciting from Maxwell Corey Blaine his full name, address, and place of employment, which was a pool parlor in Hightown, or so he said, but then again he wasn't under oath.

If Blaine was in reality breaking heads for someone linked to the Colombian cartel, as Betty Young had informed them, he couldn't very well tell the cops this was his occupation. Not if he hoped to outfox them and cut a deal later. There was no official police stenographer here as yet, and no one from the District Attorney's Office. Blaine figured the deck was stacked in his favor. The cops figured they could nail him on shooting Willis whenever the spirit moved them. Getting someone to ride uptown from the D.A.'s Office was a simple matter of making a phone call. But they were angling for bigger fish. They were looking for Murder One.

Byrnes opened with a laser beam straight to the forehead.

"Know anyone named Enrique Ramirez?"

Blaine blinked.

"Nossir," he said, "I surely do not."

"I thought you might have done some work for him," Byrnes said.

"Is that a question?" Reynolds asked.

"Counselor," Byrnes said, "could we agree on some basic ground rules here?"

"What *basic* rules did you have in mind, Lieutenant? I thought I was familiar with *all* the rules, basic or otherwise, but perhaps I'm mistaken."

"Mr Reynolds," Byrnes said, "we don't need courtroom theatrics here, okay? There's no judge here to rule on objections, there's no jury to play to, your man isn't even under oath. So why not just take it nice and easy, like the song says, okay?"

"Does the song say anything about a cop getting shot tonight?" Reynolds asked. "Which is why my client is here in custody, isn't that so?"

"Well, Counselor," Byrnes said, "if you'd let him answer my questions, we could maybe find *out* why we're here, okay? Unless you want to call the whole thing off, which is your client's right, as you know."

"For Chrissake, let him ask his goddamn questions," Blaine said. "I got nothing to hide here."

Famous last words, Byrnes thought.

Reynolds was thinking the same thing.

So was Kling.

Brown was wondering if the son of a bitch was going to claim police brutality cause he'd smacked him upside the head back there in his apartment.

Blaine all of a sudden thought he had to be very careful here because somehow they'd learned about his relationship with Enrique Ramirez, and that was a road that led directly to Guido's Pizzeria and a lot of spilled tomato sauce.

Byrnes was thinking he had to walk a very careful line here because they'd promised Betty Young sanctuary, they'd asked her to trust them, and he couldn't now reveal her name or how he'd come into possession of the information she'd given them.

"This pool parlor you work for?" he asked. "Who owns it?"

"I got no idea."

"You don't know who the *boss* is?"

"Nope. The manager pays me my check every week."

"What's the manager's name?"

"Joey."

"Joey what?"

"I haven't the faintest."

"How'd you get this job?"

"Friend of mine told me about it."

"What's your friend's name?"

"Alvin Woods. He's gone back home to Georgia."

Go find him, he was thinking.

Doesn't exist, Byrnes was thinking.

"Know a man named Ozzie Rivera?"

"Nope."

"Oswaldo Rivera?"

"Never heard of him."

"How about a man named Joaquim Valdez?"

"Nope."

"That wouldn't be the Joey who pays you your check every week, would it?"

"I don't know what Joey's last name is."

"Rivera had both his legs broken last April. Were you living in this city last April?"

"I surely was. But I don't know anything about this Ozzie Rivera or both his broken legs. That sure is a shame, though."

Like to smack him again, Brown thought.

"What were you doing on the morning of November eighth?" Byrnes asked.

Here we go, Blaine thought.

"November eighth, let me see," he said.

"Take all the time you need," Byrnes said.

"Would that have been a Saturday morning? Cause Saturday's my day off. I sleep late Saturdays."

"No, this would've been a Monday morning."

"Then I'd've been at the pool hall."

"Doing what? What do you do at this pool hall, Maxie?"

"I'm a table organizer."

"What's that, a table organizer?"

"I see to it that there's a flow."

"A flow, uh-huh. What's that?"

"I see to it that the tables are continuously occupied. So we don't have people waiting for tables or tables not being played. It's an interesting job."

"I'll bet. Did you ever hear of a man named Danny Nelson?"

"Sorry, no."

"Danny Gimp is another name he went by."

"No. Never heard of him."

"Would you be surprised if I told you he'd stiffed your boss on a minor-league dope deal ..."

"My boss? Who's supposed to be my boss?"

"Enrique Ramirez. Who owns the pool hall you work for."

"I don't know anybody named Enrique Ramirez, I already told you. Nor Danny Gump, neither."

"Gimp."

"I thought you said Gump."

"Gimp. It means a guy who limps."

"Has all this got to do with some sort of *drug* violation?" Reynolds asked.

"Two keys of cocaine," Byrnes said, nodding. "Worth forty-two large."

"You know," Reynolds said, "I really think you people should either charge my client with a specific crime or else ..."

"Ramirez paid a man named Danny Nelson to deliver two keys of coke to a dealer in Majesta," Byrnes explained genially. "Danny never showed up and neither did the coke. You don't do that to Enrique Ramirez."

"I don't know anything about any of this," Blaine said. "I especially don't know this Enrique Ramirez person, who I guess you're saying is somehow involved with dealing dope."

"*El Jefe?*" Byrnes said. "Ever hear him called that?"

"No. Is that Spanish, what you said?"

"We think *El Jefe* hired you to kill Danny Nelson," Byrnes said.

"Ooops, that's it, Lieutenant," Reynolds said.

"No, that's okay," Blaine said, grinning. "I don't know any of these people he's talking about, so just relax, it's okay. I've got nothing to worry about here. Nice and easy, okay? Like you said, Lieutenant."

Smack him right in the fuckin eye, Brown thought.

"On the morning of November eighth," Byrnes said, "did you tell a friend of yours you were going out for some pizza?"

Kling looked at him. So did Brown. The lieutenant had just come dangerously close to revealing Betty Young's identity. If Blaine walked out of here today . . .

"No," Blaine said. "What friend?"

"Excuse me, lieutenant . . .," Kling said.

"What friend?" Blaine insisted.

"A friend you told you were going out for pizza, on the morning Danny Gimp . . ."

"Lieutenant . . ."

"*Did* you tell a friend you were going out for pizza?"

"This is Betty Young, right?" Blaine said.

Oh Jesus, Kling thought. The Loot just gave her up.

"Never mind who it is. *Did* you . . . ?"

"It's that fuckin bitch Betty, ain't it? Who else could it be? What *else* did she tell you?"

"I would suggest . . ."

"If you don't mind, Counselor . . ."

"Mr Blaine . . ."

"What did you mean when you said you were going out for pizza?" Byrnes asked.

"I meant I was going out for *pizza*, what the fuck's wrong with that? Oh, I get it. She spotted me on the tape, right? She's going for the re . . ."

"What tape?" Byrnes asked at once.

Blaine suddenly shut up.

"Are we finished here?" Reynolds asked.

"Unless Mr Blaine has something else he wants to tell us," Byrnes said.

"We're finished here," Blaine said.

"You heard him. In which case . . ."

"Like what?" Blaine said.

"Come on," Reynolds said. "Let's go."

"No, like what?" Blaine insisted. "What would I want to tell you?"

"That's up to you," Byrnes said. "You think it over. Meanwhile, we're gonna hold you here for a few hours while we assemble some witnesses from the pizzeria. Run a little lineup for them, see if they can recognize you a little better in person than on that tape you were just talking about. The law allows us . . ."

"That was it, am I right? She spotted me on the tape, that fuckin bitch."

Kling was staring at the lieutenant.

They had asked Betty Young to trust them.

But the lieutenant had given her up.

"You want whose name went in with me?" Blaine asked. "Is that it?"

It was contagious.

The black man who'd been Blaine's partner on the pizzeria shivaree was a dark-skinned Colombian named Hector Milagros. They arrested him in a diner at nine that morning, having breakfast alone in a corner booth. Milagros knew there was no sense trying to force his way out of a situation where his back was to a plate glass window and he was looking at three nines as compared to his singleton thirty-eight. He asked them could he finish his eggs before they got cold. They told him they'd order more eggs for him up at the station house. Casually, he asked, "Wass thees all abou, anyways, *muchachos?*"

"We've been talking to an old friend of yours," Brown said.

"Old shooting buddy of yours," Kling said.

"Maxie Blaine," Carella said. "Remember him?"

"Mierda!" Milagros said, and stabbed his fork into one of the egg yolks. Yellow ran all over his plate.

By the time the network news broke the following day, both Milagros and Blaine had been indicted by a grand jury for the murder of Daniel Nelson. Expecting they would both be held without bail, Betty Young showed little temerity about revealing herself as the person responsible for their arrest. Ever on the prowl for promotional opportunities, Restaurant Affiliates arranged for presentation of the $50,000 reward check (blown up to gigantic viewing size) on that evening's six-thirty network news. It did not hurt that Betty Young was an attractive woman with a dazzling smile and a blameless bust. Winsomely grinning into the camera, she thanked RA, Inc. for the check she would use to buy nursing care for her bedridden mother in Florida and a new Chevy Geo for herself. She then expressed the fervent wish that those two ruthless killers would receive the maximum penalty— otherwise she'd be looking over her shoulder the rest of her life, she did not say to the television audience. Literary agents all over the city wondered if there was a book and subsequent movie in this. School children all over the United

States wept sympathetic tears into their beers and went out to buy a *nicer* pizza, hopeful they'd accidentally stumble into a Guido's killing of their own and glean a fifty-K reward as a result. Watching the show in bed, eating Chinese food with Sharyn Cooke, Kling wondered aloud if Lieutenant Byrnes had done the right thing.

"Because you know, Shar," he said, "Pete had *no* idea Blaine would suddenly open up. No idea at all. He just threw her to the lions, was what he did. After she gave us her trust."

"She didn't look so shy accepting that check," Sharyn said.

He watched her manipulating the chopsticks. She worked them like a pro, clamping them onto morsels of food as if she'd been born in Beijing. He was almost hypnotized.

"What?" she said.

"I like the way you do that."

"Yeah?"

"Yeah."

"You do it pretty good yourself, Big Boy," she said.

"I keep dropping rice."

"Just don't get it all over the bed."

"She really does have a bedridden mother in Florida, you know?"

"Reason she needs the Geo," Sharyn said. "Drive on down there to visit the old lady."

"Stop for a pizza on the way," Kling said.

"Fifty thousand bucks is gonna buy a whole lot of pizza," Sharyn said, and pincered a mushroom and popped it into her mouth. "I never won anything in my life, did you?" she said. "I grew up with my mother playing the numbers every day of the week, most she ever won was five, ten dollars. I never won a nickel."

"I won a bicycle once."

"When?"

"When I was twelve. At a street carnival."

"No kidding?"

"Yeah. One of these roulette-wheel kind of things. I still remember the number."

"What was the number?"

"Seventeen. It was black with white trim."

"The number?"

"The bike."

"Just like us," Sharyn said.

"But you know," he said, "she didn't *win* anything. This was a *reward*."

"Right, for ratting on him," Sharyn said.

"We try to discourage that sort of thinking," Kling said.

"What sort?" Sharyn said. "And who's 'we'?"

"The police. The sort of thinking that equates performing a public duty with *ratting* on somebody."

"Gee, is that whut you *po*-licemens try to do?" she said, and put her plate and chopsticks on the night table on her side of the bed, and finished her cup of tea and then slid over to him and kissed him on the mouth.

She tasted of every black woman he had ever known.

Matter of fact, she was the *only* black woman he had ever known, the only woman of *whatever* color he ever hoped to know in the near or distant future. He considered it fortunate that she felt the same way about him, that somehow in this troubled tribal universe, two people from very definitely different tribes had met and decided to give it an honest shot. He thought it miraculous, and so did she, that in the face of overwhelming odds, they were actually making a go of it. Just think of it. A little colored girl from Diamondback grows up to be a deputy police chief, and a white boy on a bicycle he won grows up to be a police detective, and in this hurried hating city, they find each other. And fall in love with each other. Go tell that to your Hutus and Tutsis, your Albanians and Serbs, your Arabs and Jews.

They both knew that the God, Country, and Brotherhood bit they'd each and separately had drummed into their heads in school wasn't quite where it was at today. They were a black woman and a white man living together in the real world. What they shared was not some idealistic democratic sentiment premised on alikeness. They knew that much of what they felt for each other had to do with identical likes and dislikes, yes, but that really wasn't all of it. They had similar senses of humor, yes, and they were in the same line of work, more or less, and yes, they had the same tastes in movies and books and plays and they both liked basketball and they both voted identically and yearned for a house and three kids if that was in their future somewhere—but this was America, you know, and so they wondered and worried about that future, and were cautious about wishing too hard for it. In the darkness of the night, where there was no color or lack of color, if they ever thought about whether their *samenesses* had created the strong and unusual bond between them, they each and separately might have concluded that it had also been their *differences*.

They were not color blind.

Any white or black person in America who told you he or she was color blind was lying.

In fact, Kling had been attracted to her *because* she was black and beautiful and he was curious, and Sharyn had been attracted to him *because* he was so goddamn blond and white and good-looking and forbidden. There were differences between them that spanned continents and oceans and spoke of jungle drums and sailing ships and slaves in chains and white men bartering in open markets and blood on the snow and blood on the stars and blood mixing with blood until blood became meaningless. These very differences brought them closer together. In each other's arms, in each other's lives, they shared an intimacy each had never known before, Kling not with any other woman, ever, Sharyn not with any other man, ever.

"A black and white bicycle, huh?" she said.

"Black with white trim."

"You sure it wasn't white with black trim?"

"I'm sure."

"You know what *trim* is?"

"I know."

"You know what *black* trim is?"

"I know."

"How come you know such dirty things?"

"How come I love you so much?" he asked.

"Sweet talker," she said.

"You love me, too?"

"Oh, *yeah*," she said.

Chapter Seven

When they went to see Norman Zimmer again, they were prepared to threaten him with a grand-jury subpoena. Instead, he seemed ready to cooperate. This was now Friday morning, the third day of December. They had last seen him on Tuesday. They assumed he'd had time since then to talk to his lawyer, and fully realized the folly of impeding a homicide investigation.

They sat in his corner office overlooking Stemmler Avenue and Stockwell Street. On The Stem, six stories below, thick traffic crawled by. Even with the windows closed, they could hear the incessant honking of horns, an annoyance specifically prohibited by law in this city. Here in the privacy of his own office, Zimmer nonetheless projected as if trying to reach the last row in the second balcony, his booming voice easily overriding the traffic noises floating up from below.

"I'm sorry I was so short with you when you popped in the other day," he said. "But we were just starting auditions, and I'm afraid I was a bit on edge. Things have calmed down a bit now. Ask me anything you'd like."

He was dressed the way he'd been on that last day of November, the suit brown this time, the shirt a sort of ivory color, the jacket again draped over his chair, the tie pulled down, the sleeves rolled up, the suspenders picking up the color of the tie again, which was a sort of rust-colored knit. *A big man*, Mrs Kipp had said. *Very big.*

"First of all," Carella said, "these rights."

"The rights," Zimmer repeated.

"Describe them."

"Long story."

"We have time."

"I'm not sure *I* do," Zimmer said, and looked at his watch the way he had on Tuesday. The detectives thought for a fleeting moment they might have to get that grand-jury subpoena after all. Zimmer took a deep breath.

"Fade in," he said. "1923. A twenty-two-year-old woman named Jessica Miles writes an autobiographical play called *Jenny's Room*. It's a big hit, it runs for three years here on The Stem. In 1928, it's turned into a musical that opens and closes in a month. End of story, right? Not quite. My partner Connie—whom you met at the auditions Tuesday? She's the one who smokes a lot?"

"The one I'm old enough to be her father," Brown said.

"That's the one. She dug up the original sheet music for the musical—this was before there were such things as cast albums, you know—and guess what? 'The score is terrific!' The book was hopeless, of course, but that could be rewritten. So she convinced me we should do it together."

"This is the same show you're doing now?" Brown asked.

"Yes," Zimmer said. "Well, I shouldn't say that. It's *essentially* the same show, yes. We've had the book rewritten, and there are several new tunes, but those are minor changes. For all intents and purposes, it's the same show, yes."

Brown was wondering why he'd want to produce a flop all over again.

"And it was based on this play called *Jenny's Room,* is that right?" he asked.

"Still *is* based on it," Zimmer said. "That's why we had to go to Cynthia Keating."

Brown looked at Carella. Carella looked back at him.

"To obtain rights to the underlying material," Zimmer said. "The *source* material. Cynthia Keating owns those rights."

Again the detectives looked stupid.

"We'd already acquired the other essential rights from the three people who'd written the musical's songs and book, but we still needed—well, wait a minute, let me correct that. The *original* creators had all passed away a long time ago. In most instances we were dealing with grandchildren, or even great-grandchildren, who'd succeeded to the rights by inheritance. But the *underlying* rights were another matter. When the musical closed in 1928, the rights to the *play* reverted back to the person who'd *written* the play—Jessica Miles. And without those underlying rights, we couldn't proceed."

"Is Cynthia Keating a grandchild?" Carella asked. "Is that it? Or a *great* ...?"

"No, Jessica Miles never married."

"Then how'd Cynthia get those rights?"

"Another long story."

"We still have time."

At first, Andrew Hale knows the woman only to talk to.

He sees her on his way in and out of the building, and they always exchange a friendly good morning or good evening, but that's it. The woman is very old, far older than Andrew, who—when he first meets her—is in his early fifties. He is still married at the time. This is long before he suffers his first heart attack. In fact, this is shortly after

he quit working at the hospital, or—to be more accurate—
got *fired* from the hospital because they thought he was too
old to be nursing, even though there were *female* nurses his
age on the ward. Fifty-three, is that old?—talk about sexism.
He guesses it's because when a man reaches a certain age, they
think of him as a dirty old man, and they don't want him
moving in and out of rooms where girls are wearing only
surgical gowns tied up the back, their behinds all showing.

He supposes the woman is in her mid-eighties, a frail
little thing who looks arthritic and possibly lame in one leg,
maybe she's diabetic, who knows? One morning, he comes
across her struggling to get a bag of groceries up to her
third-floor apartment. He asks if he can help her with that,
and she says oh, *thank* you, I'd truly appreciate it. A British
accent, he figures she's originally from England. Well, one
thing leads to another, and this and that, and the next thing
you know they're truly friends, he's making tea for her in
the afternoons, and running little errands for her, helping
her hang photographs, put up screens, dust the apartment
for her, little things like that. It makes him feel young again,
taking care of her. It makes him feel wanted and needed
again, nursing a frail old woman this way.

One day she tells him she was once a famous playwright,
did he know that? He goes Come on, what are you telling
me? She says No, it's true. When I was twenty-two years old,
I wrote a play called *Jenny's Room*, it was a big hit, may I drop
dead this very minute if I'm not telling the truth. He goes
Come on, you're *kidding* me. She goes Oh yeah? So look it
up in the library. Jessica Miles. I'm in *Who's Who in America*.

He is almost afraid to look in the book because suppose
her name *isn't* there? Suppose this is all some kind of fantasy?
Then she'd be just a crazy old lady making up things,
wouldn't she? He doesn't know if he can deal with that.
But, hey, guess *what*? His friend up there on the third floor
is a celebrity! Not only did she write the play she says she

wrote, but it was also turned into a musical five years later, whattya know about that? The play starred somebody named Jenny Corbin, who was a big star back then. When he sees her the next time, he says Well, well, well, grinning at her, and she says Was I lying? and he says I'd sure love to read that play sometime, I'd be honored.

She tells him it was originally called *Jessie's Room*, not *Jenny's Room*, because it was all autobiographical, about her coming to the city here from England and all, and her first years here working for Beneficial Loan, and the experiences she'd had with various beaux and all, and her disastrous love affair, which resulted in her vowing never to marry, all of which was in the play. But when Jenny Corbin, who was a tremendous star of the day, agreed to take the role, she also insisted they change the title to *Jenny's Room*, to make it *her* play, you see . . .

"That's terrible," Andrew says.

"Well, no, not really," Jessica says. "Because she made it a tremendous hit, you see. I mean, no one would have come to see something about *me*, but they thought the play was about *her*, you see, about Jenny Corbin the *star*, so they all flocked to the theater and I made a lot of money. And, oh, she was so *very* beautiful."

She does not have similar kind words for the producers of the musical five years later. She tells Andrew that they took a sensitive play—well, a play about Jessica herself—and turned it into something cheap and crass, with a libretto by some person born in Liverpool who'd previously written a comedy about *soccer*, can you imagine? And the words and music weren't much better. Everything had an insistent ragtime beat to it, with obvious rhymes and the crudest sort of innuendo. As an example, they took one of the play's most sensitive scenes—which Jenny performed like an angel, by the way—and turned it into a *dance* number!

"The scene where she breaks up with the one true love

of her life though she doesn't realize it at the time? A truly wonderful, touching scene, the audience cried every night when Jenny did it. But in the musical, they had colored boys and girls dancing in the background in the most suggestive manner, it was just dreadful. If I'd known what was going to happen to my little play, I'd never have given them permission."

"I would love to read it sometime," Andrew says, and Jessica goes briefly into the other room and returns a moment later with the leather-bound copy her producer presented to her on opening night.

That night, Andrew cries when he reads the scene in the play where Jessie breaks up with the one true love of her life without realizing it, though the audience does. His wife tells him to please be quiet, she's trying to sleep.

Not long after that, Jessica Miles becomes desperately ill.

He cares for her at home until it becomes apparent she must be removed to a hospital. And then, he visits her every day, often lingering by her bedside from morning to night, and sometimes throughout the night. She dies within a matter of weeks.

In her will, she leaves to him the leather-bound copy of her precious play, and something even more precious: the copyright to the play itself.

"How do you know all this?" Carella asked.

"Hale told me. A hundred times over," Zimmer said. "Of course, no one at the time expected the musical would be revived. Jessica died fourteen, fifteen years ago. For all intents and purposes, the play she left him had only sentimental value."

"Until your partner rediscovered the musical."

"Yes. We did a copyright search, found that all renewals

had been made, located the current owners, and proceeded to license the rights. You can imagine how thrilled these people were! The bookwriter's grandson works in the mail room of a publishing house in London. The lyricist's granddaughter sells real estate in L.A. And the composer's great-grandson drives a taxi in Tel Aviv! This revival is a godsend to them, an opportunity to make some very big bucks indeed. *If* the show is a hit, of course. Which I'm sure it will be," he said, and rapped his knuckles on his desk.

"When did you discover Hale had inherited the underlying rights?"

"When our lawyers did the search. We weren't expecting a problem, why would there have been a problem? In fact, we were already *proceeding*, assuming that rights to the play would follow as a matter of course. A new bookwriter was already working, we'd commissioned new songs and hired a director and a choreographer, everything was in motion. But *finding* Hale was another matter. As it turned out, he was right under our noses here in the city, but he'd moved around a lot in the past several years. Apparently he got fired from a nursing job in a hospital somewhere in Riverhead, molested a young girl in her room, or so she later said, who the hell knew? Or *cared*, for that matter? What we wanted were the rights to the mawkish little play Jessica Miles had written and inconsiderately willed to him."

"Are you saying it's not a good play?"

"It's dreadful. The only thing that put it over was Jenny Corbin in the starring role. She was the mayor's mistress at the time, you know, and quite a notorious personality. A stunning woman, from what I've been told." He hung both huge hands on the air and outlined the ripeness of her breasts, nodding in appreciation. "But we *needed* the damn thing," he said. "Without that play, we simply couldn't proceed any further." He sighed heavily, opened a cigar box on his desk, and fished a cigar from it. "Smoke?" he asked. "They're Havanas."

"Thanks, no," Carella said.

Brown shook his head.

Zimmer unwrapped the cigar, bit off one end, and struck a match. Puffing great clouds of asphyxiating smoke on the air, he waved them away with one big hand, and then settled back in his chair to puff contentedly. Without asking, Carella got up to open the window. Traffic noises flooded the room.

"Well, I went to see the old man," Zimmer said. "Never expecting a problem, mind you. Why should there be a problem? Who doesn't want to make a fortune? I told him we were reviving the musical based on Jessica Miles's play and wanted to license the rights from him. He flatly refused."

"Why?" Brown asked.

"Because he was an idiot," Zimmer said. "I tried to explain that he could make a lot of money if the show was a hit. No. I tried to tell him a hit show would play all over the United States, all over the *world!* No. At first, I thought he was holding out for a bigger advance, higher royalties. But that wasn't it."

"What was it?" Carella asked.

"He was protecting Jessica's shitty little play! Can you believe it? He said she'd been unhappy with the musical . . . well, *yes*, I said, so are *we!* That's why we're having the book rewritten, that's why we're adding new songs. No, he said. I'm sorry. She would not want the musical revived. I would be dishonoring her wishes if I let you have her play. Three *times*, I went to see him. He simply would not listen to reason." Zimmer shook his head, and blew a huge cloud of smoke at the ceiling. "So I went to see his daughter. Cynthia Keating. Mousy little housewife dominated by a legal-eagle husband who immediately appreciated how much money they could make if this show turned out to be a hit. I asked Cynthia to intercede on my behalf, go to the old man, talk some sense into him. No luck. He wouldn't budge from his position." Zimmer shook his head again, and looked across his desk at the detectives. "So I killed him," he said, and laughed suddenly, like a choir boy who'd farted during a Christmas chorale.

Neither Carella nor Brown even smiled.

"That's what you're thinking, isn't it?" Zimmer said. "That I had good reason to want him dead? Why *not* kill the stubborn son of a bitch? Be much easier to deal with the daughter, wouldn't it?"

The detectives said nothing.

"Incidentally," Zimmer said, and puffed on the cigar and then looked thoughtfully at the glowing end of it. "Cynthia *knew* her father was leaving her the rights to that play."

"How do you know that?" Carella asked.

"He told her. Said when he died she'd be getting twenty-five grand in insurance plus the rights to this miserable little play. Forgive the editorializing, but this entire matter pisses me off a great deal."

Gee, imagine what it does to *us*, Carella thought.

"Tell you what," Zimmer said. "We're having a Meet 'N' Greet tomorrow ni . . ."

"A what?" Brown said.

"Little gathering for the usual suspects," he said, and grinned. "Why don't you stop by?"

Carella wondered what had happened to those simple cases where you walked in and found a guy with a smoking gun in his fist and a bloody corpse at his feet. Zimmer had suggested that he himself was a good suspect. Carella agreed. But so was Cynthia Keating, or her greedy little attorney husband, or any one of the copyright inheritors in London, Tel Aviv, or Los Angeles. Not to mention all the people now involved with the current show—the new bookwriter and composer, the director, the choreographer,

Zimmer's partner. Anyone who wanted this show to happen could have hired the Jamaican who'd hanged Hale on the bathroom door like a wet towel.

"What time tomorrow night?" he asked.

"You want a mystery?" Parker asked them. "Here's a mystery for you."

"We don't want a mystery," Carella said.

"We already *have* a mystery," Meyer said.

"*Two* mysteries," Kling said.

"Too *many* mysteries," Brown said.

"Here's a mystery for you," Parker said. "I stop this guy the other day, he just went through a red light, I'm standing right there on the corner. I flag him down cause I'm a conscientious cop ..."

Brown blew his nose.

"... and I ask to see his driver's license and registration. So he pulls all this shit out of his wallet and his glove compartment, and guess what's there with it?"

"What?" Kling asked.

"His marriage certificate."

"His what?"

"Yeah," Parker said.

"Why's he carrying a marriage certificate?"

"That's the mystery," Parker said.

"Was he recently married?"

"No, the certificate was ten years old."

"So why's he carrying it around with him?"

"I don't know. That's why it's a mystery."

"I hate mysteries," Carella said.

The Meet 'N' Greet was supposed to start at six P.M. in Connie Lindstrom's penthouse apartment on Grover

Avenue, overlooking Grover Park, a world away from the Eighty-seventh Precinct station house, but only a mile and a half farther downtown. If Brown and Carella had gone to work that Saturday, they'd have been to the party in ten minutes. But they were coming down from their homes in Riverhead, and so they allowed themselves forty minutes, Brown picking up Carella at twenty past five. By that time, a fierce snow storm had started in the city and they hit its full force just as they were crossing the bridge over the Devil's Byte. They did not get to her building until six-thirty. As it was, they were not overly late. Most of the guests, similarly held up by the storm, were just arriving. The detectives had dressed up for the occasion, both of them wearing unaccustomed suits, Brown's blue, Carella's gray. They needn't have bothered. Half the guests were wearing blue jeans. One of them, an actor, asked them what they did. When they told him they were police detectives, he said he had once played a cop in a summer stock production of *Detective Story*.

The show's new songwriter, a man who introduced himself as Randy Flynn, told Carella that the term "Meet 'N' Greet" was usually reserved for the start of rehearsals, when the full cast met the producers and the creative team for the first time. "Connie's new in the business, though," he whispered. "She sometimes gets the lingo wrong." Flynn, a man in his sixties with several hit shows to his credit, wore a look of extreme smugness that attested to his worldwide fame. Puffing incessantly on a cigarette, he told Carella that he'd been contacted by Zimmer early in July, when they'd first acquired the rights to the original show's music from the composer's great-grandson in Tel Aviv. "He's not here tonight," he said, "but the others are."

The original lyricist's granddaughter had been flown in from Los Angeles, where she worked at Coldwell Banker selling real estate. Her name was Felicia Carr, and she was possibly thirty-three years old, a reddish-blonde wearing the only long gown in the room, a silky green number that clung to her like moss. She was listening intently to Naomi Janus, the choreographer, who had on her head the same black rustler's hat she'd been wearing this past Tuesday. Naomi was telling a man named Arthur Bragg that she planned some startlingly sexy dance sequences for the speakeasy number, whatever that was. Brown surmised that Bragg was the show's musical director, whatever *that* was. He decided there were too many people here. Felicia said she couldn't wait to see the dances, she just *loved* musicals that had a lot of sexy dancing in them.

"When did you fly east?" Brown asked her.

"Yesterday," she said. "On the Red Eye."

"And you go back when?"

"Oh, not for a while. I'm planning to do some Christmas shopping."

"This must be very exciting for you."

"Oh yes, it is!" she said. "I can't wait for it to open!"

"When will that be?"

"Next fall sometime," Naomi said. "Provided there's a theater available."

"That seems a long way off."

"Well," Naomi said, "the show's been lying dormant since it closed in 1928, so I guess it can wait a few months more."

The bookwriter's grandson was a Brit named Gerald Palmer. He was in his early forties, Carella guessed, a clean-shaven man in need of a haircut. Like the two detectives, he, too, was wearing a suit, though his seemed somewhat out of fashion, an impression possibly created by its British styling. The suit was blue, the shoes he wore with it brown. In his Cockney accent, he explained to Carella, unnecessarily, that the bookwriter wrote all the words *spoken* onstage, as opposed to anything sung or danced. "He's sometimes called the librettist," he said. "My grandfather wrote an absolutely *wonderful* libretto for the original musical. I don't know why they hired someone to rewrite it." Carella guessed he hadn't been told that the original book was "hopeless."

At just that moment, the man who'd revised the book joined them. He was tall and ungainly, in his late fifties, Carella supposed, wearing jeans, a blue shirt open at the throat, and a green shawl-collared cardigan sweater over it. "Clarence Hull," he said, and shook hands with both of them. He immediately told Palmer—almost by way of apology, it seemed to Carella—that his grandfather's libretto had been "quite artful for its day," his exact words, but that the new millennium required something more immediately engaging, which was why he'd chosen to place the show's opening not on a farm in the East Midlands, where the original had started, but instead in London, "so that the heroine isn't a simple farm girl coming to America but is instead someone rather more sophisticated moving from one big city to another, do you see?" Palmer told him that his grandfather had once written a straight play as well, "A *comedy*, actually," he said, "about soccer," which he thought might make a good musical, given the current American obsession with the sport. Hull told him flatly that the only sports musical that had ever made it was *Damn Yankees*, and then excused himself to go refill his champagne glass.

Palmer told Carella that for the past fifteen years he'd been working in the "post room," as he called it, of a publishing house called Martins and Grenville, "the last publisher in Bedford Square, d'you know it? A highly prestigious firm." He said he was thrilled they were doing his granddad's show again. "I hope it'll come to London one day," he said.

"When did you get here?" Carella asked.

"Flew over on Wednesday."

"Where are you staying?"

"The Piccadilly. Sounded a lot like home," he said, and grinned. He'd shaved too close. There were razor nicks on his chin.

"When will you be going back?"

"Not till next Sunday. I'm taking a little time here, enjoying the city. Plenty of time for work later on, eh?" he said.

Cynthia Keating was wearing a simple black cocktail dress. Her husband Robert was another of the men wearing a suit. Brown figured anyone not intimately connected with show business had dolled up for the occasion. He was beginning to feel somewhat like a horse's ass. The suit Keating had on was a severe pinstripe. He looked as if he might be trying a case for IBM. Cynthia was telling Rowland Chapp, the show's director, that the original play Jessica Miles had written was "perfectly wonderful," something Chapp accepted with a distracted nod that indicated he knew precisely how dreadful the play was. Brown wanted to go home.

Champagne and canapés were coming around on trays, served by a pair of wannabe actors who were dressed in black and white tonight, earnestly playing witty waiter and flirtatious waitress. Snow swirled past the penthouse windows, the flakes illuminated by corner floodlights that made them appear as sharp and as swift as tiny daggers.

Connie Lindstrom tapped on her champagne glass.

"I have a treat," she said. "Randy?"

There was applause, and then a hush as Randy Flynn went to the grand piano in one corner of the room, sat, and lifted the lid over the keys. Behind him, snowflakes rushed the night.

"I'm going to play the show for you," he said. "Including the three new songs I wrote. We've kept the original conceit, the entire musical takes place in Jenny's room. The window in her room is a window on the city. We see the city, we see everything happening in the city through her eyes, from her point of view."

He began playing.

Carella could not determine where any new songs had been added; to him, the music flooding the air in Connie Lindstrom's penthouse apartment sounded seamless. As Morrow sang in his raspy smoker's voice, Carella floated back to another time and place, this city in the year 1928, when everything seemed fresh and innocent to a young girl named Jenny, fantasizing in her room all the way downtown, in an immigrant area then called—as it still was—The Lower Platform.

But, oh, the differences between then and now.

Flynn sang of a young girl's yearnings and awakenings in a wondrous island bordered by confluent rivers and spanned by magical bridges. He sang of golden towers rising into the clouds, interlaced with immaculate streets, humming belowground with subways not yet sullied by time or wear. He sang of promise and hope for a population of immigrants that had brought with them customs to treasure and to nourish. As he sang, his voice became a choir of voices, the voices of a hundred tribes with as many different backgrounds, joining together in this shining new land, to become at last a single strong united tribe.

Here beyond the windows in Jenny's room . . .

Ah, what a wonderland there had been.

Flynn struck the last chord of the last dance.

It was still snowing.

Carella looked across the room to where his partner stood solid and big and black against the white flakes swirling outside. Randy Flynn rose from the piano bench, placed the palms of his hands together like a guru, and bowed in transparently false modesty, accepting applause from the assembled guests. Brown's eyes scanned the room. So did Carella's.

Almost anyone in this room could have killed Andrew Hale.

There was no way the detectives who caught the murder down in Hopscotch could have connected it with the murders uptown. No way. The first victim uptown had been a sixty-eight-year-old white man who'd been hanged from a door hook and then transported to a bed. The second one had been a nineteen-year-old black girl stabbed in the chest with a knife grabbed from her own kitchen counter. The prior ingestion of a drug called Rohypnol was the only connecting link between them—if, in fact, it *was* a link and not the sort of coincidence that plagued police work.

Except when they were reading novels, the cops in this city rarely came across serial killers. Serial killers in novels were enormously popular these days, but that did not mean they were running rampant all over the United States. Current estimates maintained that only some thirty-five to fifty of them were out there loose. In order for a murderer to qualify as a bona fide serial killer, he had to have killed three or more people within a relatively short period of time. On the other hand, a serial killer was not someone who killed Uncle George and two days later killed Cousins Mandy and Maude because they'd seen him commit the first murder. That was merely a careful murderer.

The cops in this city investigated some 2,000 homicides annually. Even if the detectives catching the downtown squeal had remotely suspected a connection between the Hale murder, the Cleary murder, and this new murder, they would not have jumped to the conclusion that a raving lunatic serial killer was loose in the city. The detectives catching the squeal early that Monday morning *might* have heard about the Hale murder from television, but they most certainly had not heard about the murder of an obscure little black girl in Diamondback. So it never once entered their minds that this new murder was somehow related to the previous two, serially or otherwise.

According to a birth certificate they found in a candy tin in the top drawer of her bedroom dresser, the victim's name was Martha Coleridge and she was ninety-eight years old. A thin, birdlike creature, she lay in her nightgown at the foot of the bed, her neck apparently broken. The detectives— an experienced First named Bryan Shanahan, and a newly appointed Third named Jefferson Long—went through the lady's belongings, sifting through browned letters and diaries, knowing they wouldn't find any clues in all this stuff, but going through the drill anyway. What they figured was that some junkie burglar had come in here, stolen the old lady's grocery money, and then snapped her neck for good measure. They kept looking through her old papers, tossing them onto the bed while the ME examined the body. One of the things they found was a blue binder with a typed label on it. The label read:

MY ROOM
by Martha Coleridge

What was inside the binder looked like some kind of play or something. They tossed it on the bed with all the other crap.

The first thing that attracted the Reverend Gabriel Foster to the case was the fact that the white suspect had been released on bail whereas his black counterpart had been denied bail and remanded to the Men's House of Detention. Same crime, same judge, two shooters, one white, one black, different disposition.

That was the first thing, but it wasn't enough to send him

running through the streets, because what he was sensing here was a change in the public mood. Whereas Maxwell Corey Blaine and Hector Milagros had at first been treated like national heroes for disposing of that vilest of human beings, the informer, they were now being pilloried as monsters or worse because a *second* informer—who was now a media darling and something of an instant heroine—had for a substantial reward turned in the white man, who had at once copped a plea and given up his partner, the black man who'd been denied bail. The world was full of no-good dirty rats these days, but Foster wasn't about to take up the banner for a pair of universally reviled murderers.

Until a pair of ambitious detectives made life easier for him.

The partners were named Archie Bingman and Robert Tracey, familiarly called Bingo and Bop by the people who lived in Hightown, where Enrique Ramirez ran his pool hall and his drug operation. They had been dogging *El Jefe's* tracks for the past year and a half now. Under the federal Racketeer-Influenced and Corrupt Organizations statute, murders committed in the furtherance of criminal enter- prise were punishable by lifetime sentences. The Colombian cartel was most definitely a racketeer-influenced and corrupt organization. If they could tie the Guido's Pizzeria murder to *El Jefe's* drug operation, he'd be sitting on his ass in Kansas for the rest of his life, Toto.

Bingo and Bop felt certain that the two shooters hadn't revealed anything that might incriminate Ramirez. The indicted pair knew well enough that the long arm of the cartel could reach into the loneliest of prison cells, and they did not long for an icepick in the eye one dark and stormy night. Better to ride the road upstate alone, do the time, and breathe easy. Besides, if the pair *had* traded Ramirez for some kind of Chinese deal, the grand jury would have already indicted him. Bingo and Bop knew of no such paper handed down.

It galled them to know that one of Ramirez's hit men was sitting downtown in custody, where any police officer with a bit of ingenuity could gain access to him and perhaps learn something about who had sent whom to shoot the hapless little stoolie neither of the detectives had ever met or used. They already *knew* who had sent Milagros to that pizzeria because it was common knowledge up here in the Eight-Nine that Milagros and his partner Blaine were two of *El Jefe*'s cleanup men. In the American criminal justice system, however, *knowing* something wasn't enough. You also had to be able to *prove* it beyond a reasonable doubt, worse luck.

That Monday night, the sixth of December, while two detectives in Hopscotch filed their DD-5 on the little old lady who'd had her neck broken, and the reverend Foster pored over that day's newspapers trying to figure out a way to turn the arrest of Hector Milagros to his advantage, Bingo and Bop drove downtown to the Men's House of Detention in its new quarters on Blanchard Street, and told the jailer on duty they were there to see the Guido's Pizzeria shooter. The jailer wanted to know on whose authority.

"We're investigating a related drug matter," Bingo said.

"You got to go through his lawyer," the jailer said.

"We already talked to him," Bop said. "He told us it's okay."

"I need it in writing," the jailer said.

"Come on, don't break 'em, willya?" Bingo said. "Where the fuck we gonna find his lawyer, this hour?"

"Find him tomorrow," the jailer said. "Come back tomorrow."

"We got something hot can't wait till tomorrow," Bingo said.

"You ever hear of hot pursuit?" Bop said.

"I never heard of hot pursuit leadin to a jail cell."

"Come on, we want to nail this cocksucker sellin dope to your kids."

"My kids are grown up and livin in Seattle," the jailer said.

"Ten minutes, okay?"

"The door was open, and you walked in," the jailer said.

Milagros was in his cell reading his Bible. One other cell in the hall was occupied by an old man mumbling in his sleep. Milagros had never seen these guys in his life, and he wondered how they'd got in here. His lawyer hadn't mentioned anything about anybody coming to see him. Far as Milagros knew, he'd be sitting on his ass here in The Catacombs till his case came to trial. The way his lawyer had explained it, you couldn't convict somebody solely on the uncorroborated testimony of an accomplice. Anyway, who was gonna believe a guy who tried to kill five cops and succeeded in hurting one of them pretty bad? Nobody, that's who. Just sit tight and you walk, his lawyer had said, which was fine with Milagros. So who were these two guys, and what did they want here, this hour of the night?

The door clicked open electrically. Bingo and Bop entered the cell, and closed the door behind them. From the far end of the corridor, the jailer threw the switch that locked it again.

Bingo smiled.

Milagros had learned a long time ago all about guys who came at you smiling.

The other one was smiling, too.

"So tell us who sent you to the pizzeria," Bingo said.

"Who the fuck are you?" Milagros asked.

"Nice talk," Bop said.

"We're two fellas gonna send your boss away," Bingo said.

"What boss you talkin abou', man?"

"Enrique Ramirez."

"Don't know him."

"Oh dear," Bingo said.

"Get the fuck outta here, I call d'key."

"The key is down the hall takin a leak," Bop said.

"I wake up dee whole fuckin jail you don' ged outta here," Milagros said.

"Oh dear," Bingo said again.

"Someone I'd like you to meet," Bop said, and yanked a nine from a shoulder holster. "Mr Glock," he said, "meet Mr Milagros."

Milagros looked at the semi.

"Come on, whass dis?" he said.

"*Dis,*" Bop said, mimicking him, "is a pistol. *Una pistola, maricón. Comprende?*"

"Come on, whass dee matter wi' you?"

"Who sent you to kill that fuckin pussy-clot?"

"Nobody. He owe us money, we go on our own."

"*El Jefe* sent you, didn't he?"

"You know who *El Jefe* is?" Milagros said, and tried a smile. "My *mama* is *El Jefe*. Thass wha' me an' my brudders call her. *Jefita.*"

"Gee, is that what you call your mama?" Bingo said.

"Is that what you call your whore mama?" Bop said.

"'Ey, man, watch your mou', okay?"

"You watch *your* mouth," Bop said, and rammed the barrel of the nine against Milagros's lips.

"'Ey, man ..."

"Eat it!" Bop said.

"Man, what you ... ?"

Bop swung the muzzle sideways across Milagros's mouth. There was the sound of something snapping. There was a spray of blood. Teeth clicked loose and spilled onto the air.

"Jesus Chri ..."

"Shhh," Bingo said.

"Eat it," Bop said again, and slid the barrel of the gun into Milagros's mouth.

"Quiet now," Bingo said.

Milagros began to blubber. His eyes were wide. Blood dribbled from the corners of his mouth, around the barrel of the nine.

"Who sent you to kill him?"

Milagros shook his head.

"No, huh?" Bop said, and cocked the pistol. "Who?" he insisted.

Milagros shook his head again.

"You ought to go see your dentist again," Bingo said, and nodded.

Bop swung the gun against Milagros's mouth.

He almost choked on his own teeth.

The jailer didn't see what had happened to Milagros until he made his rounds at midnight. Long before then, he had clicked open Milagros's cell from his end of the corridor and had watched the two detectives approaching the steel door with its bulletproof viewing window, and had let them out into the small holding room, and then out of the complex itself. Now, as he came down the corridor, the old man in the cell next to Milagros's was sitting upright on his cot, his eyes wide, but saying nothing. The jailer knew right away something was very wrong.

Milagros was lying on the floor of his cell.

There was blood on the floor, and scattered teeth, and what looked and smelled like vomit. There was also another smell because Milagros had soiled himself while the two detectives were methodically knocking every tooth out of his mouth, but the jailer didn't yet know the full extent of what had happened here, he saw only the blood and a handful of teeth in the spill of light from the after-hours illumination in the corridor.

The jailer had read enough newspapers in the past few months.

He didn't even go into Milagros's cell. He went back down the corridor, past the cell of the old man with the wide accusative eyes, and he unlocked the steel door at the far end, and locked it again behind him, and walked directly to the wall phone by the officers' station, and called his immediate superior, the Security Division captain on duty.

The jailer's story was that two detectives had come into the lockup showing a piece of paper authorizing them to question Hector Milagros. He couldn't remember their names. He'd asked them to sign in, and he assumed they both had; he hadn't looked at the log book afterward. He told the captain they'd been in the prisoner's cell for about half an hour, and that he hadn't heard anything out of the ordinary during that time. Then again, there was a thick steel door at the end of the corridor. He said he couldn't remember having seen either of the detectives down here before, nor could he remember what either of them looked like, except that one had a mustache. The duty captain figured the man was covering his own ass.

He read newspapers, too.

Lest anyone later accuse him of having delayed while a story was being concocted, he called an ambulance at once, and had the prisoner expressed to nearby St Mary's, the same hospital Sharyn Cooke had moved Willis from not four nights earlier. Then he telephoned the deputy warden of Security Division, who listened to the story from his bed at home, alternately expressing surprise and grave concern. The deputy warden in turn woke up the warden, who was commanding officer of the entire facility. The warden debated waking up the supervisor of the Department of Corrections, but finally called him at home. The Police Commissioner himself was awakened at close to three in the morning. It was he who informed the media at once, before anyone began thinking a cover-up was taking place here.

Gabriel Foster didn't hear the news until he turned on his television set the next morning.

That same morning, Carella first called Cynthia Keating's attorney to tell him he hoped he didn't have to yank her before a grand jury to get a few simple questions answered, and when Alexander started getting snotty on the phone, Carella said, "Counselor, I haven't got any more time to waste on this. Yes or no?"

"What questions?" Alexander asked.

"Questions pertaining to the rights she inherited from her father."

"In my office," Alexander said. "Ten o'clock."

They got there at five minutes to.

Alexander was wearing chocolate-brown corduroy trousers, tan loafers, a beige button-down shirt, a green tie, and a brown tweed jacket with leather elbow patches. He looked like a country gentleman expecting the local pastor for tea. Cynthia was wearing a pastel-blue cashmere turtleneck over a short miniskirt, navy blue pantyhose, and high-heeled navy patent pumps. She looked long and leggy, her dark hair styled differently, her makeup more unrestrained. Altogether, she seemed to exude an air of self-confidence that hadn't been apparent that first morning in October, after she'd admittedly dragged her father from his perch on the closet door to his new resting place on the bed. Apparently, the prospects of a hit musical did wonders for the personality. Alexander, on the other hand, seemed his same brusque, blond, blustering self.

"What do you want from my client?" he said. "Twenty-five words or less."

"Honesty," Carella said.

"That's a *lot* less," Meyer said.

Alexander shot him a look.

"She's always been honest with you," he said.

"Good," Carella said. "Then we won't have to work so hard, will we?"

"Tell me something. You don't *really* think she had anything to do with her father's murder, do you?"

Carella looked at Meyer. Meyer gave a faint shrug, a brief nod.

"She's a suspect, yes," Carella said.

"Have you shared that thought with anyone else? Anyone outside the police department, for example? Because I'm sure I don't have to remind you, if Mrs Keating is libeled . . ."

"The hell with this," Carella said. "Let's go, Meyer."

"Just a second, Detective."

"I told you on the phone I won't waste any more time with you," Carella said. "If I walk out of here empty, I go straight to the D.A.'s office. Yes, no, which? Say. Now."

"I'll give you half an hour, no more," Alexander said, and went behind his desk, and tented his hands and sat there scowling at the detectives.

"I'll make this brief," Carella said. "At the time of your father's death, you knew he'd left you the rights to Jessica Miles's play, isn't that so?"

"Yes."

"Then why didn't you tell us?"

"I'm sorry?"

"You told us about the twenty-five-thousand-dollar insurance policy . . ."

"Yes?"

"And your concern that it might contain a suicide clause ..."

"That's right. But ..."

"Why didn't you *also* mention you'd inherited the play?"

"I didn't think it was important."

"You didn't ..."

Carella turned away from her. He looked at Meyer, who said nothing. He went back to her. There was a tight, controlled look on his face. Meyer watched him.

"How much were you paid for the license to those rights?"

"That's none of your business," Alexander said.

"Okay, so long," Carella said. "Meyer? Let's go."

"Three thousand dollars for a year's option," Cynthia said at once. "And three thousand for a second year, if it hadn't been produced by then."

"What kind of royalties are you getting?"

"Same as the others."

"Which others?"

"The guy in London ..."

"Gerald Palmer?"

"Yes. And the cab driver in Tel Aviv. And the girl from Los Angeles. The redhead in the long gown. Felicity Carr."

"Felicia," Meyer corrected.

"Felicia, yes. We'll be sharing six percent of the weekly gross."

"Do you realize how much money ...?"

"Cynthia, you can end this any time you want to," Alexander said.

"And go before a grand jury?"

"I hardly think the gentlemen will convene a grand jury simply to ..."

"Do you realize how much money that can come to?" Carella said. "Six percent of the *gross*? Split four *ways*?"

"I imagine quite a lot," Cynthia said. "If the show's a hit."

"Then how can you say ...?"

He turned away from her again. Walked back. Let out his breath.

"Do you *want* us to arrest you?" he asked.

"Of course not."

"Then how can you say you didn't think it was *important*? You tell us about a lousy little insurance policy ..."

"Lower your voice, Detective. She's not in Canada."

"... but you *don't* tell us about a play that can eventually earn hundreds of thousands of dollars for you? Because you don't think it's *important*?"

"I didn't kill him."

"I think that's enough," Alexander said.

"I'm not finished."

"I said that's ..."

"*I* said I'm not finished."

"I didn't kill him."

"When did you sign over the rights to that play?"

"I did not kill my father."

"When, Mrs Keating?"

"I didn't *kill* him, damn it!"

"When?"

"Right after the will was probated."

"And when was that?"

"Two weeks after his death," she said.

Chapter Eight

Nellie Brand came to the case with a cool assistant district attorney's eye, ten years of experience in the D.A.'s office, and the hood of a ski parka pulled up over her short blondish hair. That Tuesday morning, when she was about to leave for the office, her husband suggested that perhaps she ought to dress for work a bit more conservatively than blue jeans, a heavy sweater, the ski parka, and boots. She had informed him—somewhat curtly, he thought—that there was slush on every street corner, and she wasn't heading for the Governor's ball, but thanks a lot.

Now—somewhat curtly, Carella thought—she told Lieutenant Byrnes and the detectives gathered in his office that they were premature in looking for a Murder One charge against Cynthia Keating, when all they really had on her was *maybe* Obstructing and . . .

". . . okay, I'll give you Tampering," she said. "She's admitted she moved her father's body, and that's a two-fifteen-forty, if ever I saw one. But do you really want to send her to jail for four years max? Which her attorney'll bargain down to two, anyway, and she'll be out in six, seven months? Less if she gets work release? Is it worth it?"

"We think she hired someone to kill the old man," Carella said.

"Who?"

"Some Jamaican from Houston," Meyer said.

"Has he got a name?"

"John Bridges. But the cops down there never heard of him."

"Have you tried the telephone company?"

"They have no listing for him, either."

"There's a second victim we think was maybe done by the same guy," Brown said.

"Girl danced at a go-go joint called The Telephone Company," Carella said.

"Where'd you get the name Bridges?"

"From a tulip works for Gabriel Foster," Brown said.

"He's all over the papers this morning," Nellie said. "Foster."

"We saw. *That* one's related, too."

"Which one?"

"The pizzeria shooting. Sort of."

Nellie sighed.

"Nobody says they have to be easy," Carella said.

"How is it related?"

"The informer who got killed was working for a Hightown dealer who sold cocaine and 'a lot of designer drugs,' quote, unquote. The killer used Rohypnol in both murders."

"Are you suggesting he got the rope from this Hightown dealer?"

"We don't know."

"Maybe you ought to find out, hm? Be nice to know. Who are you quoting?"

"Betty Young."

"It was our informer who led us to the gay guy, by the way."

"You think that's why he got killed?"

"Not according to Betty Young."

"That's twice."

"Former girlfriend of one of the shooters."

"Which one? The black guy they beat up Saturday night?"

"No, the other one," Kling said. "Home in his own beddie-bye."

"Betty Young, right, I saw her on television. Winner of this week's True-Blue Ex Award. What does *she* say happened?"

"She says Danny ran off with the boss's coke."

"Who's Danny?"

"Our informer."

"Bad move, stealing the boss's coke."

"Stealing the boss's *anything*."

"Now he knows," Meyer said.

"In any case, they're *not* related," Nellie said.

"Except for the rope, maybe."

"Very slender chance that in this great big city . . ."

"Well, we think of them as *sort* of related."

"You want me to bring 'sort of' charges against Cynthia Keating?"

"Way you're sounding," Brown said, "we can't bring *any* kind of charges."

"You want an indictment or a pass, which?"

"We think there's enough to take to a grand jury."

"They won't agree."

"One," Carella said, "she knew there was a twenty-five-thousand-dollar policy on the old man's . . ."

"Chicken feed."

"*Plus*," Carella went on, undaunted, "the copyright to a play she *knew* was being turned into a musical."

"Oh?"

"Yes."

"And she knew this *before* the old man got killed," Meyer said.

"When did she find out?"

"In September sometime."

"And she sold the rights two weeks after he died," Kling said.

"For how much?"

"Three thousand bucks plus ..."

"Give me a break."

"*Plus* six percent of the show's gross, split four ways."

"What does that come to?"

"One and a half percent each," Brown said.

"How do you do that?"

"Smart," Brown said, and tapped his temple.

"How much is the weekly gross?"

"On a hit musical? Enough," Carella said.

"Papa wouldn't let the rights go," Byrnes said. "The producer went to see him three times, finally asked the daughter to step in."

"Still said no."

"Why?"

"Protecting the original playwright."

"Nice."

"Or dumb, depending how you look at it."

"I say nice."

"Anyway," Carella said, "she *knew* she was going to inherit something that might bring in a whole lot of ..."

"How do you *know* she knew?"

"She admitted it."

"So she killed him. You're saying."

"Yes. Well, she *hired* someone to kill him."

"Same thing. How was the old man's health?"

"Two heart attacks in the past eight years."

"Couldn't wait for him to die of natural causes, huh?"

"The show was already in progress. They'd hired a songwriter, a bookwriter ..."

"She saw the thing slipping away."

"So she hired this Jamaican to kill him. You're saying."

"That's what we're saying."

"Went all the way to Houston to hire a hit man, is that it?"

"Well ..."

"He's from Houston, isn't that what you said?"

"That's our information, yes."

"A Jamaican," Nellie said. "From Houston."

"Yes."

"Didn't know there *were* any Jamaicans in Houston."

"Apparently, there are."

"My point is ... this woman's a housewife, right?"

"Yes."

"How the hell would she know how to hire a hit man? In *Houston*, no less."

"Well ..."

"Yeah, tell me."

"Well ..."

"I'm listening."

Nobody said anything.

"Tell me about this second murder. You think the housewife arranged that one, too?"

"No."

"Just the first one."

"Yes."

"So tell me about the second one."

"The Jamaican went partying before he flew home," Brown said. "Got into some kind of scuffle with this little girl does occasional tricks at a go-go joint downtown."

"What kind of scuffle?"

"Don't know. But he stabbed her."

"Why?"

"Some kind of scuffle."

"The old man was hanged, right?"

"Right. But Rohypnol figures in both cases. And we've

got a witness who saw the girl with this Jamaican. He's got a distinctive knife scar on his face, he's easy to spot."

"So," Nellie said, "what we seem to have here is an old man killed for money, in effect, and a snitch killed for the same thing, in effect, and a go-go girl killed for we don't know what, but if she was turning tricks, we can euphemistically say love, which are two pretty good motives for murder, wouldn't you say, love and money? I would say so."

The detectives said nothing.

"All we need now is a *fourth* murder," Nellie said.

"Bite your tongue," Meyer said.

"You think the housewife's only behind one of them, huh?"

"Yes."

"She hired this mysterious Jamaican to kill her father . . ."

"He's not so mysterious, Nellie. We've got clean descriptions of him from two different people."

"Scar on his face, you said."

"Yes."

They were all wondering who'd tell her about the tattoo on his penis. They let it slide. Carella sort of smiled.

"But you can't find him," Nellie said.

"Not yet."

"Not here, and not in Houston, either."

"That's right. But we've got him linked to the father, and also the go-go dancer."

"He branched out, right? Started free-lancing, so to speak."

"Nobody likes a smart-ass, Nellie."

"Sorry. I'm just trying to see how I can possibly go for an indictment on this without making a fool of myself."

"We think it's strong, Nellie."

"*I* think it's pie in the sky. I thank you for the journey uptown," she said, and picked up her handbag. "It's always a pleasure to see how the other half lives. But if you want me to bag this lady for you, here's what you'll have to do. One, it would be very nice if you could find the Jamaican with the knife scar and whatever other identifying mark you're all smirking about. But that would be too good to be true. Lacking the trigger man himself—so to speak, since what we're looking for is a hangman and a knifer—I suppose you'll have to find some evidence that shows how a housewife with a lawyer husband, God forbid, could have got in touch with a Jamaican hit man. Did she phone him in Houston? Or perhaps Kingston? Did she pick him off the Internet? Did she pick him up in a bar? Did she write to him in prison? Show me some evidence that *ties* her to him, whoever he may be—and don't tell me he isn't so mysterious, Steve, I think he is very damn mysterious. If you guys *really* believe he got the rope from this guy in Hightown—and really, that sounds *so* far-fetched—then find *out* if he did, and get some better information on him than you already have, something that'll *lead* you to him. When you have all that, you know where to reach me. Toodle-ooo, fellas," she said, waggling her fingers at them, and then tossed the hood of her parka up over her head and walked out.

Lorraine Riddock could hardly contain her excitement.

She was nineteen years old, a redheaded sophomore at Ladd University, not two miles uptown, working part-time for the Reverend Foster since the beginning of the school term. What she did, mostly, was stuff envelopes and run the postage-meter machine, but she'd taken the job because she was a political science major who strongly believed in the reverend's program of Truth and Justice. During the past two days—ever since the brutal beating of Hector Milagros—Foster had allowed her to sit in on some of the strategy meetings, and so she truly felt she had contributed to the plan he was about to announce this evening.

The three white men on the reverend's tactical committee called themselves "The Token Honkies," which even Foster found amusing, though normally he avoided any expression, white *or* black, that might be considered racist. There were street blacks who casually tossed around the word "nigger," as if it didn't carry with it centuries of hateful baggage, using it instead as if it were a salutation similar to "brother" or "sister." Here in the offices above the church, however, Lorraine had never once heard that word, certainly not from any of the whites but not from any of the blacks, either. It was a word she herself had never used in her lifetime. She scarcely noticed—and certainly didn't care—which of the men or women here tonight was white or black, misnomers in any case. White was the color of snow. Black was the color of coal. Nobody here even remotely fit either of those descriptions.

"They're ready for you now, Rev," someone said, and Lorraine turned to see Walter Hopwell walking over from the mobile television crew. He was wearing his trademark black jeans and black turtleneck sweater, a tan sports jacket over them. His bald head seemed scarcely less shiny than the gold earring in his left ear lobe.

"Eleven o'clock news," someone behind her whispered.

Lorraine glanced at her watch. It was now close to nine, so this had to be a taping. Hopwell handed Foster a hair brush, which he turned aside.

"The flowers look a bit wilted, Rev," one of his aides said. "You might want to distance yourself from them."

Foster took a few steps sideward, moving as gracefully as the boxer he once had been, gliding toward where a framed photograph of Martin Luther King hung on the wall. A blonde wearing a dark blue jacket and a gray skirt stepped closer to him, asked her microphone, "Do we need another level?," and then chanted, "One, two, three, hello, hello, hello, okay? Want my advice?" she asked Foster.

"Always welcome," he said.

"Lose King. They'll be looking at his picture instead of you."

"How can we do that?" Foster asked.

"Try this, Will," she said into her microphone. "On me for the intro, then in close on the picture of King, and slide off it to the reverend." She waited a moment, and then asked, "How's that look?" She listened to her ear button, said, "Okay, great," and then told Foster, "You've got both now, Reverend, ain't I smart? Say a few words for a level, could you?"

"One, two, three, four," Foster said.

"Thanks," she said. "I'll do the intro, then we'll pan off King and on to you. Say when, Jimmy," she told somebody.

"Let me put another cake in here," Jimmy said. "We're almost out."

She waited while he changed cassettes, and then said, "Okay, ten seconds, please. Standby, people."

A girl wearing earphones started the countdown out loud, "Ten, nine, eight, seven, six ..." and then fell silent as she continued counting down the seconds on her fingers, her hand stretched toward the reporter, five, four, three, two, one, and pointed her index finger directly at her as a red light popped on the camera.

"This is Bess MacDougal here at the First Baptist Church in Diamondback, where the Reverend Gabriel Foster has called a press conference."

The camera panned past the King photograph and came to rest on Foster in a medium shot, a solemn somewhat angry look on his face. Rivers of rain ran down the window behind him.

"I don't care what color you are out there," he said,

"you have to believe that what the Mayor said today was untruthful and unjust. Truth and justice! That's all there is, and all we need to know!"

"Yes, Rev!" someone shouted.

"The Mayor said that it was not any of his detectives who marched into The Catacombs downtown on Saturday night and beat up Hector Milagros, and that is not truth! The Mayor said that Hector Milagros is a self-confessed murderer and not entitled to the pity of the people of this great city, and that is not justice!"

"Right on!"

"I don't care if you are some kind of belligerent black man, all he needs is a gun ..."

"Tell 'em, Rev!"

"I don't care if that's the kind of bellicose person you are, or whether you are an abstemious soul goes smiling at white folks and behind their backs wishes they were dead ..."

"Oh Lordy!"

"Whatever kind of African-American you are, rich or poor, whether you a doctor or a homeboy, whether you clever or dim, whether you a telephone operator or somebody scrubs floors on her hands and knees the way my mama done when I was coming along in Mississippi, I know in my heart and in my soul that there is not a single one of you out there tonight—black *or* white—who is not *appalled* by what happened to that man while he was in custody and entitled to protection!"

The cheers were deafening.

Bess MacDougal listened and watched, waiting for her back-to-studio cue.

"So tonight, I am making this promise to you. Starting at eight tomorrow morning, when the shifts change, there will be people marching outside every police precinct in this city! And thousands of us will be marching outside The Catacombs downtown, to raise our voices in protest, and to demand an investigation that will lead to the arrest of the two detectives responsible for this brutal act against a helpless black man in custody! We will not desist until we know the truth! We will not desist until there is justice! Truth and justice! That's all there is, and all we need to know!"

The girl with the earphones pointed to Bess again.

"You've been listening to the Reverend Gabriel Foster," she said, "here at the First Baptist Church in Diamondback. This is Bess MacDougal. Back to you, Terri and Frank."

There was the sound of laughter, black and white, the sound of the rain lashing the windows, the noisy swagger of the television crew wrapping up. Bess MacDougal told Foster what a lovely, heartfelt speech that was, and shook his hand, and went to join her crew. Lorraine walked over to where a reporter from *Ebony* was asking Foster if he would mind posing for a photo outside in the rain . . .

"Under an umbrella, of course," she said, smiling up at him. "What I had in mind for the caption was something like 'Let it come down!'"

"Second murderer," Foster said at once. *"Macbeth."*

"Referring, of course, to the blue wall of silence," the reporter said.

"I realize. Give me ten minutes. I'll meet you down-stairs."

Lorraine extended her hand to him.

"That was wonderful," she said,

Foster took her hand between both his.

"Thank you, Lorraine," he said.

Until that moment she hadn't even realized he knew her name. She felt a sudden rush of blood to her face, the telltale curse of being a redhead with a fair complexion. Blushing to her toes, she dropped his hand and backed away. Walter Hopwell called her name, "Lorraine? Some coffee?" One of the television crew called to Bess that they had a breaking story downtown, and all the TV people rushed out, leaving only the mere newspaper and magazine reporters, and Foster's people, black and white, and the rain, and the long night ahead.

She was waiting on the corner in the rain, a flimsy umbrella over her head, half the spokes broken, the rain coming down as if it would never stop, when all of a sudden a dark blue automobile pulled up to the curb and the window on her side rolled down.

"Lorraine!" a man's voice called.

"Who's that?" she said, bending to look into the car.

"Me," he said. "Do you need a lift?"

She walked over to the car, peered in more closely.

"Oh. Hi," she said.

"Get in," he said. "I'll drive you home."

"The bus'll be here any minute."

"It's no trouble."

"Only if it's on your way."

"Get in before you drown," he said, and leaned across the seat to throw open the door. She slid onto the seat, closed the umbrella, swung her legs inside, and then pulled the door shut behind her.

"Boy oh boy," she said.

"Where to?"

"Talbot and Twenty-eighth."

"At your service," he said, and put the car in gear, and pulled it away from the curb. The windshield wipers snicked at the rain. The heater insinuated warm air onto her feet and her face. The car felt as warm and as safe as a cocoon.

"How long were you waiting out there?" he asked.

"Ten minutes, at least."

"This time of night, you never know when a bus is coming."

The digital clock on the dashboard read 10:37.

"I wouldn't mind," she said. "But this *weather!*"

"Snow, rain," he said, "what's coming next? And it isn't even winter yet."

"Oh, I *know*," she said.

"How'd you like tonight?"

"It was wonderful."

"I could see you were enjoying yourself."

"I love working for him, don't you?"

"I surely do."

"Did you ever see him do a TV taping before?"

"Once or twice. He's an incredible person."

"I know, oh, I know."

They fell silent, anticipating the precinct protests tomorrow morning, awed by the fact that they both worked for this marvelous human being who was doing so much for race relations in this city. Lorraine had been assigned to a precinct all the way out in Majesta. She wasn't even sure she knew where it was.

"I hope it won't be raining," she said. "Tomorrow."

"Or snowing," he said. "Snow would be even worse."

"Where will you be?"

"The Fifth. Down in The Quarter. Near Ramsey U."

"My building's just up ahead," she said. "On the right."

"Okay."

He eased the car to the curb, looked at the dashboard clock. It read 10:52.

"Damn," he said. "I'm going to *miss* it."

"I'm sorry?"

"The news. It goes on at eleven. I'm sure he'll be the lead story."

"Oh," she said. "Yes. Oh, that's too bad."

"Well, there'll be other stories."

"Why don't you ... well ... would you like to come up? Watch it with me?"

"It's late," he said. "Tomorrow's a big day."

"If we don't hurry, we'll *both* miss it," she said.

He parked and locked the car, and they dashed through the rain to her building, her spindly umbrella virtually useless now, the rain relentless. Once inside the small apartment, she went immediately to the television set and turned it on, and then asked him if he wanted a beer or anything.

"Help yourself, they're in the fridge," she said, and pointed toward the tiny kitchen, and then went into the bathroom across the hall. He took two bottles of beer from the refrigerator, found a bottle opener in the top drawer of the kitchen counter, and uncapped both bottles. He found two glasses in the cabinet over the sink, and poured beer into each of them. Glancing toward the closed bathroom door, he took a pair of blister-packed white tablets from his jacket pocket, and popped both of them into one of the glasses.

He was sitting on the couch in the living room when she joined him a moment later. The news was just coming on. As he'd suspected, the Gabriel Foster announcement was the lead story. He handed her one of the glasses.

"Thanks," she said.

"This is Bess MacDougal at the First Baptist Church here in Diamondback ..."

"There it is," she said.

"Cheers," he said.

"There *you* are! Oh, look, there you *are!*"

"Cheers," he said again.

"There's *me*, too! *Look!*"

"... has called a press conference."

The pan shot over the photograph of Martin Luther King worked exactly as Foster might have hoped, forging a dramatic pictorial link between the slain civil rights leader and himself. They both fell silent as he began speaking.

"I don't care what color you are out there," he said,

"you have to believe that what the Mayor said today was untruthful and unjust. Truth and justice! That's all there is, and all we need to know!"

"Yes, Rev!" someone shouted.

"Look at him," Lorraine said.

"Beautiful."

"The Mayor said that it was not any of his detectives who marched into The Catacombs downtown on Saturday night and beat up Hector Milagros, and that is not truth!"

"Character is what comes through."

"Sincerity."

"Character and sincerity, right."

"The Mayor said that Hector Milagros is a self-confessed murderer and not entitled to the pity of the people of this great city, and that is not justice!"

"Right on!"

"I don't care if you are some kind of belligerent black man, all he needs is a gun . . ."

"Tell 'em, Rev!"

"I don't care if that's the kind of bellicose person you are, or whether you are an abstemious soul goes smiling at white folks and behind their backs wishes they were dead . . ."

"Oh Lordy!"

"Whatever kind of African-American you are, rich or poor, whether you a doctor or a homeboy, whether you clever or dim . . ."

"Cheers," Lorraine said at last, and raised her glass.

"Cheers," he said.

". . . whether you a telephone operator or somebody scrubs floors on her hands and knees . . ."

They clinked glasses and drank.

There were at least three dozen people marching back and forth and chanting in front of the station house when Arthur

Brown got to work on Wednesday morning. A black man carrying a sign reading TRUTH AND JUSTICE gave Brown a dirty look and said, "I wouldn't go in there I was you, brother."

"I work here, brother."

"You should fine another job."

Brown walked right on by, and up the familiar steps, and past the uniformed officer standing on the top step in front of the scarred wooden doors flanked by green globes with the numerals 87 on each. Sergeant Murchison, sitting behind the muster desk said, "They still dancing out there?"

"Looks like," Brown said, and started up the iron-runged steps leading to the second-floor squadroom.

Actually, he didn't know *how* he really felt about those people outside marching and yelling. He knew it was wrong for two detectives to have gone in there and beaten up a prisoner in custody, white *or* black. But that man down there in The Catacombs worked for a dope dealer and the job he performed for him was the same as what had *happened* to him: he beat people up. Sometimes *killed* them, in fact, like he'd done to Danny Nelson. The question Brown had to ask— and this was a question the reverend Foster *never* asked— was whether the man had been beaten up cause he was black or just cause he was an evil piece of shit. Wasn't no way you could learn the truth of *that* situation till you found the deuce of dicks who'd gone in there for whatever reason. Way Brown figured it, you let somebody beat up *any* black man just cause he was black, then next time it could be your *own* ass. He knew there were white sons of bitches in this world would think nothing of laying a pipe upside his head just for his color alone, he knew that. But he was a cop. And in his day and time, he had clipped many a *black* son of a bitch coming at him, and in those instances color'd had nothing to do with anything. Nor had he regretted it. That was the truth. Justice was another story.

First thing he saw on his way into the squadroom was a redheaded girl sitting at Bert Kling's desk.

Meyer told him she was waiting for somebody from the Rape Squad.

She didn't look like a cop at all, much less someone here to talk to Lorraine about a rape. She was in her mid-thirties, Lorraine guessed, with black wedge-cut hair and brown eyes behind designer eyeglasses, a slender woman of medium height wearing what looked like a naval officer's greatcoat, hatless and gloveless though the temperature outside this morning was in the low twenties and the wind was blowing fiercely. A blue leather shoulder bag dangled from a strap over her left shoulder. Lorraine guessed there'd be a pistol in it if she was a cop, though she didn't look at all like a cop. "Miss Riddock?" she said, and extended her hand, "I'm Detective Annie Rawles." They shook hands briefly. "Let's go down the hall, okay?" she said. "Be a bit more private."

Lorraine nodded and followed her through the gate in the slatted wooden railing, and then down the corridor to a door marked INTERROGATION on its upper frosted-glass panel. There were no windows in the room. They sat at a long table scarred with cigarette burns. A mirror hung on one wall. Lorraine wondered if it was a one-way mirror. She wondered if anyone was watching and listening beyond the smudged apple green wall.

"Want to tell me about it?" Annie said.

The girl did not look like your average rape victim. Usually, there was a stunned demeanor, a glazed look to the eyes. Usually, the shoulders were slumped, the fingers inter-laced as if in prayer, the knees pressed together defensively, a shamed expression on the face. Instead, Lorraine Riddock's eyes were filled with anger, her mouth a tight little line across her face, her fists clenched. When she spoke, her voice was clear and resonant.

"I was raped," she said.

"When did this happen?"

"Last night."

"What time?"

"I don't know."

"You don't ..."

"Sometime after eleven o'clock."

"Where, Miss Riddock?"

"My apartment."

"How'd he get in the apartment?"

"I invited him in."

"Was this a date?"

"No. We work together."

"Tell me what happened."

"I don't know what happened."

"You don't ..."

"I don't remember. But I know I was raped."

"Were you drinking, Miss Riddock?"

"Yes."

"How much did you drink?"

"All I had was a beer. We were drinking beer while we watched television. Reverend Foster had done an interview earlier that evening. We were watching it on television."

"Reverend Foster is?"

"Gabriel Foster. Who's protesting all over the city this morning. Don't you know Gabriel Foster? I should be in Majesta right now."

"So you were watching television ..."

"Yes."

"And what happened?"

"I don't remember."

"But you say you were raped."

"Yes."

"If you can't remember anything . . ."

"There was blood," Lorraine said. "When I woke up this morning. In my bed. On the sheet. I'm not due for two weeks," she said. "It wasn't my period. Anyway, it wasn't that much blood. Someone raped me," she said.

"Lorraine . . ."

"I'm a virgin," she said. "I was raped."

A female doctor at Morehouse General examined Lorraine and discovered a freshly ruptured septate hymen and multiple genital lacerations indicative of forcible entry. A nurse prepared two vaginal-smear slides, gathered samples of whatever loose hairs she could comb from Lorraine's pubic area, clipped comparison samples of Lorraine's own pubic hair, and then did an acid phosphatase test on a swab from Lorraine's genital area. The immediate purple reaction indicated presumptive presence of semen. They were still well within the seventy-two-hour testing limit for Rohypnol: they found in her urine sample the metabolite that indicated exposure to flunitrazepam.

Annie Rawles herself went to make the arrest.

Annie spotted him easily among the forty or so men and women marching in the bitter cold outside the Fifth Precinct. Like all the others, he, too, was carrying a sign that read TRUTH AND JUSTICE. Like all the others, he, too, was chanting the words over and over again. But he was the only white man in the group. Lorraine Riddock had described Lloyd Burton as a somewhat nerdy type wearing eyeglasses, some five feet, nine or ten inches tall, with brown hair, brown eyes, and a zitty complexion. He fit the picture exactly.

Annie fell into step beside him.

"Mr Burton?" she said.

He turned, startled.

"Yes?" he said.

"Lloyd Burton?"

"Yes?"

Their breaths clouded the brittle air between them.

"You're under arrest, sir," she said.

A black woman marching behind him said, "You goan 'rest him, you better 'rest me, too."

"Not unless you committed rape, ma'am,' Annie said, and yanked a pair of cuffs from her shoulder bag, and began reciting Miranda.

She questioned him in the same room where three hours earlier Lorraine Riddock had described him. He had a somewhat reedy, high-pitched voice that resonated irritatingly in the small windowless space. In the adjoining room, Lieutenant Albert Genetti, Annie's immediate superior on the Rape Squad, watched through the one-way mirror, listening intently.

"Where were you last night at eleven o'clock?" she asked Burton.

"Home watching television," he said.

"Where's home?"

"637 South Third."

"Anyone with you?"

"No, I live alone."

"Sure you weren't up here on Talbot and Twenty-eighth?"

"Positive."

"1271 Talbot?"

"No."

"Apartment 3D?"

"Don't know it."

"Watching television with a girl named Lorraine Riddock?"

"No, I wasn't. I was home alone."

"You know Lorraine, don't you?"

"Yes, I do. But I wasn't with her last night."

"Well, you were with her at the First Baptist Church, weren't you?"

"Yes, but not later. Not at eleven o'clock, which is what you asked me."

"You were present at Gabriel Foster's press conference, weren't you?"

"Yes, I was."

"The television tape substantiates that."

"I know. I saw it."

"Lorraine's standing right there next to you. On the tape."

"I know."

"Where'd you see it? The tape."

"On the news that night. At home."

"Didn't you drive Lorraine home after the press conference?"

"Yes, I did."

"Didn't you go up to her apartment at a little before eleven last night?"

"No, I dropped her off downstairs."

"Didn't you go up to her apartment to watch the eleven o'clock news?"

"No, I went home to watch it."

"Didn't you sit drinking beer with her while you watched the news?"

"No, I went home to watch it."

"Didn't drink beer with her?"

"No."

"Didn't drop two tabs of rope in her beer?"

"I don't know what that is, rope."

"Where'd you get the rope, Mr Burton?"

"I don't know what rope is."

"Mr Burton, you know we're permitted to take your fingerprints, don't you?"

"Well, no, I don't think you are. If you plan to do that, I want to change my mind about having a lawyer here."

"You can have a lawyer anytime you want, but it won't change the fact that we're allowed to take your fingerprints. If you want to call your lawyer ..."

"Truth and Justice has its own lawyers."

"Good, go call one of them. You want to make this a political issue, fine. All *I* want to do is charge you with first-degree rape."

"Then I'd better call a lawyer right now."

"Good, I'll get you a phone. And if it'll make you feel more comfortable, I won't take your prints till he gets here. What I'd like to do, you see ..."

"You already told me. You'd like to charge me with first-degree rape."

Yes, you rapist bastard, Annie thought.

"That's the plan," she said. "But first I want to compare your prints against whatever we get from a pair of beer bottles in Lorraine Riddock's kitchen."

Burton's face went pale.

"Forget something?" she asked.

Junius Craig was one of a staff of five black attorneys employed by Truth and Justice. Alone with Burton, he informed him that "engaging in sexual intercourse with a female incapable of consent by reason of being physically helpless" constituted violation of Section 130.35 of the Penal Law, defined as Rape in the First Degree, a Class-B felony punishable by a minimum of three to six and a max of six to twenty-five. He suggested that if Burton for a moment believed his fingerprints might match the latents on the beer bottles in the victim's kitchen, or if he thought for a further moment that samples of his pubic hair might match anything they'd recovered from the girl's pubic area, or if— as yet another possibility—he felt DNA testing might come up with a positive match between his semen and anything they'd swabbed from the girl's vagina . . .

"And make no mistake," he warned, "they *are* going to get those samples from you. My guess is they'll seek a court order . . ."

"Make them get a court order for my fingerprints, too," Burton said.

"They won't need one. In fact, under Miranda they won't need one for the samples, either. But they'll play it safe because they snatched you from a line of civil rights marchers. So what do you say?"

"About what?"

"About any of these possibilities."

Burton did not answer.

"Because if you think any of them *are* possibilities, I suggest we start shopping a deal right now. Twenty-five in a state pen is a long time."

"She wanted it as much as I did," Burton said.

"You're lucky you're white," Craig said.

"Anyway, Walter Hopwell gave me the rope," Burton said.

They had him so doped up he couldn't even remember his own name, but oh how sweet was the release. One swift kick of the needle and all the throbbing pain in his thigh disappeared, and all at once he was floating far far away on clouds of sweet contentment, floating. He tried to remember how long he'd been a cop, but he couldn't even remember how he'd got shot tonight. Last night? Two nights ago? What case had they been working? He tried to remember how *many* cases the Eight-Seven had worked over the years, but he couldn't even remember where the precinct was. He lay in his hospital bed smiling, trying to remember, conjuring victims and villains alike, cataloguing the cases by their key characteristics, then arranging them alphabetically to achieve some semblance of order, smiling as he worked it through, pleased with what a smart detective he was, even though he'd got himself shot—until he lost his place and had to start all over again. Well, okay, how many *had* there been? Ten, twenty? Who knows, he thought, easy come, easy go. Forty maybe? Who's counting? Who remembers, who even cares, I got *shot!* I deserve a medal or something just for *being* here. *Two* medals if I die.

I remember Marilyn Hollis.

I remember loving Marilyn Hollis. I remember poison, I remember those sons of bitches shooting the love of my life, killing Marilyn Hollis. If I should die here in this place in this minute in this bed . . .

There must be fifty at least, don't you think?

At least.

Let's dance, Marilyn.

Marilyn?

Would you care to dance?

May I have this last dance with you?

Bryan Shanahan, the detective who'd caught the Martha Coleridge murder downtown, could find no indication that anything had been stolen from the old lady's apartment. So he had to assume someone had broken in there *looking* for something to steal and—when he hadn't found anything— had turned on the old lady in rage. That sometimes happened. Not all your burglars were gents. Matter of fact, in Shanahan's experience, not *any* burglars were gents.

He went back to the apartment that Wednesday afternoon without his partner, first of all because he didn't want the burden of answering a rookie detective's interminable questions, and second because he thought better when he was alone. This wasn't what he would categorize as a difficult case, some junkie burglar breaking in and messing up. At the same time, it wasn't a simple one because the killer—whoever he was—hadn't left anything for them to go with. No latents, no stray fibers or hairs—which in any case wouldn't have done them any good unless they caught somebody to run comparisons on.

Maybe he went back alone because it annoyed him that somebody had killed a lady old enough to die without any outside help. Or maybe he went back alone because while he was reading Martha Coleridge's play he'd fallen half in love with the farm girl who'd migrated to America from England's East Midlands. Maybe her play had given him a little insight into age and aging, death and dying. Looking down at the fragile old lady with the broken neck, he'd never once considered that once, a long time ago, she might have been a spirited and beautiful nineteen-year-old who'd come to this city and discovered a world beyond her bedroom window. For a long time now, a corpse had been only a dead body to Bryan Shanahan. All at once, reading Martha's play, a corpse became a human being.

So he went through the apartment yet another time, alone this time, savoring his aloneness, searching for the young girl in the old lady's belongings, hunting for brown photographs or handkerchiefs lined with lace, mementos from Brighton or Battersea Park. On a shelf at the back of her closet, he found a satin-covered box that once might have contained sachets, the fabric faded and threadbare, the little knob on the lid dangerously loose to the touch. There were letters in the box, all tied with a faded red ribbon. He loosened the bow and began reading.

The letters had been written by someone named Louis Aronowitz. The ink had turned brown over the years, and the writing paper was brittle. Shanahan almost feared turning pages, lest they would snap as easily as had the old lady's neck. The letters had all been written in 1921, two years after Louis returned to New York from the war, a year after Martha sailed from Southampton to America. The letters chronicled a love affair that started in April of that year and ended in December, just before Christmas. It was Martha who'd ended it. Quoting her in a letter dated December 21, Aronowitz wrote, "How can you say you see no future in a relationship between a Christian girl and a Jew? I love you! That is the future, my darling!" His last letter was written on New Year's Eve. It told her that he was going back to Berlin, where his parents had been born, and where "a Jew can call himself a Jew without fear of being judged different from any other man. I will love you always, my Martha. I will love you to my very death."

Clearly, the letters formed the basis of the love story Martha used in her play the following year. But juxtaposed to her heart-wrenching tale of a doomed love was the contrapuntal story of a young girl finding a new life in a rich and vibrant city: the world beyond the windows in her room. Shanahan gently closed the lid on the brittle, fading box. There had been nothing in it that told him who might have killed the old lady.

But there was another letter.

He found it in a folder of paid bills. The letter was typewritten. Shanahan sat in an easy chair under a lamp with a fringed shade, and read it in the fading light of the afternoon.

My name is Martha Coleridge, author of a play titled *My Room*, which I wrote in 1922, and which was performed for one week only at the Little Theater Playhouse on Randall Square in September of that year. I am enclosing a copy of the program. I am also enclosing a copy of the play itself for your perusal. I do not know your separate personal addresses, so I am sending all of this to Mr Norman Zimmer's office for forwarding.

I recently learned from an article in *Daily Variety*, the theatrical and motion picture journal, that a musical based on a play titled *Jenny's Room* is being readied for production next season. Your name was listed among the others involved in one way or another with the pending production.

I wish you to know that in 1923, when the play *Jenny's Room* opened to spectacular success, I wrote to its alleged author, a Miss Jessica Miles, and warned her that I would bring suit against her on charges of plagiarism unless I was substantially rewarded for the work from which her play had derived, namely *my* play, enclosed. She never replied to my letter and I did not have the means at that time to pursue the matter further.

However, since reading the *Variety* piece, I have contacted several lawyers who seem interested in taking the case on a contingency basis, and I am writing to all of you now in the hope that together or separately you will wish to make appropriate compensation to the true creator of the work that will be engaging you all in the weeks and months to come. Otherwise, I shall be forced to initiate litigation.

I close in the spirit of artistic endeavor that embraces us all.

Cordially,

Martha Coleridge
Playwright

Martha Coleridge's letter had been written on November 26, the day after Thanksgiving. Stapled to it was a copying service bill dated November 27. There was another bill on that same date, from Mail Boxes, Etc. who had packed and mailed all the material to Norman Zimmer. A separate sheet of paper with his mailing address on it was stapled to a list of names and addresses to whom copies of the material were to be forwarded. The names on that list were:

Constance Lindstrom, Co-Producer
Cynthia Keating, Underlying Rights
Gerald Palmer, Book Rights
Felicia Carr, Lyrics Rights
Avrum Zarim, Music Rights
Clarence Hull, Bookwriter
Buddy Flynn, Composer
Rowland Chapp, Director
Naomi Janus, Choreographer

When Norman Zimmer's secretary told him two detectives were here to see him, he expected Carella and Brown again. Instead, there was a big redheaded cop named Bryan Shanahan and his shorter curly-haired partner named Jefferson Long, both of whom worked out of the Two-Oh precinct downtown. Shanahan did all of the talking. He told Zimmer they were investigating the murder of a woman named Martha Coleridge, and then they showed him the letter she'd written and asked if he had received a copy of it. Zimmer looked at the letter and said, "A crank."

"*Did* you receive a copy of this letter?" Shanahan asked.

"Yes, I did."

"When, sir?"

"I don't remember the exact date. It was after Thanksgiving sometime."

"Did you respond to it?"

"No, I did not. I told you. The woman's a crank."

"If you didn't contact her, how can you know that for sure, sir?" Shanahan asked.

Zimmer was beginning to get the measure of the man. One of those bulldog types who came in with a preconceived notion and would not let go of it. But he'd said they were investigating the woman's *homicide*. So attention had to be paid.

"Whenever there's a hit play," he said, "or movie, or novel—or *poem* for all I know—someone comes out of the woodwork claiming it was stolen from an obscure, unpublished, unproduced, undistinguished piece of crap scribbled on the back of a napkin. It's *Dadier's Nose* all over again."

"Sir?"

"*Le Nez de Dadier*, a play written by a Parisian scissors grinder named Henri Clavère, in the year 1893, four years before Edmond de Rostand's play opened. *Cyrano de Bergerac*, hmm? Well, Clavère brought suit for plagiarism. He lost the case and drowned himself in the Seine. If I responded to every lunatic who feels his or her work was later appropriated, I wouldn't be able to do anything else."

"But you are, in fact, producing a show called 'Jenny's Room', aren't you?" Shanahan asked.

Jaws clamped tight on the idea already formed in his mind, whatever that idea might be. His partner standing by deadpanned, listening, learning. Zimmer wanted to kick both of them out on their asses.

"Yes," he said patiently, but unwilling to conceal the faintest of sighs. "I *am* co-producing a show titled 'Jenny's Room', that is a fact, yes. It is also a fact that the show has nothing to do with this pathetic woman's play."

"Have you read her play, sir?"

"No, I have not. Nor do I intend to."

"Then how do you know there are no similarities between her play and the play 'Jenny's Room', upon which your musical . . ."

"First of all, the play wasn't even *called* 'Jenny's' Room' when it was written. It was called 'Jessie's' Room'. And 'Jessie's' Room' was a highly autobiographical play written by a woman named Jessica Miles . . ."

"So I understand."

". . . and not anyone named Margaret Coleridge."

"*Martha* Coleri . . ."

"What*ever* her name is."

"Whose play is also highly autobiographical."

"Oh, is it?"

"Yes. *My Room.* The play she wrote. Which she claims was stolen by Jessica Miles."

"How do you know it's autobiographical?"

"I read it."

"I see. Did you *know* this woman?"

"Not until I read her play," Shanahan said.

"You knew her when she was alive?"

"No, sir, I did not," Shanahan said. "I got to know her after I read her play. It's a very good play."

"I see. You're a theater critic, are you?"

"There's no need to get snotty, sir," Shanahan said, and his partner blinked. "A woman was killed."

"I'm sorry about that," Zimmer said. "But I'm getting tired of detectives coming in here with their questions. What the hell am I producing? The Scottish Play?"

"What detectives?" Shanahan asked, surprised.

"What's the Scottish play?" his partner asked.

"To ask about Martha Coleridge?"

"No, to ask about Andrew Hale."

"I'm sorry, who's . . . ?"

"Tell you what," Zimmer said. "Go talk to your colleagues, okay? Carella and Brown. The Eighty-seventh Precinct."

"What's the Scottish play?" Long asked again.

Chapter Nine

The detectives were waiting in the lobby of Fitness Plus when Connie Lindstrom walked out early Thursday morning, her mink coat flapping open over black tights and Nike running shoes as she sailed past to start her working day. Her eyes opened in surprise when she saw Carella and Brown sitting on the bench. She broke step, stopped, looked at them, shook her head, and said, "What now?"

"Sorry to bother you again," Carella said.

"I'll bet."

"Ever see this?" he asked, and handed her a copy of the letter Shanahan had passed on to him late yesterday afternoon. Connie took it, began reading it, recognized it at once, and handed it back to him.

"Yes," she said. "So?," and hurried past them to the exit door.

They came down the steps and into the street, Connie leading, glancing at her watch, walking quickly to the curb, looking up the avenue for a taxi. It was eight-thirty in the morning on a very cold day, the sky bright and cloudless overhead, the streets heavy with traffic. At this hour, it was almost impossible to catch a free cab, but the buses were packed as well, and getting anywhere was a slow and tedious process. Connie kept waving her hand at approaching taxis, shaking her head as each occupied one flashed by.

"I have to be downtown in ten minutes," she said. "What*ever* this is, I'm afraid it'll have to ..."

"Woman who wrote that letter was murdered," Carella said.

"Jesus, what *is* this?" Connie said. "The Scottish Play?"

"What's the Scottish Play?" Brown asked.

"We have to talk to you," Carella said. "If you want a lift downtown, we'll be happy to take you."

"In what?" she said. "A police car?"

"Nice Dodge sedan."

"Shotgun on the back seat?"

"In the trunk," Brown said.

"Why not?" Connie said, and they began walking toward where Carella had parked the car, around the corner. She was in good shape; they had to step fast to keep up with her. Carella unlocked the door on the driver's side, clicked open all the other doors, and then threw up the visor with the pink police notice on it. Connie sat beside him on the front seat. Brown climbed into the back.

"Where to?" Carella asked.

"Octagon," she said. "You've been there."

"More auditions?"

"Endless process," she said. "I don't know this woman, you realize. If you're suggesting her murder ..."

"When did you get her letter, Miss Lindstrom?"

"Last week sometime."

"Before the Meet 'N' Greet?"

"Yes."

"How'd you handle it?"

"*Dadier's Nose*," she said, and shrugged.

"What's that?"

"Too long a story. Too long a *nose*, in fact. Suffice it to say that plagiarism victims surface whenever anything smells of success. I turned the letter over to my lawyer."

"Did he contact her?"

"She. I have no idea."

"You didn't ask?"

"Why should I care? We're talking about a play written in 1922!"

"We're also talking about a play that seems to inspire murder."

The car went silent.

Connie turned to him, her face sharp in profile.

"You don't know that for sure," she said.

"Know what?"

"That the two murders are in any way connected. I suppose you'd both take a fit if I smoked."

"Go right ahead," Carella said, surprising Brown.

She fished into her bag, came up with a single cigarette and a lighter. She flicked the lighter into flame, held it to the end of the cigarette. She breathed out a cloud of smoke, sighed in satisfaction. On the back seat, Brown opened a window.

"I know what it looks like," she said. "Hale refuses to sell us the rights, so he gets killed. Woman writes a letter that could seem threatening to the show, and *she* gets killed. Somebody wanted both of them dead because the show *must* go *on*," she said, raising her voice dramatically. "Well, I have news for you. The show doesn't always have to go on. If it gets too difficult or too complicated, it simply does *not* go on, and that's a fact."

"But the show *is* going on," Brown said. "And that's a fact, too."

"Yes. But if you think any of the professionals involved in this project would *kill* to insure a production ..." She shook her head. "No," she said. "I'm sorry."

"How about the amateurs?" Carella asked.

✫   ✫   ✫

Sometimes it was better to deal with professionals.

A professional knew what he was doing, and if he broke the rules it was only because he understood them so well. The amateur witnessed a murder or two on television, concluded he didn't have to know the rules, he could just jump in cold and do a little murder of his own. The amateur believed that even if he didn't know what he was doing, he could get away with it. The professional believed he had *best* know what he was doing or he'd get caught. In fact, the professional knew without question that if he didn't get better and better each time out, eventually they'd nail him. The irony was that there were more amateurs than professionals running around loose out there, each and every one of them thriving. Go figure.

The way Carella and Brown figured it, there were four amateurs involved in the musical production of *Jenny's Room*, and three of them were still here in this busy little city. The fourth was somewhere in Tel Aviv, driving his taxi through crowded streets and hoping a bus bomb wouldn't explode in his path. There was nothing that said an Israeli cab driver couldn't have hired a Jamaican from Houston to hang an old man in his closet and later break an old lady's neck, but that sounded like the kind of stuff a neophyte might devise. Distance also would have disqualified Felicia Carr from Los Angeles and Gerald Palmer from London had they not both been here in the city when Martha Coleridge had her neck snapped.

Cynthia Keating always loomed first and foremost.

Mousy little Cynthia, who'd hoisted her father off that bathroom door hook and lugged him over to the bed. Dear little Cynthia, who'd been worried about a suicide clause depriving her of a lousy twenty-five grand when there were hundreds of thousands to be coined in a hit musical?

They already knew where they could find Cynthia

Keating. They knew that Palmer was staying at The Piccadilly because he'd mentioned it at Connie Lindstrom's party. From the ever helpful Norman Zimmer, they learned that Felicia Carr was staying with a girlfriend here in the city. Because both Felicia and Palmer were leaving for their respective homes this weekend and time was running out, they split the legwork into three teams.

Whether a person was guilty or not, he or she always seemed surprised—and a little bit frightened—to find policemen standing on the doorstep. Felicia Carr opened the door to her girlfriend's garden apartment in Majesta, saw two burly men standing there flashing badges, opened her big green eyes wide and asked what seemed to be the trouble, Officers?

"We're investigating a homicide," Meyer said, because that often caused amateurs to wet their pants.

"A double homicide, in fact," Kling said genially. "May we come in, please?"

"Well ... sure," Felicia said.

They followed her into a spacious, sunny living room overlooking the Majesta Bridge not far in the distance. The furniture was still wearing summer slipcovers, the fabric all abloom with riotous red and yellow and purple flowers against a background of large green leaves. The summery decor, the sun glaring through the big windows made the day outside appear balmy. But the temperature was in the low twenties, and the forecasters had predicted more snow either late tonight or early tomorrow morning.

Felicia told them she was just on her way out ...

"So much to see here," she explained.

... and hoped this wouldn't take too long.

"Though I'm sorry to hear someone got murdered," she added.

"Two people," Kling reminded her.

"Yes, I'm sorry."

"Miss Carr," Meyer said, "can you tell us where you were this past Sunday night?"

"I'm sorry?"

"This past Sunday night," he repeated.

"That would've been the fifth," Kling said helpfully.

"Can you tell us where you were?"

"Well ... why?"

"This is a homicide investigation," Meyer said, and smiled encouragingly.

"What's that got to do with me?"

"Most likely nothing," Kling said, and nodded regretfully, as if to say *I* know you had nothing to do with these murders, and *you* know you had nothing to do with them, but we have to ask these questions, you see, that's our job. But Felicia Carr was from the motion picture capital of the universe. She had seen every cop movie ever made, every cop television show ever broadcast, and she wasn't about to get snowed by a song-and-dance team doing a dog-and-pony act.

"What do you mean, most *likely*?" she snapped. "Why do you want to know where I was on Sunday night? Is that when someone got killed?"

"Yes, Miss," Kling said, trying to look even more sorrowful, but the lady still wasn't buying.

"What is this?" she said. "Los Angeles? The LAPD Gestapo?"

"Do you know a woman named Martha Coleridge?" Meyer asked. Bad Cop suddenly on the scene. No more smile on his face. Bald head making him look like an executioner with an ax. Arms folded across his chest in unmistakably hostile body language. Blue eyes studying her coldly. Didn't know he was dealing with Wonder Woman here, who'd sold three houses in Westwood only two weeks ago.

"No, who's Martha Coleridge?" she asked. "Is she the person who got killed last Sunday? Is that it?"

"Yes, Miss Carr."

"Well, I don't know her. I never heard of her. Is that enough? I have to leave now."

"Few more questions," Kling said gently. "If you can spare a minute or so."

Good Cop with the flaxen hair and the hazel eyes and the cheeks still glowing from the cold outside, gently and persuasively trying to lead the lady down the garden path, not taking into account that she was from Tinseltown, USA, where if people ever walked anywhere they actually waited on street corners for lights to change.

"I don't think you're allowed to do this," she said. "Barge in here and ..."

"Miss Carr, have you ever been to Texas?" Meyer asked.

"Yes, I have. *Texas*? What's Texas got to ...?"

"Houston, Texas?"

"No. Just Dallas."

"Do you know anyone named Andrew Hale?"

"No. Yes. I never *met* him, but I know his name. Someone mentioned it."

"Who mentioned it?"

"Cynthia, I think. He was her father, wasn't he?"

"How did she happen to mention it?"

"Something about underlying rights? I really can't remember."

"But you say you don't know anyone named Martha Coleridge."

"That's right."

"Didn't you get a letter from her recently?"

"What?"

"A letter. From a woman named Martha Coleridge. Explaining that she'd written a play called ..."

"Oh yes. Her. I sent it back to Norman. Are you telling me *she's* the same person who got killed?"

"Norman Zimmer?"

"Yes. Is she the one . . . ?"

"Why'd you send it to him?"

"I figured he'd know what to do about it. He's the producer, isn't he? What do I know about a crazy old lady who wrote a play in 1922?"

"Excuse me," Kling said politely. "But what do you mean you sent it *back* to him?"

"Well, it was addressed to me care of his office. He had it messengered to me here. I mailed it back to him."

"Didn't try to contact Miss Coleridge, did you?" Meyer asked.

"No, why would I?"

"Didn't write to her, or try to phone her . . ."

"No."

"Didn't you find her letter at all threatening?"

"Threatening?"

"Yes. All that stuff about starting litigation . . ."

"That has nothing to do with me."

"It doesn't?"

"That's Norman's problem. And Connie's. They're the ones producing the show."

"But if the show got tangled up in litigation . . ."

"That's not my problem."

"It might not get produced," Kling said reasonably.

"So what?"

"Come on, Miss Carr," Meyer said sharply. "There's lots of money involved here."

"I've got a good job in L.A.," Felicia said. "It'll be nice if *Jenny's Room* happens. But if not, not. Life goes on."

Not if you're Martha Coleridge, Meyer thought.

"So can you tell us where you were Sunday night?" he asked.

"I went to a movie with my girlfriend," Felicia said, sighing. "The woman whose apartment this is. Shirley Lasser."

"What'd you see?" Kling asked casually.

"The new Travolta film."

"Any good?"

"The movie was lousy," Felicia said. "But I like him."

"He's usually very good," Kling said.

"Yes."

"Do you find him handsome?"

"Extremely so."

"What time did the show go on?" Meyer asked, getting back in character.

"Eight o'clock."

"What time did you get home?"

"Around eleven."

"Girlfriend with you all that time?"

"Yes."

"Where can we reach her?"

"She's at work right now."

"Where's that?"

"You guys kill me," Felicia said.

The sky was beginning to cloud over as they headed uptown. Decked out for Christmas as she was, the city petulantly demanded snow. Store windows were decorated with fake snow, and there were fake Salvation Army Santas shaking bells in front of fake chimneys on every other street corner. But this was already the ninth of December and Christmas Day was fast approaching. What the city needed now was a real Santa soaring over the rooftops, real snow falling gently from the sky above. What the city needed was a sign.

"I think she was telling the truth," Kling said.

"I don't," Meyer said.

"Where was she lying?"

"She gets a letter threatening legal action, and she forgets the woman's *name?*"

"Well . . ."

"Says she never heard of her, quote, unquote. Then all at once, comes the dawn! Oh yes, *now* I recall," he said, doing a pretty fair imitation. "Martha Coleridge! She's the one who wrote a letter that can only deprive me of early retirement." He snapped the mobile phone from its cradle, held it out to Kling. "Call this Shirley Lasser," he said, "tell her we're on the way. Six to five her pal's already been on the pipe, telling her they saw a Travolta movie together last Sunday night."

Kling began dialing.

"I wonder which one it was," he said.

Knowing that Jamaicans slept ten, twelve to a room, Fat Ollie Weeks did not consider it beyond the realm of possibility that a Jamaican visitor from Houston, Texas, might have crashed with friends or relatives now residing in this fair city, ah yes. Further knowing that the Jamaican in question had picked up Althea Cleary in a diner in the Eight-Eight, he took a run at the precinct's own Jamaican enclave, The Forbes Houses on Noonan and Crowe—and came up empty. Undaunted, but unwilling to do a door-to-door canvass of the city's six *other* Jamaican neighborhoods, he headed for the largest of them, downtown in the Three-Two Precinct.

Here in the old city, narrow, twisting little streets with Florida-sounding names like Lime, Hibiscus, Pelican, Manatee, and Heron ran into similarly cramped little lanes and alleys called Goedkoop, Keulen, Sprenkels, and Visser, named by the Dutch when the city was new and masted sailing ships lay in the harbor. Them days was gone forever, Gertie. Running eastward from the Straits of Napoli and Chinatown, Visser Street swerved to the north into what used to be an area of warehouses bordering the River Harb. Too far uptown to be considered Lower Platform, not far enough downtown to be a part of trendy Hopscotch, the newly erected projects here were officially called The Mapes Houses, after James Joseph Mapes, a revered former Governor of the state.

All of the city's projects were rated by the police department on a one-to-five scale ranging from "uncertain" to "chancy" to "risky" to "unsafe" to downright "hazardous." The Mapes Houses were classified a middling three on the Safety Factor scale, although foot patrolmen assigned to the area considered this a conservative ranking. The cops of the Three-Two dubbed the project "Rockfort," after a seventeenth-century moated fortress on the easternmost limits of Kingston, but perhaps that was only because eighty percent of the residents here were Jamaican.

On Fat Ollie Weeks's scale of personal safety, Rockfort ranked a dismal eight, which in his lexicon meant shitty, mon. He went in there alone early that Thursday afternoon, but only because it was broad daylight a few weeks before Christmas. Otherwise, he'd have requested backup and a SWAT team. Abandoning his usual swagger, which he felt might be a liability here among the Jamaican brethren, ah yes, his manner became almost obsequious as he went from door to door asking after a man some six foot, two or three inches tall, with a fawn-colored complexion, deep brown eyes, wide shoulders, a narrow waist, a lovely grin, and a melodic Jamaican lilt to his voice. He did not mention the blue star tattooed on the suspect's penis because many of the people he spoke to were women, and many of the men considered themselves Christians.

He did not strike pay dirt until three that afternoon, by which time it was beginning to snow and the skies above were dark enough to cause him to consider going back uptown.

✳   ✳   ✳

Cynthia Keating did not seem surprised to find Carella and Brown on her doorstep yet another time. She didn't even threaten calling her lawyer. She asked them to come in, told them they had ten minutes, and then sat opposite them, crossing her legs and folding her arms across her chest. It had begun snowing, and the window behind her was alive with wind-driven flakes.

Carella got directly to the point.

"A woman named Martha Coleridge," he said, "mailed some letters to Norman Zimmer's office, asking that they be forwarded. One of them was addressed to you, as owner of the underlying rights to *Jenny's Room*. With it was a photocopy of a play Miss Coleridge herself had written. Did you ever receive that play and the accompanying letter?"

"Yes, I did."

Progress, Carella thought.

"How'd you feel about it?"

"Concerned."

"Why?"

"Because it seemed to me there *were* similarities between her play and *Jenny's Room*."

"What kind of similarities?"

"Well, the premise, to begin with. An immigrant girl comes to America and falls in love with someone of another faith while at the same time she's falling in love with the city itself—which she finally chooses over the man. That's identical in both plays. And the conceit. We see her love affair with the city through the window of her room, which is really a window to her heart. That's the same, too. Reading it was . . . well . . . alarming."

"So what'd you do?"

"I called Todd. He . . ."

"Todd Alexander?"

"Yes. My lawyer. He advised me to forget about it."

"And *is* that what you did?"

She hesitated for the briefest tick of time. Carella caught the hesitation, and so did Brown. Their eyes revealed nothing, but they had caught it. Her fleeting inner debate apparently led to a decision to tell the truth.

"No, I did not forget about it," she said.

But the truth inevitably led to another question.

"What did you do instead?" Brown asked.

Again, the slight hesitation.

"I went to see her," Cynthia said.

The detectives did not know why she was telling the truth—if indeed this was the truth. The woman they were here to inquire about was dead, and anything that had transpired between her and Cynthia Keating could neither be confirmed nor contradicted. But the path of evident truth was the one Cynthia seemed to have chosen, and they thanked God for small favors and plunged ahead regardless.

"When was this?" Carella asked.

"The day after I received the play. I called her, and we arranged to meet."

"And when was that?"

"The Thursday before Connie's party."

"Where'd this meeting take place?" Brown asked.

"Her apartment. Downtown on Sinclair."

"What'd you talk about?"

"Her letter. The play. I wanted to find out exactly what she had in mind."

"How do you mean?"

"Her letter said she was looking for 'appropriate compensation.' I wanted to know what she considered appropriate."

"You went there expecting to deal, is that it?"

"As I told you, I was concerned. Her play couldn't have been a fake, she'd sent us a program with the name of the theater on it, the date the play opened, how could she have faked all that? And if she *wasn't* faking, then her play was the model for *Jenny's Room*. There was no question in my mind about that."

"So you went there to deal?"

"To explore a deal."

"Even though your lawyer advised against it."

"Well, lawyers," she said, and dismissed the entire legal profession with a wave of her hand.

"What *did* she have in mind exactly?" Brown asked.

"A cash settlement of one million dollars."

"She asked you for a *million* dollars?"

"That was the total sum she wanted from *all* of us. The ten people she'd sent the letter to. A hundred thousand from each of us."

"What'd you tell her?"

"I told her I couldn't speak for the others, but that I'd give it some thought and get back to her. I had no intention of doing that. I thought her demand was absurd. Todd was right. I shouldn't have gone there in the first place."

"Did she seem serious about that price?"

"Non-negotiable, she told me. One million dollars."

"Did you talk to any of the others about this?"

"Yes."

"Who?"

"Norman Zimmer and Connie Lindstrom. They're our producers. I should have turned it over to them from the beginning."

"What'd they say?"

"Forget it. Same as Todd."

"How about the others who received the letter? Did you talk to any of them?"

"No."

"None of the creative team?"

"No."

"The other rights holders?"

"Felicia and Gerry? No."

"Didn't mention it to them at the Meet 'N' Greet?"

"No."

"Even though you'd met with Miss Coleridge just a few days earlier?"

"I didn't see any need to."

"How come?" Brown asked.

"I told you. I'd been advised to forget about it. So I forgot about it." She shrugged airily. "Besides, it was a party. The hell with her."

"What'd you expect would happen?"

"I had no idea. If she sued, she sued. But I wasn't about to hand her a hundred thousand dollars I didn't even *have*."

"Ever see her again after that Thursday?"

"No."

"Didn't go back to talk to her again?"

"No."

"Didn't call her?"

"No."

"Had no further contact with her, right?"

"Right."

"Do you know she's dead?"

Cynthia was either stunned into silence or else was hesitating again, debating whether or not to tell the truth.

"No," she said at last. "I didn't know that."

"It was in the papers," Brown said.

"I didn't see it."

"On television, too," he said.

"So *that's* why you're here," she said.

"That's why we're here."

"You still think . . ."

She shook her head, fell silent.

"You're wrong," she said.

Maybe they were.

☆   ☆   ☆

"The one with the scar, yes," the woman said.

It came out "Dee wan wid dee scah, yes."

"You know him?" Ollie said, astonished. He'd been pounding leather for close to two hours now.

"I seed him here dee projec," the woman said. "But I doan know him cept for dat."

The woman was frying bananas at the kitchen stove, tilting the frying pan from one side to the other to spread the butter. A pot of greens in garlic and oil was simmering on another burner. Something succulent was roasting in the oven, too. The woman was barefoot, wearing a loose-fitting smock with a floral design, a matching pink kerchief on her head. The kitchen was small and tidy, the cooking smells overpowering. Ollie was suddenly very hungry.

"What's his name, would you know?"

"Never heerd his name," the woman said.

"Where'd you see him?"

"Aroun dee projec, like I say."

"What are those?" he asked. "Fried bananas?"

"Yes, mon, fried bananas, wot you tink?"

"How do they taste?"

"Mon?"

"Them fried bananas."

"You lak to taste one?"

"They sure look good."

"They be done soon," she said.

Ollie watched the butter bubbling around them in the pan. His mouth was watering.

"Any idea where in the project?" he asked.

"Playin dee saxophone," she said. "You wann summa dis now?"

She moved the pan to an unlighted burner, forked one of the bananas onto a dish and handed fork and dish to Ollie. He speared the banana, swallowed it almost whole. Hands on her hips, smiling in satisfaction, she watched him.

"That's really good," he said.

"Yah," she said. "Still later, they be mo better. I serves em wid vanilla ice cream."

He was hoping she'd offer him another one, with or without ice cream, hot or cold, but she didn't. He put the disk back on the counter, wiped the back of his hand across his lips, and said, "He's a musician, huh?"

"No, but he play dee saxophone," the woman said, and laughed.

"Where'd you hear him play?"

"Dee rec room," she said.

Gerry Palmer was packing for London when they got to his hotel room at four that Thursday afternoon.

"Not leaving till Sunday night," he said, "but I like to be ready well in advance."

The room was on the tenth floor of The Piccadilly, far less fashionable than the hotels in the sidestreets off Jefferson Avenue, and not close enough to The Stem to be considered convenient to restaurants or shows. Carella had some dim recollection that the place used to be a riding academy in the not-too-distant past, before the new mayor started cracking down on hookers using hot-bed hotels for their swift transactions. The place still had a look of seedy weariness about it, the drapes and matching bedspread a trifle shabby, the arms on both easy chairs beginning to look a bit threadbare. Carella sat in one of those chairs, Brown in the other. Palmer stood on the far side of the bed, facing them, carrying clothes from the dresser and the closet to his open suitcase on the bed.

A brown suit, a canary-colored shirt with a white collar, a fresh pair of Jockey shorts, brown socks, and a brown silk tie were laid out neatly on the bed. Palmer explained that he'd set them aside for when he went out to dinner and a play tonight. He named the play—which neither of the detectives had seen, or even heard of—and explained that Norman Zimmer had arranged for house seats at the Ferguson Theater, all of this in the Cockney accent that made him sound like a bad imitation of an Englishman.

"So to what do I owe the honor of this visit?" he asked.

"Know a woman named Martha Coleridge?" Brown said.

"Know *of* her," Palmer said, "but I can't say I've had the pleasure."

"Did you receive a letter from her recently?"

"Oh indeed I did."

"Accompanying a play called *My Room*, and a copy of the opening night program?"

"Yes. All that. Indeed."

"What'd you think of it?" Carella asked.

"Can't say I read the play. But I thought the letter quite interesting."

"What'd you do about it?"

Palmer was carrying some five or six folded shirts from the dresser to the bed. He stopped, looked across the bed at the detectives, and said, "*Do* about it? Was I *supposed* to do something about it?"

"Didn't the letter seem threatening to you?"

"Well, no, actually. I simply took her for a barmy old lady," Palmer said, and began arranging the shirts in the suitcase.

"Didn't find her at all threatening, huh?"

"Was I *supposed* to find her threatening?" Palmer said, and managed to look surprised, and amused, and at the same time somehow challenging, like a kid making a cute face for grandma and grandpa, his blue eyes opening wide, his mouth curling into an impish little grin. Again, Carella had the feeling he was imitating someone, perhaps a comic he'd seen on a music hall stage, perhaps a silly comedian in a movie. Or perhaps he was merely stupid.

"Did you call her or anything?" Brown asked.

"Lord, no!" Palmer said.

"Didn't think it was worth a call, huh?"

"Certainly not."

"Did you talk to either Cynthia Keating or Felicia Carr about it?"

"No. I didn't."

"Mention it to Mr Zimmer? Or his partner?"

"I may have, yes."

"When was that?"

"That I mentioned it to them? At the party, I would imagine."

"Didn't call either of them before the party, huh?"

"No. Was I *supposed* to ring them?"

"No, but how come you didn't?"

"Well, let me see. The material was forwarded to me from Mr Zimmer's office, you know. So I assumed he already *knew* what it was about. In which case, there was no need to call him, was there?"

Again the impish, somewhat insulting raised eyebrows and grin that said, Now, really, this is all quite elementary stuff, isn't it, chaps? So why are we getting all in a dither about it, eh? Brown felt like smacking him right in the eye.

"Didn't you feel this woman was endangering the show?"

"Of *course* I did!"

"*And* a possible future windfall?"

"Of *course!*" Palmer said. "But she wanted a hundred thousand dollars from each of us! A hundred thousand! She could just as easily have asked for a hundred *million.* I shouldn't have been able to give her *either* sum, don't you see? Do you know how much I earn in the post room at

Martins and Grenville? Seven thousand pounds a year. That's a far shout from a hundred thousand dollars."

Again the raised eyebrows. The wide blue eyes. The lop-sided grin. Brown was doing the arithmetic. He figured seven thousand pounds came to about ten-five a year in dollars.

"So you just let it drop," he said.

"I just let it . . ." A shrug. "Drop, yes. As you put it." A pursing of the lips. "I simply ignored it."

"And now she's dead," Brown said, and watched him.

"I know," Palmer said. "I saw the news in one of your tabloids."

No widening of the big blue eyes this time. No look of surprise. If anything, there was instead a somewhat exaggerated expression of sorrow. More and more, Carella felt the man was acting a part, pretending to be someone a lot smarter, a lot more sophisticated than the underpaid mailroom clerk he actually was.

"How'd you feel when you read the story?" he asked.

"Well, I shouldn't have wanted the woman to *die*, certainly," Palmer said. "But I must admit we're all much better off this way." And raised his eyebrows again, and widened his eyes, no grin this time, just a look that said Well, don't you agree? He closed the lid on his suitcase, jiggled the numbers on the combination lock, and dusted his hands in dismissal.

"There," he said.

"What time do you leave on Sunday?" Brown asked.

"The eight o'clock flight."

"Then there's still time."

"Oh? For what?"

To nail you, Brown thought.

"Catch a matinee," he said. "Lots of Saturday matinees here."

"London, too," Palmer said, almost wistfully.

✳   ✳   ✳

The person in charge of giving out the keys to the project's recreation room was an old black man who introduced himself solely as Michael, no last name. People seemed to have no last names these days, Ollie noticed, not that he gave a damn. But it seemed to him a person should be *proud* of his last name, which was for Chrissake only his heritage. Instead, you got only first names from every jackass in every doctor's office and bank. And now this keeper of the keys here, telling him his name was Michael, served him right he'd been born a shuffling old darkie.

"I'm looking for a Jamaican got a knife scar down his face, a tattooed star on his pecker, that plays the saxophone," Ollie said.

The old man burst out laughing.

"It ain't funny," Ollie said. "He maybe killed two people."

"That ain't funny, all right," Michael agreed, sobering.

"See him around here? Some lady told me he played his saxophone in here."

"You mean the guy from London?" Michael asked.

They were all sitting in the squadroom, around Carella's desk, drinking the coffee Alf Miscolo had brewed in the Clerical Office. Ollie was the only one there who thought the coffee tasted vile. Over the years, the others had come to believe the coffee didn't taste too bad at all, was in fact the sort of gourmet coffee one might find in little sidewalk cafes in Paris or Seattle. Ollie almost spit out his first sip.

He was there to tell them what he had learned downtown at Rockfort. The four detectives listening to him were Carella, Brown, Meyer, and Kling, who'd been dogging various aspects of this case for what seemed forever but was in actuality only since October 29. Ollie felt somewhat like a guest on a talk show. Carella was the host, and the others were earlier guests who'd moved over to make room for Ollie when he'd come on to exuberant whistling and thunderous applause. Brown and Meyer were sitting on chairs they'd pulled over from their own desks. Kling was sitting on one corner of Carella's desk.

This was a nice cozy little talk show here, with the temperature outside hovering at somewhere between twenty and twenty-two degrees Fahrenheit, which came to six or seven below zero Celsius, more or less, good to be inside on a night like tonight. The clock on the squadroom wall read a quarter past five, or 1715, depending on your point of view. Ollie had called from downtown right after he'd spoken to Mr Michael and then again to the lady who'd offered him another banana, asking Carella to wait for him, he'd be right there. That had been at ten to four. The snow had delayed Ollie, what can you do, an act of God, he explained. It was still snowing, the flying flakes spattering against the squadroom windows like ghosts desperately seeking entrance.

"The way I understood it," Ollie said, "Bridges was there with his cousin for a week or so at the beginning of November. Rec room guy remembers him coming in to practice his saxophone. I figure this was after he done the Hale murder and before he flew back home."

"The rec room guy told you all this?"

"Not about the murder, that's my surmise. He didn't know anything about that."

"Then what?"

"The cousin, the sax, him flying back home."

"Did you talk to the cousin?"

"Knocked on the door, no answer. But I figured this was important enough to get moving on it right away. Which is why I'm here."

"Who told you the sax player's name was John Bridges?"

"The rec room guy."

"And told you he'd flown back home to Houston?"

"Yes and no," Ollie said, and grinned.

"Let us guess, okay?"

"He did *not* fly home to Houston, Texas."

"Then where *did* he go?"

"Euston, *England.* Sounds the same, ah yes, but it's spelled different. E-U-S-T-O-N. That's a locality, is what they call it in London. I went back to my lady who cooks fried bananas ..."

"Huh?" Carella said.

"A lady in the project, her name is Sarah Crawford, she cooks great fried bananas."

Ollie felt he now had their complete attention.

"She's Jamaican, she told me all about Euston and also King's Cross—which is a nearby ward, is what they call it in London—where there are lots of hookers, drug dealers, and train stations. She didn't know Bridges personally, but his cousin told her he lived in Euston. So that's it, ah yes," Ollie said. "You know anybody else from London?"

They were waiting outside the Ferguson Theater when Gerald Palmer showed up for the eight o'clock performance that night. He was wearing a dark blue overcoat over the brown suit, canary-colored, white-collared shirt, and brown silk tie they'd seen on his bed earlier that day. His hair and the shoulders of the coat were dusted with snow. He opened his blue eyes wide when he saw Carella and Brown standing there near the ticket taker, waiting for him. There was a blond woman on his arm. She looked puzzled when the detectives approached.

"Mr Palmer," Carella said, "would you mind coming along with us?"

"What for?" he asked.

"Few questions we'd like to ask you."

As if trying to impress the blonde—or perhaps because he was merely stupid—Palmer assumed the same wide-eyed, smirky, defiant look they'd seen on his face earlier.

"Awfully sorry," he said. "I have other plans."

"So do we," Brown said.

The blonde accepted Palmer's gracious offer to go see the play alone while he took care of this "silly business," as he called it, still playing the Prime Minister dealing with a pair of cheeky reporters. All the way uptown, he kept complaining about the police in this city, telling them they had no right treating a foreigner this way, which of course they had every right in the world to do, the law applying equally to citizens and visitors alike unless they had diplomatic immunity. They read him his rights the moment he was in custody. These were vastly different from those mandated in the UK, but he had no familiarity with either, as he explained to them, never having been in trouble with the law in his life. In fact, he could not understand why he seemed to be in police custody now, which was the same old song they'd heard over the centuries from ax murderers and machine-gun Kellys alike.

Out of deference to his foreign status, they sat him down in the lieutenant's office, which was more comfortable than the interrogation room, and offered him some of Miscolo's coffee, or a cup of tea, if that was his preference. In response, he affected his Eyes Wide Open, Eyebrows Raised, Lips Pursed in Indignation look again, and told them there was no need to presume stereotypical behavior, in that he rarely drank tea and in fact much preferred coffee as his beverage of preference, redundantly sounding exactly like the sort of Englishman he was trying *not* to sound like.

"So tell us, Mr Palmer," Carella said. "Do you know anyone named John Bridges?"

"No. Who is he?"

"We think he may have killed Andrew Hale."

"I'm sorry, am I supposed to know who Andrew Hale is?"

"You're supposed to know only what you know," Carella said.

"Ah, brilliant," Palmer said.

"He's from Euston."

"Andrew Hale?"

"John Bridges. Do you know where Euston is?"

"Of course I do."

"Know anyone from Euston?"

"No."

"Or King's Cross?"

"Those aren't neighborhoods I ordinarily frequent," Palmer said.

"Know any Jamaicans in London?"

"No."

"When did you first learn Andrew Hale was being difficult?"

"I don't know anyone named Andrew Hale."

"He's Cynthia Keating's father. Did you know he once owned the underlying rights to *Jenny's Room?*"

"I don't know anything about him or any rights he may have owned."

"No one ever informed you of that?"

"Not a soul."

"Then you're learning it for the first time this very minute, is that right?"

"Well . . . no. Not precisely this very minute."

"Then you knew it before now."

"Yes, I suppose I did. Come to think of it."

"When *did* you learn about it?"

"I really can't remember."

"Would it have been before October twenty-ninth?"

"Who can remember such a long time ago?"

"Do you remember *how* you learned about it?"

"I probably read it in a newspaper."

"Which newspaper, do you recall?"

"I'm sorry, I don't."

"Do you remember when that might have been?"

"I'm sorry, no."

"Was it a British newspaper?"

"Oh, I'm certain not."

"Then it was an American paper, is that right?"

"I really don't know what sort of paper it was. It might have been British, I'm sure I don't know."

"But you said it wasn't."

"Yes, but I really don't remember."

"How well do you know Cynthia Keating?"

"Hardly at all. We met for the first time a week ago."

"Where was that?"

"At Connie's party."

"The Meet 'N' Greet?"

"Why, yes."

"Never talked to her before then?"

"Never. Am I supposed to have spoken to her?"

"We were just wondering."

"Oh? About what?"

"About when you first spoke to her."

"I told you . . ."

"You see, after we learned Mr Bridges was from London . . ."

"Big city, you realize."

"Yes, we know that."

"If you're suggesting he and I might have known each other, that is."

"But you said you didn't."

"That's right. I'm saying the population is even larger

than it is here. So if you're suggesting I might have known a *Jamaican*, no less, from Euston or King's Cross ..."

"But you don't."

"That's right."

"And you never met Cynthia Keating, either ..."

"Well, not until ..."

"The party at Connie Lindstrom's, right."

"That's correct."

"Never even spoke to her before then."

"Never."

"Which is what made us wonder. When we were going over our notes. After we learned Mr Bridges ..."

"Oh, you take notes, do you? How clever."

"Mr Palmer," Carella said, "it might go better for you if you stopped being such a wise ass."

"I didn't realize it was going *badly*," Palmer said, and raised his eyebrows and opened his eyes wide and smiled impishly. "I was merely trying to point out that scads of people are from London, that's all."

"Yes, but not all of them are linked to Cynthia Keating's father."

"I never met Andrew Hale in my life. And I'm certainly not *linked* to him, as you're suggesting."

"Mr Palmer," Carella said, "how did you know Martha Coleridge wanted a hundred thousand dollars from each of you?"

The blue eyes went wide again. The eyebrows arched. The lips pursed.

"Well ... let me think," he said.

They waited.

"Mr Palmer?" Carella said.

"Someone must have told me."

"Yes, who?"

"I can't remember."

"You didn't talk to Miss Coleridge herself, did you?"

"Of *course* not. I never even *met* the woman!"

"Then who told you?"

"I have no idea."

"Was it Cynthia Keating?"

Palmer did not answer.

"Mr Palmer? It was Cynthia Keating, wasn't it?"

He still said nothing.

"Did she also tell you her *father* owned the underlying rights to the play?"

Palmer folded his arms across his chest.

"And was refusing to part with them?"

Palmer's look said his carriage had just run over an urchin in the cobbled streets and he was ordering his coachman to move on regardless.

"I guess that's it, huh?" Carella said.

Palmer took an enameled snuff box from the pocket of his brocaded waistcoat, disdainfully opened the box, and sniffed a pinch of snuff into each nostril.

Or so it seemed to the assembled flatfoots.

They called Nellie Brand and spelled out what they thought they had. At the very least, they figured they were cool with conspiracy to commit first-degree murder. Nellie advised them to pick up Cynthia Keating and bring her in. She herself got there in half an hour. It was seven thirty-five on the face of the squadroom clock, and it was still snowing outside.

They brought Cynthia in ten minutes later. Todd Alexander came to the party at ten past eight. He promptly informed them that his client would not answer any questions and he warned them that unless they charged her with something at *once* she was marching right out of there.

It now remained to see who would blink first.

✳   ✳   ✳

"I wouldn't be so hasty, Todd," Nellie said, "You stand to make a lot of money here."

"Oh? How do you figure that?"

"I plan to consolidate the two murders. This'll be a very long trial. I hope your client has a gazillion dollars."

"Which two murders are you talking about?" Alexander asked.

"First off, the murder for hire of Mrs Keating's father ..."

"Oh, I see, murder for hire." He turned to Cynthia and said, "Murder for hire is first-degree murder."

"Tell her what she's looking at, Todd."

"Why waste my breath? Is that what you're charging her with? Murder One? If so, do it."

"What's your hurry? Don't you want to hear me out? I can save your life," Nellie said, turning to Cynthia. "I can also save you a lot of money."

"Thanks," Cynthia said, "but my life's not in danger ..."

"Don't kid your ..."

"... and I'll be rich once *Jenny's'* ..."

"The penalty for Murder One is lethal injection," Nellie said. "I'm offering you a real bargain discount."

"What exactly do you think you have?" Alexander asked.

"I've got an old man standing in the way of what your client perceives as a fortune. I've got a bird brain in London who looks at it the same way. The two conspire to ..."

"Mrs Keating and somebody in *London*, are you saying?"

"A *specific* somebody named Gerald Palmer. Who also stands to make a fortune if this show is a hit."

"And they conspired to kill Mrs Keating's *father*, are you saying?"

"That's our surmise, Todd."

"A wild one."

"The Brits have been known," Nellie said.

"Sure, Richard the Second."

"Even more recently."

"You're saying ..."

"I'm saying the pair of them found a Jamaican hit man named John Bridges, brought him here to America ..."

"Oh, please, Nellie."

"The Metropolitan Police are checking his pedigree this very minute. Once they get back to us ..."

"Ah, Sherlock Holmes now."

"No, just a detective named Frank Beaton."

"This is all nonsense," Cynthia said.

"Fine, take your chances," Nellie said.

"What do you want from her?"

"Her partner and the hit man."

"That's everybody."

"No, that's only two people."

"What do you give her in return?"

"Is this *me* you're talking about?" Cynthia asked.

"Just a second, Cyn," Alexander said.

"Never mind just a second. If she had anything, she wouldn't be trying to strike a deal here."

"You think so, huh?" Nellie said.

"What can you give us?" Alexander asked.

"She rats them out, I drop the charge to Murder Two. Twenty to life as opposed to the Valium cocktail."

"Go to fifteen," Alexander said.

"Twenty. With a recommendation for parole."

"Come on, at least give me the minimum."

"Fifteen can come and go without parole," Nellie said. "And then twenty, and thirty, and forty, and still no parole. Before you know it, your lady's in there for the rest of her life. Take my advice. Twenty with a recommendation."

"She'd be *sixty* when she got out!"

"Fifty-seven," Cynthia corrected.

But she was thinking.

"On the other hand, you can always roll the dice. Just remember, you're looking at the death penalty. You'll sit on death row for five, six years while you exhaust all your appeals—and that'll be it."

"Recommend parole after fifteen," Alexander said.

"I can't do that."

"Twenty just isn't sweet enough."

"How sweet is the cocktail?" Nellie asked.

Chapter Ten

It is Palmer who makes the first contact, toward the end of
September.

He tells Cynthia on the telephone that he's had a
transatlantic call from Norman Zimmer, who's producing
a musical based on *Jenny's Room,* is she familiar with ...?

"Yes, he's been in touch," Cynthia says.

"I hate to bother you this way," he says, "but from
what I understand, the project may be stalled because of
your father's intransigence."

"Yes, I know."

"It does seem a shame, doesn't it?" he says. "All these
people who'd stand to earn a little money."

"I know," Cynthia says.

"Couldn't you talk with him?"

"I have," she says. "He won't budge."

"It does seem a pity."

"He's protecting Jessica, you see."

"Who's that?"

"Jessica Miles. The woman who wrote the original
play. He feels she wouldn't have wanted the musical done
again."

"Really? Why's that?"

"Because it was so awful."

"Oh, I don't think so, do *you*? I've read my grandfather's book, and I've also heard the songs. It's really quite good, you know. Besides, they're having new songs written, and a new book, and—well, it's truly a shame. Because I think it has a really good shot, you know. I think we can all become quite rich, actually. If it's done."

There is a crackling on the line.

She tries to visualize London. She has never been there. She imagines chimney pots and cobblestoned streets. She imagines men with soot-stained collars and women in long hour-glass gowns. She imagines Big Ben chiming the hour, regattas on the Thames. She imagines all these things. And imagines going there one day.

"Couldn't you please talk with him again?" Palmer says.

It is she who makes the next call, sometime early in October. He has just come home from work, it is seven o'clock there in London, only two in the afternoon here in America. He tells her he works for "the last of the publishers in Bedford Square," a line she surmises he has used often before. In fact, there is something about the way he speaks that makes everything sound studied and prepared, as if he has learned a part and is merely acting it. A lack of spontaneity, she supposes, something that makes whatever he says seem artificial and rehearsed, as if there is nothing of substance behind the words.

"Have you seen him again?" he asks.

"Several times," she says.

"And?"

"Dead end."

"Mmm."

"He won't listen to reason. He says the play is a sacred trust . . ."

"Nonsense."

"It's what he believes."

"She must have written it in the year dot."

"Nineteen twenty-three."

"Norman tells me it's bloody awful."

"My father thinks it's simply *wonderful*."

"Well, as the old maid said when she kissed the cow ..."

"It's a shame this had to come along just *now*, though. The opportunity, I mean. To have the musical revived."

"How do you mean?"

"Well ... ten *years* from now would have been so much better."

"I don't under ..."

"Never mind, I shouldn't have said that.

"I'm sorry, I still don't ..."

"It's just ... my father isn't in the best of health, you see."

"That's too bad."

"And *I* certainly don't have the same problems he has."

"Problems? What ... ?"

"With the play. With it being done as a musical. I have no emotional ties to Jessica Miles, you see. I never even *met* the woman. What I'm saying is I don't give a *damn* about her play. In fact, I'd *love* to see the musical revived."

"But what's ten years from now got to ... ?"

"My father's leaving the rights to me."

"Oh?"

"To her play. When he dies. It's in his will."

"I see."

"Yes."

There was a long silence.

"*But*," she said. "It *isn't* ten years from now, is it?"

"No, it isn't," Palmer says.

"It's now," she says.

"Yes," he says. "So it is."

He calls her again on the eighteenth of October. It is

midnight here in America, he tells her it's five A.M. there in London, but he hasn't been able to sleep.

"I've been thinking a lot about your father," he says.

"Me, too," she says.

"It seems *such* a pity he won't let go of those rights, doesn't it? Forgive me, but have you made your position absolutely clear to him? Have you told him *your* feelings about having this musical done?"

"Oh, yes, a thousand times."

"I mean . . . he *must* realize, don't you imagine, that the moment he's passed on . . . forgive me . . . you'll do bloody well what you *like* with the play. Doesn't he realize that?"

"I'm sure he does."

"It does seem unfair, doesn't it?"

"It does."

"Especially since he's in bad health."

"Two heart attacks."

"You'd think he'd hand over the play *immediately*, why wouldn't he? With his blessings. Here you are, Cynthia, do with it as you wish."

"His only child," Cynthia said.

"One would think so."

"But he won't."

"Well, when they get to be a certain age . . ."

"It isn't that. He's just a stubborn old fool. Sometimes I wish . . ."

She lets the sentence trail.

He waits.

"Sometimes I wish he'd die tomorrow," she says.

There is another silence.

"I'm sure you don't mean that," he says.

"I suppose not."

"I'm sure you don't."

"But I do," she says.

*　　　*　　　*

There is a Jamaican named Charles Colworthy who works in the mail room with Palmer, and he knows another Jamaican named Delroy Lewis, who knows yet another Jamaican named John Bridges, who by all accounts is what they call a "Yardie," which Palmer explains is British slang for any young Jamaican male involved in violence and drugs.

"I wouldn't want him hurt," Cynthia says at once.

"Of course not."

"You said violence."

"He's assured me it will be painless."

"You've met him?"

"Several times."

"What's his name?"

"John Bridges. He's quite ready to do it for us. If you still want to go ahead with it."

"I've given it a lot of thought."

"So have I."

"It does seem the right thing, doesn't it, Gerry?"

"Yes."

There is a long silence.

It all seems to be happening too quickly.

"When . . . when would he do it?"

"Sometime before the end of the month. He'll need an introduction. You'd have to arrange that."

"An introduction?"

"To your father."

"Is he black?"

"Yes. But very light skinned."

"I don't know any black people, you see."

"Very pale eyes," Palmer says. "A lovely smile. All you need do is introduce him. He'll take care of the rest."

"It's just that I don't know any black people."

"Well . . ."

"I wouldn't know what to say."

"Just say he's a friend of yours from London."

"I've never been to London."

"A friend of a friend, you could say. Who'll be there for a few days. Who you wanted your father to meet. Is what you could say."

"Why would anyone want to meet my father?"

"You could say he once worked in a hospital here. Just as your father did. That would give them something in common. I'll give you the name of a hospital here in London."

"I've never introduced my father to anyone in my life."

"It would just be to put him off guard."

"He'd be suspicious."

"Just someone you'd like him to meet. A nurse. Just as your father was."

"He won't hurt him, will he?"

"No, no, you needn't worry."

"When did you say it would be?"

"Well, he'll come as soon as we authorize it. He'll want half of his fee beforehand, half after it's done."

"How much did he say?"

"Five thousand."

"Is that a lot?"

"I think it's reasonable. Dollars, that is. Not pounds."

"I wouldn't want him hurt," she says again.

"No, he won't be."

"Well."

"But I have to let him know."

"What do *you* think we should do?"

"I think we should go ahead with it. Twenty-five hundred dollars is a lot of money to me, but I look upon this as a serious investment ..."

"Yes."

"... an opportunity to advance myself. I can't speak for

you, of course ... but ... I've never really had very much in my life, Cynthia. I work in the post room, I don't get invited to very many balls at Windsor. If this show is a hit, everything would change for me. My life would become ... well ... glamorous."

"Yes," she said.

"I think we should do it," he said. "I truly do."

"Well then ..."

"What I'll do, if you agree, I'll give John my half of the fee just before he leaves London, and you can pay him the rest when he's done it. There in America. Afterward. Would you be happy with that?"

"I guess so."

"Shall I call him then?"

"Well ..."

"Tell him we're going ahead with it?"

"Yes."

Now, sitting in the lieutenant's office with her lawyer and the detectives, she lowers her eyes and says, "John was very charming. He and my father hit it off right away. But he caused me a lot of trouble later. Because he said it would look like an accident, and it didn't."

Gerald Palmer called the British Consulate the moment the cops told him what charges they were bringing against him. The consul who came over was named Geoffrey Holden, a somewhat portly man in his mid-forties, stroking a bristly mustache that made him look like a cavalry colonel. He took off his heavy overcoat and hung it on a corner rack. Under it, he was wearing a somber gray suit with a vest and a bright yellow tie. He told Palmer this was his first DBN of the week, which letters he jovially explained stood for Distressed British National.

"Murder, eh?" he said. "Who'd you kill?"

"I haven't killed *anyone*," Palmer said. "Don't be a bloody fool."

"Let me explain how American law works," Holden said. "If you actually hired someone to kill someone else, then you're as guilty as the person pulling the trigger. Murder for hire is first-degree murder, and the penalty is death by lethal injection. They use Valium. A massive dose that stops the heart. *Conspiracy* to commit murder is another A-felony. If you did either or both of these things . . ."

"I didn't."

"I was about to say you'd be in very deep trouble. *If* you did these things. Which you say you didn't."

"That's right."

"Being British is no excuse, by the way. It doesn't entitle you to immunity."

"I don't need immunity. I haven't done anything."

"Well, good then. D'you know anyone named John Bridges?"

"No."

"They seem to think you know him."

"I don't."

"How about a man named Charles Colworthy?"

Palmer's eyes opened wide.

"Supposed to work with you at Martins and Grenville. Good publishers, eh? D'you know him?"

Palmer was thinking it over.

"The way they have it," Holden said, "Colworthy knows someone named Delroy Lewis, who put you in touch with this Bridges chap to whom you and Cynthia Keating together paid five thousand dollars to kill her father. But that isn't so, is it?"

"Well, I *know* Colworthy, yes. But . . ."

"Ah, you do?"

"Yes. We work together in the post room. But I certainly didn't hire . . ."

"That's good. I'll just tell them they've made a mistake."

"Where'd they get those names, anyway?"

"From the woman."

"What woman?"

"Cynthia Keating," Holden said, and hooked his thumbs into his vest pockets. "She's ratted you out."

Palmer looked at him.

"But if you had nothing to do with this . . ."

"Just a minute. What do you mean? Just because she gave them the name of someone I *work* with . . ."

"The other man as well. Delroy Lewis. The one leading directly to Bridges. Who killed her father."

"Well, the only one *I* know is Charlie. He's the one I work with. I may have mentioned *his* name to her. In casual conversation. If so, she must have contacted him on her own."

"Ah," Holden said, and nodded. "To ask if he might know anyone who'd help kill her father, is that it?"

"Well, I . . . I'm sure I don't know *what* she asked him."

"Called London to arrange his murder, is that how you see it?"

"I don't see it any way at all. I'm merely trying to explain . . ."

"Yes, that *you*, personally, had nothing to do with this."

"Nothing whatever."

"So Mrs Keating is lying to them. *Has* lied to them, in fact. She's accepted a deal, you see. They've dropped the conspiracy charge and lowered the murder charge to second degree. Twenty to life, with a recommendation for parole." Holden paused. "They might even offer you the same deal. Then again, perhaps not."

Palmer looked at him.

"Because of the related murder."

Palmer kept looking at him.

"They seem to think you did *that* one personally. The old lady. Martha Coleridge. I have no idea where *she* fits into the scheme of things, but apparently she was threatening a plagiarism suit. Do you know the woman I mean?"

"Yes," Palmer said.

"That would constitute a second count of first-degree murder," Holden said, and stroked his mustache. "So I doubt if they'd offer you the same deal, after all."

"I'm not looking for a deal."

"Why should you be? You haven't done anything."

"That's right."

"I'll just tell them to forget it."

"Of course. They have no proof."

"Well, they have the woman's confession. Which implicates you, of course. And our chaps may get something more from Bridges, if ever they find him. They're looking for him now, apparently. In Euston. He lives in Euston."

Palmer fell silent again.

"You won't be granted bail, you realize," Holden said. "You're a foreigner implicated in murder, no one's going to risk your running. In fact, till the dust settles one way or another, they'll want your passport." He sighed heavily, said, "Well, I'll see about finding a lawyer for you," and went to the corner where he'd hung his overcoat. Shrugging into it, buttoning it, his back to Palmer, he said, "You wouldn't possibly have anything to . . . *offer* them, would you?"

"How do you mean?"

Holden turned toward him.

"Well," he said, "I must tell you, with the woman's confession, they have more than enough for an indictment. It'll go worse for you if they catch up with the Jamaican and flip him as well, but even so they've got a quite decent case."

"But I haven't done anything."

"Right. Keep forgetting that. Sorry. Let me talk to them." He opened the door, hesitated, turned to Palmer again, and said, "You wouldn't know anything about this little black girl who got stabbed up in Diamondback, would you?"

Palmer merely looked at him.

"Althea Cleary? Because they like to tidy things up, you see. If you can tell them anything about *that* murder . . . they're not trying to implicate you in it, by the way, they seem to think the Jamaican did that one all on his own. Got into some sort of argument with the girl, lost his temper. Whatever." His voice lowered. "But if he mentioned anything about it to you . . . perhaps before he went back to London . . . it might be worth a deal, hm?"

Palmer said nothing.

His voice almost a whisper, Holden said, "He's just a Yardie, y'know."

Palmer sat as still as a stone.

"Well, I suppose not," Holden said.

It suddenly occurred to him that the man was simply very stupid.

He sighed again, and went out of the room.

In the squadroom, they were speculating about what *might* have happened to Althea Cleary.

"She takes the Jamaican back to her apartment," Parker suggested. "He drops the rope in her drink, figures he's home free. But while he's waiting for it to take effect, she casually mentions she's a working girl and this is gonna cost him two bills. He's offended because he's never had to pay for it in his life, male *or* female. So he stabs her."

"That's possible," Brown said, "but you're forgetting something."

"What's that?"

"He's gay."

"He's bi."

"He *thinks* he's bi."

"He wouldn'ta been there if he *wasn't* bi," Parker insisted.

"He gets into the apartment," Brown said, undaunted, "drops the pills, and starts moving on her. Trouble is he's gay. She doesn't excite him. He can't *perform*. So he loses his temper and jukes her."

"Well, that's a possibility," Meyer said, "but something else could've happened, too."

"What's that?"

"Bridges drops the pills, right? Five minutes or so, the girl starts feeling funny. She accuses him of having put something in her drink. He panics, grabs a knife from the counter, lets her have it."

"Yeah, maybe," Kling said, "but here's what *I* think happened. He gets in the apartment . . ."

"Who's for pizza?" Parker asked.

"They profile a Yardie as someone who enters the country carrying a forged or stolen British passport," Carella said. "Usually—but not necessarily—he's a black man from Jamaica, somewhere between the ages of eighteen and thirty-five. He's either got a record already . . ."

"Does Bridges have one?" Byrnes asked.

"Nobody by that name in their files. They said he may be a new kid on the block, there's a constant flow. Most of them are in the drug trade. Getting rope would've been a walk in the park for him."

"Is he wanted for anything?"

"Not by the Brits. Not so far, anyway."

"Give him time," Byrnes said.

"Meanwhile, he's running around London someplace."

"Or Manchester."

"Or wherever. Actually, we don't need him, Pete. Nellie says the overt act is enough."

"Conspiracy and the overt act, yes."

"Which she's already got."

"So let the Queen's mother worry," Byrnes said.

Ollie felt very nervous, like a teenager about to ask for a first date. He dialed the number on the card she'd given him, and let the phone ring three, four, five . . .

"Hello?"

"Miss Hobson?" he said.

"Yes?"

"This is Detective Weeks. We talked about piano lessons, do you remember?"

"No. Detective *who*?"

"Weeks. Oliver Wendell Weeks. I was investigating the murder of Althea Cleary, do you remember? Big Ollie, they sometimes call me," he said, which was a lie. "I wanted to learn five songs, remember?"

"Oh. Yes," she said.

"I *still* do."

"I see," she said.

"I got a list we can pick from," he said.

"Did you find him?"

"Who do you mean, Miss Hobson?"

"Whoever killed Althea."

"He's in London just now. We're leaving it to the bobbies there, they're supposed to be very good. When can we start, Miss Hobson?"

"That depends on which songs you want to learn."

"Oh, they're easy ones, don't worry."

"That's so reassuring," she said drily. "But which ones are they exactly?"

"Guess," he said, and grinned into the mouthpiece.

They had no idea they were in the middle of a race riot until it was full upon them. Until that moment, they'd been peacefully watching television and drifting off to sleep, Kling knowing he was due back in the squadroom at eight tomorrow, Sharyn knowing her day would start at about the same time in her office at 24 Rankin Plaza, neither anticipating an explosion, each surprised when it came.

A panel of talking heads was offering its collective opinion on the war, the election, the wedding, the crash, the trial, the disaster, the game, the *whatever* because in America, it wasn't enough merely to present the news, you then had to have half a dozen commentators parading their thoughts on what the news had just been all about. Over the background din, Kling was telling Sharyn there'd been an extraordinary number of people informing on other people in this case they'd just wrapped, a veritable chorus of rats singing to whoever would listen, when all at once a blond woman on the panel said something about the "so-called blue wall of silence," and Sharyn said, "Shhh," and someone else on the panel, a black man, shouted that the blue wall of silence wouldn't be holding in the Milagros case if the victim had been *white*, and someone else, a white man, shouted, "This poor *victim* you're talking about is a *murderer!*" and Kling said, "Milagros is one of the guys I mean," and Sharyn said "Shhh" again, when all he'd wanted to say was that Hector Milagros had been given up by Maxie Blaine who'd been given up by Betty Young in a case virtually defined by perpetual snitchery.

"You don't know whether those men who went in there were white *or* black!" someone on the panel shouted.

"You don't even know if they were actually *cops!*" someone else shouted.

276

"They were *cops* and they were *white!*"

"I'll bet they were," someone else said, but the voice wasn't coming from the television set, it was coming from the pillow next to Kling's. He turned to look at her.

The blonde on television very calmly said, "I do not believe that any police officer in this city would maintain silence in the face of such a brutal beating. The police ..."

"Oh, come off it," Sharyn said.

"... simply don't *know* who went in there, that's all. If they knew ..."

On the television set, the black man said, "The guy who let them *in* knows."

"Every cop in this *city* knows," Sharyn said.

"I don't," Kling said.

And now there was a veritable Babel of voices pouring from the television set in a deluge of conflicting invective that rose higher and higher in volume and passion.

"Instead of maintaining their ridiculous posture of ..."

"There are black cops, too, you know. I don't see any of *them* ..."

"Would *you* come forward if ...?"

"You're asking them to be *rats.*"

"It's not informing if the person ..."

"Milagros was in custody!"

"He's a criminal!"

"So are the cops who beat him up!"

"A murderer!"

"... almost killed him!"

"He's *black!*"

"Here we go," Kling said.

"*That's* why they beat him up!"

"Hang on, honey," Sharyn said.

Together, they huddled against the angry voices.

At last, Kling said, "Wanna dance?"

About the Author

Ed McBain is the only American to receive the Diamond Dagger, the British Crime Writers Association's highest award. He also holds the Mystery Writers of America's coveted Grand Master Award. His books have sold over one hundred million copies worldwide, ranging from his first bestselling novel, *The Blackboard Jungle*, to the recent bestseller *Privileged Conversation*, both written under his own name, Evan Hunter, which he used on his screenplay for Alfred Hitchcock's *The Birds*. His most recent 87th Precinct novel was *The Big Bad City*. He lives in Connecticut with his wife, Dragica.